THE VICTORIAN TIME TRAVELLER

JAMES D QUINTON

a xplosive book

First published in 2010
Second edition published in 2012
by Xplosive Books

Copyright 2010 James D Quinton
All rights reserved

A CIP catalogue record for this book is available from
the British library

ISBN 978-0-9567823-0-4

'Good evening brothers and sisters, friends and neighbours, vibrations in the mind of the one true God, whose name is love.'

- Bill Hicks

'And suddenly, like light in darkness, the real truth broke in upon me; the simple fact of Man, which I had forgotten, which had lain deep buried and out of sight; the idea of community, of unity.'

- Ernst Toller

'Love is all we have, the only way that each can help the other.'

- Euripides

'God has no religion.'

- Mohandas Karamchand Gandhi

'Respect for another man's opinion is worthy. It is the realization that any opinion is valuable, for it is the sign of a rational being.'

- Robert Sargent Shriver, Jr

Foreword

I still recall that day, almost eighteen months ago, when I found in the bottom drawer of my great aunt's bureau, the manuscript of the book you are holding in your hands now. It had been three months since her death from a heart attack at the age of ninety-eight.

Harriet Tretheway was an eccentric. She was my late grandmother's sister, and unlike my grandmother, she never married or had children. When we were growing up my sister and myself would see her at least once a week, and she would entertain us with tales of her wild youth and her time working as a nurse during World War Two.

Following her death the unfortunate task of clearing her modest semi-detached property fell to my mother. I, of course, volunteered my services. My aunt had a great deal of 'things', which she'd accumulated on her travels. Slowly we made progress. Many of her belongings had to be taken to charity shops, as despite our fond memories of the items, we simply had no room for it all.

I remember approaching the bureau, a beautiful antique piece of furniture that my sister had been left in the will, with trepidation, fearing that its four drawers would be filled with bric-a-brac that would take hours to sort. I started at the bottom. The drawer was stiff; the wood had expanded, probably due to excess water dripping from a nearby plant stand. Eventually I pulled it open and was greeted with the site of a stack of sheets. The loose leaves on top were old bills, some dating from the 1950s. Beneath however, I found a faded, stained, bundle of paper tied up with string. I immediately felt that this was something interesting, but I certainly wasn't expecting what I found.

Aside from being aware that he was a pre-eminent scientist of his day, as a family we know very little about the gentleman who apparently wrote this text.

From what my mother can remember, my grandmother and great aunt did not know much of him themselves. Once, when my mother made an attempt at a family tree, my grandmother recounted a story about Harriet and herself visiting their paternal uncle in a sanatorium. She had been five when their parents and uncle's wife, Joyce, had made that strange trip. In fact it was one of her earliest memories. She recalled a feeling of great sadness. This would have been roughly 1915. At the time of writing I have been unable to track down any documentation on my great, great uncle, aside from the photograph below, but my investigation is ongoing. I do know that he passed away in 1917 and is buried in a family plot in a church graveyard in Norfolk, England.

Upon reading the text, my immediate thought was that this was some kind of joke. Indeed my family thought the same. Perhaps my aunt's final jape? But I really can't believe that. True, her imagination was lively, but this goes beyond anything she ever told us. To dismiss this bizarre possibility we have had the paper analysed, and it has been radiocarbon dated to the early twentieth century. Remarkable as it is, we can only conclude that this document is true, as true as it was for the man writing it in 1900.

Some of the document was badly damaged. We found woodworm at the bottom of the bureau and it seemed they had at some time made their home in the manuscript. So I took on the task of transcription, filling in the damaged parts using, like my great, great uncle before me, a 'literary liberty'.

It is really impossible to quantify the implications of what is written in this book. Although my family and myself aren't at all religious, after reading and believing this manuscript, we are sure that our lives will never be the same again. Of course some will say this is a hoax, or perhaps that though there may be something veridical in it, it is simply a confused, drug-induced vision. I do, however, wonder what my great aunt and my great, great uncle's wife thought of it. I suppose we will never know, but it would not be surprising if they thought he had lost his mind.

In a further twist, I believe, although my family do not agree, that in photo published here he is holding a copy of this very book in his hands. Presenting a rather interesting paradox: could he have seen his own story in print before he'd even written it?

Finally, our simple hope in publishing the manuscript is that the message my great, great uncle left us can be espoused.

- James D Quinton, UK, 2010

∞

This is not my story, although in many ways it is, but I write it for one person, you Joyce, my darling wife. Will you ever read it, and more importantly, if you do, will you believe me?

Beloved, this is my attempt to make sense of what I experienced, what I learnt, and what I saw. As you can imagine I have had a great deal of time for reflection.

Let me begin by stating that this journal is based on the testimony of a sole individual. I have written his story as a narrative, as Mr Dickens may have done, as I consider it the most effective way of showing you what did, or should I say, will, happen. I have used creative licence to bridge, and subsequently, embellish, the gaps in my knowledge. So, in some sections that follow, I am taking a literary liberty - but it is with a guided sincerity that I do so. You will also be unfamiliar with some of the late twenty-first century terminology, but darling, you are an acute woman. I write, describing the period in which this account is set, as precisely as I can. If I find myself with enough spare paper, although they have only given me what looks to be one hundred or so sheets and one pot of ink, I will add an appendix, listing the innovations and giving an explanation to their particular purpose.

In the future many novels featuring fictional time travel tales will be published; I have read many and enjoyed few. The most notable, is, naturally, Mr Wells' 'The Time Machine'. I must say that I hardly know the man and have certainly not discussed the subject with him at any great length. I therefore, in the event that these pages are discovered after my death, wish to distance myself completely from any similarities; the most distinguishing feature being of course, his is fantasy, whereas my story is, for the most part, factual (I will say that I did take great pleasure in his book).

Like Mr Wells, I was trained in the sciences, as you know, but unlike Mr Wells I do not feel I am a natural to the art of writing, although I will attempt to be as florid and descriptive as possible. I have learnt much from reading twentieth and twenty-first century 'classics'.

It was in a back-street drinking establishment over the course of two weeks that he told his story. When we first met he had been there all day, for in the future it is legal, and indeed encouraged, to frequent the parlours, or 'bars' as they are known, twenty-four hours of the day. At that point I had already enjoyed many trips into the future, always assured that I could return to you a few moments after I left. The past held little interest to me, although I did go back and observe Boyle, Newton, Lavoisier and Volta. I yearned to see what was to come, what was to be. I spent a great deal of time immersing myself in the culture, marvelling and witnessing the innovations that were to come: the automobile, the aeroplane, the advances in medicine and science, the atomic bomb, and the Internet. They put people on the moon and Mars.

Initially, I had wanted to visit myself forty years hence, but the mechanics of the capsule were not, at first, as specific as I had hoped, and on that opening journey I found myself wandering unknown streets, *dressed incongruously*, in a *very* unfamiliar time.

But now to my final adventure, for it is that which I wish to illustrate for you.

1

Through the recently cleaned pane of glass of a second floor bedroom window of a semi-detached house, a young woman looked out, peering left and right.

Kristina was waiting for Tobias, her boyfriend. He was always late, she was used to that, and although she thought that if you were purposefully waiting for someone or something to arrive, it would take longer, she still did so, whilst checking her long red hair for split ends.

The large round numbered clock on her yellow painted bedroom wall struck a quarter past six. She killed time, as she stood by the window, listening to music on the digital radio that she had been given at Yuletide. She hummed along to each song irrespective of genre or style.

After cutting off a strand of damaged hair she was shocked to see a familiar figure walking up the quiet suburban street on which she and her parents lived. The man was middle-aged with black hair that was side-parted harshly. He wore a pair of brown-rimmed glasses and was dressed in a smart two-piece dark grey suit with a white shirt and blue tie. He appeared, for all intent and purpose, to be an office worker on his way home from work, but she had seen him before. First, just out of the corner of her eye at a store; then, sitting a few rows back on the bus as she travelled to college; nothing significant, coincidence maybe, but he'd begun appearing more notably; brushing past her in a crowded shop, holding her gaze whilst striding down the opposite side of the street, and now here he was, strolling, with apparent nonchalance, past her home.

Apprehension swept through her. Kristina immediately took a step back, but lent forward just enough to be able to observe. The man continued on; Kristina assumed he was going to go by. She moved closer to the window, but he suddenly, gazed up, and with a friendly confident smile, waved. Surprised and scared she jumped away and sat down on her bed. Every day, she thought to herself. Weirdo. She bit her fingernails considering, as she chewed, what to do. Kristina looked at herself in the mirror. She could see why someone would want to stalk her. She was always getting asked out and had done some modelling in the past, but this was a little creepy. She should tell her parents, but maybe that was over-reacting. Perhaps she should be flattered. She edged herself to the window; the man had moved on and was now at the top of the road. Kristina's attention focused back on her boyfriend as Tobias' red Ford came into view, passing the man and speeding up to her house. The vehicle slid to a stop. She smiled, the unwanted attention from the stranger promptly forgotten. Rushing downstairs she shouted goodbye to her parents who were watching television in the living room. "Don't be late," her mother called back. Kristina replied by slamming the front door behind her.

Outside she couldn't help but take a look to see where the man was; he was still at the end of the street, just about to go around the corner and out of her line of vision. In that moment he twisted, and made direct eye contact. Kristina was transfixed and a sharp shiver of discontent shot through her body. She quickly broke the stare and hopped into the car.

"Hey." Tobias turned down the music blaring from his player and attempted to give Kristina a kiss on the lips. She didn't respond. "Are you okay? Sorry I'm late."

"What?"

"A kiss?"

"Oh, sorry." She leant over and gave him a peck on the cheek.

"Is that it?"

"Did you see that guy? You passed him."

Tobias looked to where Kristina was pointing, but there was no one there. "I didn't see anyone."

"The one in the grey suit?"

Tobias smiled. "Nope." He put the car in gear and slammed his foot down on the accelerator.

"Oh, you're useless." She glanced around. He had gone.

"I thought we could go up to the cliffs?"

"Yeah, if you like. No funny business, Mr!"

"Oh, would I try anything like that?"

They shot each other mischievous smiles.

As they got closer to the sea they saw the sun disappearing on the horizon, turning the sky crimson.

Tobias drove them to their usual secluded spot, half way down a dirt track that cut alongside a farmer's field and overlooked the English Channel. In-between unkempt trees and bushes they embraced under the approaching night sky.

Kristina sighed as she broke away from Tobias' lips. "Mmm, this is almost perfect."

"Almost?" Tobias moved in for another kiss.

She giggled. "Yes, almost!"

"What can I do to make it perfect?"

"Well, it would be nice if we had our own place, or at least somewhere more comfortable to go."

"Yeah, I know. My parents are a bit strict about this sort of thing and we know what your parents are like!"

"Hmm. Anyway, never mind that right now."

The two once again embraced, rapt in each other, their lips locked with fervour.

It was a brief few seconds of snapping branches that tore their bodies apart.

"What was that?" Kristina asked, wide-eyed and wary.

"Probably a fox or something." Tobias wound down the passenger side window and stared out into the woods behind them. "I can't see anything. We must have been here for ages."

Kristina checked her watch. "We have!" She brushed back her matted hair. "I guess we should get going."

"Yeah, I guess." Tobias tucked his shirt back into his jeans.

As they were composing themselves, the car shook with a sudden violent vibration. Something had hit it. They both looked in the wing mirrors and out of the windows. It was then that Kristina saw the man, *that* man, heading towards the driver's door with his fists clenched and his eyes glazed over with fierce insanity.

Kristina urged to Tobias to lock his door. The tone of her voice made him do as he was told; he fumbled for the catch, but he was not quick enough. The door was ripped open. Tobias was effortlessly hauled from the vehicle and thrown on to the sandy earth.

"Tobias!"

The man snarled at Kristina and pointed a stiff finger at her. "You're mine!" His eyes seemed to be on fire, two spheres of deep red burning in his skull.

Kristina could do nothing; she had frozen in fear. Tobias pulled himself off the ground and valiantly, and without thought, launched himself at the man. The assailant twisted from the car and turned his attention to Tobias. He grabbed the boy by the neck and flung him back into the driver's seat. By this time Kristina had willed herself to come to her boyfriend's aid. The man felt Kristina's light blows on his back. Half turning, and with one hand, he shoved her, sending her flying at least ten metres into some bushes, which abruptly broke her fall. The man leaned over Tobias, evading his desperate attempts at attack, and released the handbrake. He punched Tobias hard in the face, slammed the door shut and made his way to the rear of the vehicle, where he gave it a kick, denting the bumper. It began to roll. From among the nettles and bracken Kristina could only watch in horror as the car went over the edge of the cliff. There was no explosion, just an enormous crash that sent birds flying from the trees.

The man began to advance on Kristina, whose trembling body, filled with absolute terror, was attempting to get out of the undergrowth. "You're mine!" His mouth was foaming and his eyes were flaming. "You're mine!"

∞

Every story has to start somewhere. This is where I have chosen to begin. How it relates to the rest of the tale will become apparent later. This section, like others to come, is one I have left my own imagination to construct, based on what I was told. I cannot be certain that it actually took place as I have written, but nobody, except those present, would know what really happened on that terrible night.

Now, to return to the tale and once again I adopt the style contemporary to the period of which I write; it now seems to come quite naturally to me.

2

The heat permeated every pore of the skin, producing droplets of perspiration that glistened in the midday sun. Dan stood, dressed in cut off jeans and a khaki coloured shirt, wiping the stinging sweat from his brow. He watched his fellow workers shovelling earth. They'd been here three weeks now, contracted to excavate a large, remote area of jungle in Thailand, where road access for heavy machinery was impossible. Whilst his colleagues dug and shifted soil with no knowledge of reason, he did know, or at least thought he knew. Unlike some of the others he hadn't been indentured in a seedy bar, nor was he a gap year traveller or a down on his luck local. He'd purposefully signed on, hoping that what was being searched for would not be found.

"Hey dude, are you taking a break?" Jones asked, one of the ten men and women at work.

"What?"

Jones shook her head, unhooked a bottle attached to her belt and took a gulp of water. "Dan, you can be one distant dude sometimes."

Dan lunged his shovel into the soil. "Sorry, miles away."

"Yeah me too, miles away from home that is. Still, with the money we're making here, I'll soon be back!"

"Where's home again?"

"Detroit," she replied, with a wide gap toothed grin, "motor city. Well, was once."

"Never been to the States." Dan piled a heap of dirt at the top of their trench. "I've been everywhere else, but not the States."

"You gotta, gotta go. Come over and visit! I know everybody."

Dan chuckled to himself. "I will, I will."

"Now that's a promise, right?"

He shook his head at Jones' ardour. "Of course."

"If it wasn't for getting caught with that ganja at the airport by those damn 3D image scanners, I'd be there right now with my man. We'd be in a downtown bar drinking." Jones paused. "And, well, you know."

"Sure."

"Hey, you got anyone special back home in Engerland?"

"Nah, I move around a lot."

"That loner baloney went out years ago, Dan."

"You're a great teacher."

"You bet I am."

Dan shook his head again.

Out of the jungle, an open top jeep came into sight, driven by a woman in her late twenties. She had long blonde hair that was scraped back into a ponytail and matched her golden tanned skin; she was wearing dark brown shorts and a white shirt, unbuttoned to her chest, with sleeves rolled up high on her arms.

"Hey, there's that Anya," Jones remarked.

Dan nodded and watched. She parked and headed into the archaeologists' camp, which had been named Gath. It consisted of a congregation of twelve large tents from where they lived and worked. The labourers' camp was situated on the edge of the site, where they'd been hidden away like second-class citizens.

"She looks stressed," Dan replied.

"Wouldn't you be if you were hired to find something and hadn't found it?"

Dan and Jones watched Anya through the gaps between the huge canvas tents. The site's osteologist, Clarke, a bearded, slightly overweight Englishman, approached her. He indicated to a large wooden bench in the centre of the camp. Anya's shoulders dropped and she held one hand to her temple. She wore no make-up, it was pointless in this environment, but she was naturally beautiful. Cosmetics would have detracted from her innate charm. After a few seconds she looked up, wearily nodded her head, and accompanied Clarke. Dan's eyes followed the pair over to a laptop that was open on the table. Anya saw her two employers' faces staring out at her from the paper-thin monitor. Dan looked intently at Anya, who had her arms crossed defensively. He cautiously concentrated hard, examining her moving lips....

"Good morning Dr Roberts," began one of the men, who called himself Lowell.

"Hello," she replied, her intonation South American. She tried to express a smile after her greeting.

The two men were, as always, dressed in black suits. They quickly engaged in a heated discussion.

"Three weeks isn't a great deal of time," Anya tried to explain to the other man on the screen, Keller, as he questioned her about the project's lack of progress.

"But what about the months of preparation and planning, Dr Roberts?" Lowell asked. The shorter of the two, his angular face jutted forwards.

"Our employer, the man who is paying you Dr Roberts, is understandably very disturbed at this continued delay."

Anya rubbed her forehead in frustration. "Look." She picked up and unfolded a map. "There is this area. It's a little off the original information you and your boss gave us, we'd have to run some preliminary geophysical tests...."

"Excellent, Dr Roberts." Keller said. Lowell gave him an approving nod. "You must open a trench there immediately."

"Well, what about the current ones?" she asked, taken aback by their vehemence.

"Close them. I'm...." Lowell paused. "We're sure this is it, Dr Roberts."

"Look, I've never been involved in such a bizarre...."

"Dr Roberts, aren't you being paid extremely well?"

"The money wasn't what attracted me to this project."

"No," Lowell mocked, "of course it wasn't."

"Keep us informed, Dr Roberts."

Keller and Lowell's unnerving image lingered for a few seconds on the monitor before disappearing.

"Maybe they know something we don't?" Clarke said, in his thick West Country accent.

"Who knows?" Anya closed the laptop. "But they've certainly put some effort into this, assembling the world's foremost archaeologists with all the most up-to-date technology."

Clarke nodded his head. "And despite that we still haven't found anything!"

"This is a large site."

"Yes, but they seem to know that we're looking in the wrong places."

Anya kicked at the soil. "Well, perhaps we're finally getting somewhere."

"Hey you." Dan looked up. An outline was blocking the sun. It was one of the other archaeologists, a Frenchman named Larouche. "You're not paid to stare into space."

Dan smiled at him. "I think you're going to be called any second."

"Mr Larouche." Larouche glanced over his shoulder to see Anya hurriedly making her way towards him. "We're opening another trench."

"Huh? Another one? When?"

"Right now. We're stopping all other digging."

Anya and Dan exchanged glances as she reached Larouche's side.

Jones wiped her face. "Phew, glad to get a break."

"All right men, women," Larouche said. The other workers threw down their tools and began ascending from the shallow channel.

"Will you help me mark out the new area?" Anya asked Larouche.

"Naturally."

"Need any help?" Dan asked, climbing out of the ditch.

"No," Anya snapped. "Sorry, I mean, no thank you. You can all take a break whilst we mark out the new trench," she said, addressing the other workers, before giving Dan one final fleeting look and heading, map in hand, further into the jungle.

"I'm sure she likes you really." Jones gave Dan a slap on the back. "Come on, time to play some cards."

The setting sun turned the day to dusk, which was now slowly turning to night. The site was lit with solar-powered lights and burning torches that sent shadows dancing on the surrounding dense foliage. Dan stood at the edge of the camp looking out into the formidable forest. He played with the cigarette in his hand, running it in-between and over his fingers.

"Do you smoke?" asked a light feminine voice from behind him.

Dan turned to see Anya walking towards him. "Not usually." He flicked the cigarette away.

"I don't mind."

"Just needed something to do with my hands."

"Oh?"

"I don't like sitting around doing nothing."

"Don't you get tired?"

"Sometimes."

"We'll have to work you harder." Anya smiled and began to turn away.

"Would you like a beer?"

"Beer? Where did you get that from?"

"One of the others paid the guy who delivers the supplies from the village to bring them in."

"I wondered why you lot weren't complaining about these conditions that much."

"The heat?"

"And the rest."

"So, beer?"

She considered his proposal for a few seconds. "Okay, if you're offering."

"I'm offering."

Anya smiled again. Dan walked to his tent, lifted the canvas flap and from a cooler box packed with ice, pulled out two bottles of beer. He uncapped the bottles with a sharp twist and passed one to her.

"Thanks." Anya took a swig. Dan did so as well, watching her wipe her mouth as some of the liquid escaped the seal between her lips and the rim. "That's good." She dried her hands on her tan coloured shirt.

"It sure is," Dan said, holding the bottle up and noticing he'd already necked half the contents. "Quite beautiful." He took a none-too-subtle glance at her legs.

"Pardon?"

"Thailand. The jungle," Dan said, covering his remark and pointing out towards the vegetation.

She swatted a mosquito. "Yes, I suppose. So, what brings a man like you out to a place like this?"

"Money?"

"I can't believe that. We, they, pay a pittance."

"True. Perhaps I'm interested in archaeology?"

"Are you?"

Dan shrugged his shoulders, took another swig of beer and held Anya's gaze. "Maybe, more than I was." She blushed and ran her finger up the bottle, catching a bead of condensation running down it. "What about you? I hear the money is good for you guys."

"How would you know that?"

"People talk."

"Right…. Well, I assure you, I'm here strictly for the archaeology."

"I heard that too. Anyway, who are they?"

"Huh?"

"You said *they* pay a pittance."

"These two guys, they call themselves Lowell and Keller. I thought you would have known that too?"

"Oh, I know their names, but who are they?"

Anya scuffed the surface of the soil with her right boot. "I'm not too sure. You seem to be pretty clued up, what else do you know?"

"What we're here to find."

Anya almost choked on her mouthful of beer. "How do you

know that? The labourers weren't told. Only a few of us know and we're all sworn to secrecy."

"I wish I hadn't said anything."

Anya moved closer to him, her eyes widened; she looked aggrieved and surprised at Dan's knowledge. "Has someone talked?"

"No."

Dan thought back to the conversations he'd overheard and the information that had brought him to Thailand in the first place. Anya continued to stare into his eyes, trying to see either the truth or lies behind them. She couldn't tell. But she did see something there, and what she saw was darkness. She nervously took a step back.

"What?" Dan noticed Anya's face turn from anger to alarm.

"You know...." She turned towards the jungle and swilled the remaining beer around in its bottle. "I grew up in Sonora in Mexico."

"Nice country."

"You've been?"

"Yes, once, no twice, it was a few years ago."

"Oh. Anyway, when I was a little girl I'd watch my grandmother practising Candomblé, slaughtering chickens as an offering to Olodumare. I saw the same look in the eyes of those women and men possessed as I do in yours." Dan didn't say anything. "You're surprised?"

"I am."

"I was three when I left. My father, he was Amercian, won custody of me, but I rememeber what I saw, that look...."

"I'm not sure what to say."

Anya smiled. "There's something else to you, isn't there?"

"Maybe."

"Maybe?"

"Yeah. So what else can you tell me about this dig?"

"You know I can't tell you anything."

"Apparently so, but not even...." He raised his now empty bottle. "Two friends, over a beer?"

"Friends? I hardly know you."

"We can change that, I'm sure." Dan went in closer.

"Anya."

They turned to see Larouche marching towards them.

"Where did you get that?" Larouche asked, pointing at the bottle of beer Dan was holding.

"The beer?"

"Yes, the beer."

13

"The beer tree?"

"Don't take that tone of voice with me."

"It's okay, Claude." Anya downed the last of the liquid. "A couple of beers aren't going to end the world."

Larouche shot Dan a look of disdain. "Right. They're online."

"Lowell and Keller?" Dan asked.

"How do you know?"

"He doesn't know anything." Anya handed Dan her empty bottle. "I'd better not keep them waiting." She brushed past Larouche, leaving him and Dan to outstare each other.

"Remember you're only here to dig."

Dan nodded slowly.

The two men parted, Larouche heading back to Gath, and Dan to his tent.

Dan took out another bottle of beer from the cooler, opened it and took a mouthful. He faced the forest again and allowed himself to think of his past, but he blinked quickly, dropping the shades on those memories. Then the thought of Anya entered his head and of what she had said. At least there didn't seem to be anything sinister about her. Possibly she didn't realise the implications of what they were here to find. He wondered if his admission would compromise his position on the dig. Anya hadn't mentioned it to Larouche, but she could have done and still might do. Perhaps, he hoped, she had taken a shine to him. He had to remind himself that he wasn't there for romance, although he couldn't help trying to initiate something.

It had become dark. Dan, now with a half empty whiskey bottle in his hand, looked out on the glade and listened intently to the nighttime sounds of the jungle. He thought that he should've followed Anya and Larouche back to their camp to hear what Lowell and Keller had to say. The sudden halt in digging earlier in the day had been playing on his mind. Lowell and Keller had seemed almost too optimistic that the new trench would yield. Tomorrow could bring the project to its end. They could uncover what they'd been looking for, and Dan didn't quite know what he was going to do if they did.

3

Melted ice water, thrown from the cooler box, woke Dan. He bolted upright.

"Hey," Jones said, "get up."

Dan groaned, pulled himself up from the now wet sheet he'd been sleeping under and saw her at the entrance to his tent.

"Had one too many of those beers I got you?"

"A few, and a bottle of whiskey or two."

Jones laughed. "Man, I don't know how you do it. Well, it's time to get to work. You missed breakfast."

"You could have woken me earlier."

"What? Do I look like your maid?"

"No, of course not. Sorry."

"Aw, I saved you a couple of sausages actually." She handed him a paper towel parcel.

"Cheers, Jones, I appreciate it." Dan took and unwrapped it. Inside were two lukewarm sausages. He picked one up and began to eat.

"Not the best in the world, and I dare not think what the meat might be." Dan smiled at her between chews. "But what do I care? Anyway, better hurry up, there's a buzz about the place."

"Right."

"See you in a minute?"

"Yeah, in a minute."

Jones left. Dan finished the sausages and laid back down on his camp bed, closed his eyes and wondered what the day would bring.

When Dan joined the others fifteen minutes later, he saw that the new trench had been marked out with red spray paint on the ground. Dan spotted Anya talking with Clarke and Larouche; she gave him the briefest of glances before returning her eyes to the map they were studying.

"What's the hold up?" Dan asked Jones, who was playing cards with some of the other labourers.

"Geophys has broken. You would have thought they'd surveyed that area when they first arrived."

Dan checked out Jones' hand and pointed to the jack of diamonds. "I don't think it was on their original map. We're on the edge of the main site."

"Thanks. How do you know that?" She placed the card down on the wooden box they were sitting around, and won the game to the frustration of her opponents.

"Must've overheard it."

Before they could start digging, the new area had to be geophysed. An H-shaped frame walked over the ground would take magnetic images and create a map showing outlines of anything beneath the surface. A solid concentration of activity would indicate the best place to open a trench.

"Any idea how long it's going to take?"

"They haven't said anything. Oh, is it just me or is it really hot today, hotter than normal?"

Dan wiped the sweat from the back of his neck. "Every day is hot."

"Yeah, ain't that true." Jones dealt out the cards to four others.

"You're not cheatin' are you, Jones?" Antonio asked, one of the labourers.

"Hey, what do you mean?"

Antonio pointed at Dan. "Just that every time he turns up, you win."

"He must bring me luck," she replied, sorting out her hand.

Dan took a look at them. "And she's got another good one guys."

"Oh what!" Antonio flung his cards down on the box.

Dan smiled, stepped past them and headed towards the marked out trench. He squatted down and picked up a handful of soil.

"Hey you!" It was Larouche. Dan looked up to see the Frenchman bearing down on him. "What do you think you're doing?" Dan let out an exasperated sigh, shook his head, and let the soil fall through his fingers; he stood and faced Larouche. "What are you doing?"

"Is there a problem?" Dan asked, trying to cover his irritation.

Larouche squared up to him. "Your attitude."

"*My* attitude?"

"Yeah, I've been watching you."

"I'm flattered."

"What?"

"Claude," Clarke said, appearing behind the Frenchman, engrossed in the PDA in his hands and unaware of the confrontation, "take a look at these readings."

"Geophys fixed?" Dan asked.

"Oh, yes, yes," Clarke said. Larouche took the PDA without breaking eye contact with Dan. "We can finally get the trench dug!"

"Maybe some hard work under this scorching sun will knock some respect into you."

Dan didn't reply. He turned away and went back to his fellow workers.

Half an hour later Dan, Jones and the others excavated the ground, as the archaeologists patiently looked on.

The sun glared down, the temperature was well over forty degrees and the heat was taking its toll. A few, including Antonio, had reached a point of exhaustion and sat in the shade of the jungle's trees. Dan, Jones and four others continued to shift soil.

"Hey," Anya said. She stood over Dan offering him a bottle of water. He took it.

"Cheers." Twisting the cap off, he took a large mouthful and then passed it along to Jones.

"There's more if you want."

"I know we've been going through them."

"Don't want you getting dehydrated. This heat is unbearable."

"Tell us about it," Jones said.

"Are you sure you can continue?"

"This is what we're paid to do."

Just as Dan finished his sentence another labourer collapsed. Dan and Jones rushed to help the man, a young Scot called Andy who, like Jones, had served time for drug possession.

"That's it," Clarke yelled, throwing his arms up in the air and walking towards the trench, "these conditions are not acceptable."

"That's what they're paid for."

"Don't be ridiculous, Claude."

"And what do you think they will say?"

"Look, it's up to Anya, she's the team leader."

Larouche and Clarke turned to Anya who wiped the sweat from her face. She looked at Dan and the remaining workers.

"Okay, let's take a break."

"What about Lowell and Keller?" Larouche replied.

"I'll deal with them." Anya began walking towards the camp.

"On your head be it."

Dan gave Larouche a broad smile. Larouche's face contorted. Dan thought he was going to say something, but he clenched his teeth and headed back to Gath. Dan climbed out of the six-foot deep hole, picked up a half full bottle of water and poured the sun-warmed contents over his head.

"How is he?" he asked Jones, who was tending to Andy.

"He'll be all right."

"Bring him over to our medical tent," Clarke said.

"Okay." Jones put one of Andy's arms over her shoulder and Dan took the other one over his.

The pair followed Clarke into the camp. Larouche watched Dan and Jones haul Andy into the medical tent, where he joined two others.

"Thank you. I'll see to him," Clarke said.

"Right," Dan replied.

Ducking down to leave the tent, Dan stopped and waited for Jones to join him. Then they both had a good look around the usually off-limits encampment.

"Almost like a home away from home," Jones said.

Aside from the medical tent, there was a small shower block, and a canteen, which had a metal chimney poking out through the canvas roof, with a row of benches outside; the labourers, in contrast, were served from pots on an unsteady table. A small solar-powered generator hummed smoothly. There were also two shacks that had 'men' and 'women' written across their wooden panels in chalk; the hired hands took their chances in a designated jungle clearing. Dan saw Anya standing next to a wooden bench on which various pieces of equipment were scattered. She stared into a computer monitor.

"Oi!" Larouche shouted, annoyed at their presence.

Jones smirked. "I think he means you." Dan sighed.

"Get out of here," he said, flinging his arms in the air.

Jones shook her head at Larouche's attitude. "Come on."

Dan stood his ground. He was watching Anya who was fiddling with the laptop, presumably trying to put a video call though to Keller and Lowell. He wanted to get a look at them. But the oncoming frame of Larouche blocked his view.

"Are you deaf? Get out of here." He pointed towards the exit.

Dan twisted, winked at Jones, then turned swiftly back and punched Larouche in the jaw. He flew backwards, landing on the ground. Everyone in the compound looked on.

"Nice punch, dude," Jones said, slapping Dan on the back.

Larouche squirmed in pain, holding the right side of his face where Dan's clenched fist had impacted.

"What do you think you're doing?" Anya cried, rushing over to Larouche.

Dan noticed behind her that the connection to Lowell and Keller had been made and the two men were staring out, wondering what was going on.

"He deserved it," Jones remarked.

Anya stared at Dan. Clarke and two other archaeologists helped Larouche to his feet.

"You're off this dig!" Larouche shouted. He spat out some blood. "And don't think you're getting paid!"

Anya examined her colleague's wound and then looked up at Dan. "You'd better go."

"Come on, man," Jones muttered.

As they left Dan took a final glance towards the laptop; the two faces of Lowell and Keller gazed intently out, questioning what was going on. Their mouths moved, but the volume was muted.

"He was asking for that," Jones said, "if you're going to go out, go out in style."

"Yeah, I guess."

"What's wrong?" You're not going to miss this place are you?"

"No, but I shouldn't have done that."

"Why not? The job?"

"No, shouldn't have let him provoke me." He paused, as if he were searching. "But I did enjoy it, maybe a bit too much."

"Ah, don't worry about it. I'm going to miss you, though, but you're going out a hero! We all wanted to sock that guy!"

Back with the other workers Jones wasted no time in telling them about the incident. They all cheered and laughed as Jones re-enacted the event, the gleeful noise no doubt reaching Larouche's ears over in Gath.

After a few minutes of frivolity, Dan and Jones broke off from the group and walked back to Dan's tent.

"Well, it was great to know you." Jones held out her hand.

"You too."

"Are you leaving now?"

"As soon as I'm packed."

"In this heat?"

"I'll be okay. It's not far to the village. I'll put an order in for some more beer to come with the next supply truck."

"Okay, we'd all appreciate that."

"I hope you make it back to the States."

"Oh, I will, and if you ever find yourself over there, look me up."

"I will."

The pair hugged.

"Take care, dude." Jones pulled away and clapped him on the arm.

"You too."

Jones turned and made her way back. Smiling, Dan went into his tent. Wiping the sweat away from his face, he resigned himself to packing, and the walk to the village. He looked down at the icebox and wished he still had some beer left. He picked up his rucksack and began putting his meagre possessions inside.

A short controlled cough made him glance up. Anya stood at the entrance to his tent.

"That was stupid thing to do." Dan didn't respond. "Really stupid."

"What did Lowell and Keller say?"

"They're not interested in a pathetic spat. They want that trench dug."

"I bet."

"We're going to do it tonight, it will be cooler."

"Good idea. What did the geophys come up with?"

"It's looking good. Although, it looked good before and we only found animal bones."

"And what if you find what you're looking for?"

"Well, we'll be able to prove their existence beyond doubt. What would be so wrong with that?" Dan again remained quiet and carried on packing. "Why are you here?" Anya asked.

"I don't know. What does it matter? Let's just say I had a personal interest."

"A personal interest? I don't understand."

"It's better that you don't." He pulled the drawstring on his now full rucksack.

"Where will you go?" Anya enquired, even though she sensed he wasn't going to elaborate any further.

"Anywhere. Home."

"And where's home?"

"A long way away."

"Okay. Look, I reckon I could get you back on board."

"Don't bother."

"You do the work of two men, financially you being here makes sense."

"Right."

"Fine, well I think I can get you your pay at least." Dan nodded and put the remainder of his things into the external pockets of the bag. "I'm going to miss you," she said, half to get his attention away from his packing and half because she meant it.

Dan looked into her dark brown eyes. "Yeah," he replied, acknowledging her admission as his own.

Anya moved closer. She stared up at the man in front of her. He was at least six and a half feet tall, his short hair dark brown with red flecks that appeared natural rather than dyed. His physique was impressive, muscle under taut skin. His face was solid with razor sharp blue eyes that she knew concealed mystery. Acting on instinct she drew herself up on her tiptoes and kissed his lips, wrapping an arm around the back of his neck to hold herself to him. She broke away when Dan's warm, chapped lips didn't reply. Anya looked at him again, wondering why he didn't react. Dan met her eyes and ran a conciliatory hand through her hair.

"I...." he said, looking for words that wouldn't come.

Anya moved forward again and kissed him. Dan, who had thought about Anya's touch for weeks, couldn't help but embrace her, his concupiscent nature taking over. It wasn't long before the pair fell back on to Dan's camp bed. Outside, in the shade, the workers played cards, a few tried to tune a radio into a station, and the sun was as unrelenting as ever.

After spending the majority of the afternoon gambling, the labourers, who had agreed to start the new trench in the relative cool of the evening, finally began digging. The camp was lit by filament and flame. Larouche, his mouth swollen from the earlier fracas, stood beside the hole with Clarke. The geophys suggested that there was a level of high resistance, a dark patch on the PDA screen, around ten feet from the surface. Jones and the others, including those who had suffered from exhaustion earlier in the day, dug into the earth.

"Careful now," Clarke said, pacing around.

"Of course," Antonio replied, "we're professionals."

The men and women laughed.

"Enough of that!" Larouche said through his bruised jaw.

"Hey, you cut yourself shaving?" Jones asked.

Everyone laughed again.

"Shut up, shut up all of you!"

"Mr Larouche," Anya said, walking towards the ditch.

"Where have you been, Anya?" Clarke asked. "We were worried."

"Just...." She paused, thinking of an excuse. "Just tidying up some loose ends. What's the problem?"

"Nothing," Larouche said, watching the labourers work.

"Good. We wouldn't want to lose any more hard working people."

Larouche didn't respond. He just stood, trowel in hand, waiting for something to be uncovered.

The excavating continued for some time. Clarke tried to engage Anya in a discussion but she was a million miles away. Larouche had abandoned his trench-side vigil and was trying to chat up one of their younger female colleagues.

"I've hit something," Andy suddenly shouted.

Larouche swiftly broke away from his conversation with the girl. "Everyone stop," he ordered.

Anya and Clarke both took deep breaths and looked down into the hole.

"Let me see." Larouche descended the nine-foot depth on the ladder propped up inside the trench. He dropped to his knees and started scraping away at the spot Andy pointed to.

"What have you got?" Clarke asked.

"Hang on." The Frenchman continued unearthing as everyone watched on. "Yes, we have something. Everyone out." The workers climbed out. As always they were replaced when the interesting stuff occurred.

"What have you got?" Clarke asked again.

"I think it's a skull."

"Wonderful!"

"We've seen that before," Anya said.

Larouche stood, so that the pair could see. The torch that lit the area revealed the vault of a cranium.

"Looks promising," Clarke commented, rubbing his hands together.

"Interesting," Anya said, "we might be on to something, at last."

"Just a few more minutes and I think I'll have it." Larouche guided the trowel around the bone, slowly exposing more.

"Be careful!" Clarke told him.

Larouche glanced up. "I have done this before."

"Yes, yes, of course."

Everyone stood waiting to see what Larouche would uncover.

"It is a skull and it's gigantic."

"I can't believe it," Anya replied.

The workers looked on, oblivious to what was being discovered.

"This could be the archaeological find of the," Clarke said, "well, *the* archaeological find."

"I've got it, I've got it!" Larouche delicately lifted the bones from the ground. "It's perfect!"

"Oh my," Anya said.

"Careful!" Clarke said, moving forward and bending down to take the object from Larouche.

The labourers were now talking amongst themselves, amazed at what they were seeing before them.

"Goliath…." Clarke muttered, but he was interrupted by an anxious voice from behind them.

Dan emerged from the jungle. "What have you found?"

"What are you doing here?" Clarke asked.

Anya looked surprised. "Dan."

"Dan!" Jones exclaimed.

"What have you found?" he asked, his tone grave and serious.

"You? What are you doing here?" Larouche said, climbing out of the ditch.

"What have you found?" he repeated, but then he saw the large humanoid skull in Clarke's hands. "Oh no."

There was a silence as everyone looked on in amazement. Then, from the forest, a succession of rustles emanated, and two men emerged from the night. It was Lowell and Keller.

"What are you two doing here?" Anya said, shocked at the men's sudden and unexpected appearance.

"Good evening, Dr Roberts," Keller replied. They trod out from the undergrowth.

"Where did you come from?" Clarke asked.

"We've been waiting for this moment," Lowell told them.

Anya was lost for words. "Yes, but…."

"This is what we've been looking for, Dr Roberts," Keller said.

"We know that," Larouche replied, equally surprised to see the two men.

Lowell laughed. He pointed at the skull. "This hoax?"

"Hoax?"

"A bit elaborate but needs must. Events are, quickly, coming to pass," Keller said. "Our plans are falling behind."

"What are you talking about?" Anya asked, confused at the situation unfolding in front of her.

"Yes, we've been hunting for lost treasure, haven't we… *Daniel*. We had to be sure it was you." Lowell's eyes burned into Dan's. Everyone was focused on them. Dan broke Lowell's gaze and cursed.

"What are you talking about?" Larouche asked.

But Lowell and Keller weren't interested in answering any more questions. The charade was over.

"Men!" Lowell shouted. At his order twenty or so figures, masked, dressed in black and armed with machine guns, appeared from the darkness and encircled the area.

"What is going on?" Anya demanded.

The other archaeologists and the labourers stood bewildered and frightened.

Keller looked firmly at Dan. "We've found what we've been looking for."

"Take him alive," Lowell ordered. "No one else leaves."

4

Dan dropped to one knee and with his right hand swept up a handful of dirt from the ground. As he rose, he blew on the soil sending a cloud of earth spiralling outwards, blinding those round him. He grabbed Anya's arm and she watched in amazement as he absorbed the flame from one of the torches around the perimeter of the camp into his palm, and sent it, high-powered and white-hot, into the trench where it exploded. He then dragged Anya towards her jeep, as Lowell and Keller's men started firing.

"Alive remember," Lowell shouted.

Dan and Anya didn't look back as they made for the vehicle; he moved with determination, Anya staying close behind him out of fear. Reaching the jeep they threw themselves into the front seats. Dan grabbed Anya's hand. She screamed. He extended her forefinger and pressed it on to the ignition screen. The engine turned over. He slammed his foot down on the accelerator. The vehicle leapt forward, but not fast enough to outrun the torrent of bullets that rained down on it.

Dan cried out in pain. Anya saw him clutching his right shoulder, blood trickling through the gaps between his fingers.

"They shot you. That's blood. Oh my God," she spluttered.

As they sped away they could hear the screams and desperate pleas of those left behind over short controlled bursts of gunfire.

The speeding jeep hugged the narrow jungle dirt track, with Dan turning the steering wheel one handed.

"They'll be coming after us," Dan warned a still shocked Anya. "Damn." He punched the wheel. "I shouldn't have been so...."

"What?" Anya said. "What is going on? Who are you? What happened back there?"

"Are you okay?"

"Okay?" She tried to catch her breath. "Just what the hell is going on? How did you do that with the flame?" He stayed silent, glancing into the rear-view mirror. "Who are you?"

Dan took his eyes off the road. Her face was twisted in torment. He wondered how he could answer that in a single sentence whilst driving one handed at speed through dense Thai jungle, probably being pursued by gunmen. It had taken him years to find out and to come to terms with the knowledge of his true self. He wished he could explain it to her. "I know you have questions. But can we make some distance between us and them first?"

Anya just stared at him, then nodded. She settled back, wiped the perspiration from her face, and then noticed that Dan was now driving with both hands. The wound to his shoulder had stopped bleeding; it appeared to have almost healed.

They weren't far enough away, he thought, but the jeep's electric-powered battery had run down.

Dan surveyed the area as Anya sat rigid in the passenger seat. "Well, I think we may have crossed into the Erawan National Park. Would you mind getting out so I can get this thing off the track?"

Anya slid silently out and stood arms folded as she watched Dan manoeuvre the vehicle into a line of trees. It disappeared into the undergrowth.

"Come on, we've got to keep moving. We'll head up into the mountains. That should give us a good vantage point to see if anyone is following, and it'll make it harder to be tracked. I'm glad you had a torch." Dan started to walk but sensed Anya wasn't. "Come." He held out his hand.

"I'm not going another millimetre until I get some answers."

Dan sighed. "This isn't the time, but what I can tell you is that those men back there will kill us."

"Me maybe, but not you." Anya strode past, indicating to his shoulder.

Dan glanced down at the wound that was now just a scar. He flicked the torch on and they began to make their way towards the base of the mountain.

The pair hiked slowly forwards in silence. The path they were attempting to follow was slight and precarious. Both of them struggled in the dimness, as gravel and rocks slipped beneath their feet. The one saving grace was that they couldn't see how far down they'd fall if they went over.

"How long have we been walking for?" Anya asked, breaking the quiet.

"I'm not sure, a few hours?"

She dropped to her knees. "I'm so tired, and confused."

"Come on, we must keep moving."

"Why?"

"Because they'll kill us."

"Who are they?"

"You wouldn't believe me if I told you." Dan looked down at Anya's exhausted face. "Okay, we'll take five minutes."

Anya exhaled and shifted herself into an alcove in the rock. Dan joined her, placing the torch, which was ominously fading, between his feet.

"You'd better turn that off."

"Yeah, you're right."

The couple sat in darkness on the mountain face. In the distance the first few moments of the breaking dawn were just visible. Shards of light were breaking out from beneath the night sky.

"This could be quite breathtaking."

"Yes. Can you hear that?"

"What?"

"Sounds like a waterfall."

They both listened and they heard the distinctive sound of water cascading over rock and hitting water. There was the wildlife too; birds, insects, and mammals, alive and making their own sound in and around the rich vegetation.

Dan and Anya awoke startled. It was light. Birds had shot up from the trees below and they could feel the reverberation of blades that was synonymous with an approaching helicopter. And sure enough their eyes were drawn to an object getting nearer to them.

"Oh no," Dan said. "I don't believe it. We fell asleep."

Anya looked towards the craft. "Is that...?"

"Of course it is."

Dan quickly got to his feet, pulling a still heavy-eyed Anya up with him, and they made their way along the path, now fully aware of the drop beside them.

The helicopter was closing in fast; they'd been spotted.

"Now we're trapped!" Anya shouted, as they arrived at the sloping summit of the mountain.

"It's okay, they can't land." Dan looked around for inspiration.

Anya screamed as the chopper swooped down on them.

They could now both clearly make out the pilot flanked by Keller and Lowell. Lowell was taking aim with a rifle.

Dan watched Lowell line up his shot. "Anya!"

In slow motion Dan saw the bullet leave the barrel of the gun; it spun forward, cutting through the air. Dan followed its trajectory, to its point of impact, and before he could utter another word of warning, Anya fell, wide-eyed but lifeless, to the ground. The shot had struck the centre of her temple.

Dan rushed to her. The helicopter descended, churning up dust that swirled like a sand storm.

He held Anya in his arms. "I'm sorry." He ran a hand over her eyes to close them.

Lowell and Keller jumped the remaining few feet.

Dan stood and turned to face the men.

"You're a hard man to find," Keller said, "but we knew you existed." He gave a self-satisfied smile.

"Yes, we did," Lowell said, "and you've done well to keep yourself hidden for so long. It must be hard, having your abilities and living like a vagrant, a drifter...."

Dan didn't reply. He was fighting to control his emotions.

"Anyway, we thought our little charade might pay off," Keller told him. "You couldn't resist finding out, could you?"

"We can give you a life, Daniel, a marvellous one. The one that you were born for."

Dan said nothing. As they were speaking he had been slowly backing towards the mountain's edge. He peered down at the fast flowing river that ran along the bottom of the rock face.

"It is time you became what you are, young man. You have a great future ahead of you. We all do." Keller held his hand out.

"I'll pass," Dan replied impassively. Then he launched himself over the precipice.

∞

I must now interject and reveal a terrible secret to you. As I wrote before, you are a keen woman. You will remember, some months ago, that you displayed concern for my welfare. You rightly pointed out that

I was looking haggard, tired, and older than my thirty-seven years. I brushed your aspersions aside, as you will recall. There's no easy way to write this. Darling, I lived for a decade between the years two thousand and one and two thousand and eleven; over one hundred years into your, our, future, and I returned to you, just minutes after I had left. Yes, I spent ten years away. It wasn't intentional; the capsule developed a fault. No, it didn't take ten years to fix, a mere matter of months. Initially I was plagued with guilt for leaving you, and frightfully fretted, but I soon became rather attached to the period, which I was forced, at first, to live in. I learnt so much. If only you could have witnessed it, I feel you would have felt awe and shock in equal measure.

I know now that it was during that ten-year period that the seeds were being sown for the appalling future events I was, at that point, yet to see. I should explain the political landscape at the very end of the twenty-first century. For decades a right-wing axis had been stretching itself across the globe, originating in Europe and then spreading to all the major powers. The world was affluent, and with that prosperity came a mindset of self-centredness and a total disregard for those who were less fortunate (the view was that it was somehow their own fault), and a thinking that all the opulence had come through man's own achievements and dominance, which it had, but at a severe cost.

Let me start with that most blessed of festivals, and your favourite time of year, Christmas. At the end it is little more than an excuse for over-indulgence. The celebration became a three-day splurge of consumption: drinking, eating and spending. Money had replaced the true meaning of Christmas, or Yuletide, as it was now called. 'Good will to all men' meant nothing, as around the world millions starved. On those three days, more than at any other time of year, it was customary to attend a huge shopping centre – gone in the future are those independent shops we know and love; the greengrocer, the baker, the butcher, the milliner, the blacksmith, the cobbler and dozens of others that are so abundant locally, on every street in Britain, and the world. Now there were out-of-town centres - giant metal structures that stretched for miles and miles and contained a multitude of 'branded' outlets, each in competition with the other, baying for the shopper's money. There was nothing that could not be bought, or for that matter, sold. Consumerism was God. Greed was God. Want was God. In just this one facet, man had become separated from what made him human, and with his new-found riches he had no intention of turning back.

A movement, known under a variety of self-important names, was responsible for the traditional Christmas being abandoned, its second meaningful victory after the rejection of BC and AD in favour of BCE and CE – Before Common Era and Common Era (prior to this their successes had been psychological – their hatred was slowly being absorbed into the public consciousness). This campaign group comprised, at first, academics, writers and journalists, and had grown alongside the political shift rightwards that I mentioned above (you will recall my stern conviction that Jesus was the first socialist – and I am correct about that by the way). At the outset it appeared unconnected, but the none-too-subtle attacks on faith increased to encompass all beliefs; there was a fundamental hatred of religion that went beyond atheism to anti-theism. The by-line of the anti-theist movement's literature read: *religion is for the weak – enjoy yourselves.* Blasphemy days were held annually. All of the ills of the world were laid at religion's feet. For religion brought rules, even if those rules were affirming guides and not obstructions to living a contented life. These factions claimed intellect, science and the arts as theirs, a counterfeit postulation designed to demonstrate to the population that religious persons were somehow inferior mentally, that their belief was a failing of their logical reasoning, that they were, in effect, stupid, and incapable of creativity and unwilling to embrace the advances in knowledge. It was an impure invention, yet a successful coercion, cementing in the general public's minds that religion was backward, and held no solutions to problems; only preservation of the self would achieve that. They also successfully inferred that faith was on a par with the paranormal and superstition, mediums and psychics.

Governments, eager to control the thoughts and actions of their citizens, saw religion as a problem. Eventually right-wing policies and the views of the anti-theists merged; a marriage made in totalitarianism. Simultaneously there had been a shift to the fundamental side of faith that, in the public's eyes, showed religion to be totally incompatible with the everyday. It was also intolerable for the majority, and quite rightly so, to be subjected to faiths which curtailed equality. These, as I have now come to realise, were double bluffs made by the enemy and his agents, acting to bury the true message, which, as you know, is love. Fortunately another new movement, one blessed by God, was growing.

But I am digressing terribly. I hope I might have given you an idea as to the climate and frame of mind of many in those late twenty-first century years and the decades preceding it.

5

The late night London streets sparkled with a thin veneer of autumn rain and illumination from moonlight. A small puddle had formed between two cracked paving stones; its surface shimmered before being broken as a foot landed in it.

Simon and Sunayani walked hand in hand, each dragging a suitcase on wheels that bumped over the uneven pavement.

Their two-week honeymoon in Spain had gone quickly, something which they realised as they were greeted with the usual everyday sight of the neighbour's cat sitting on the doorstep of their terraced house.

"Hello, Kitty," Sunayani cooed. She bent down and stroked the animal.

"Looks like she missed you," Simon said, reaching over them to unlock the front door.

"Yeah, and the bowls of tuna. Have we got any?"

"No, I don't think so."

"Sorry puss. Can you wait till tomorrow?"

The cat squeaked.

Simon laughed. "I'd take that as a no."

"Sorry, Kitty. I'll get you some tomorrow, I promise."

The cat, sensing defeat, trotted across the pavement and started rubbing itself against a lamppost.

Simon entered the house. "Come on, I'm knackered."

"See you later and mind the road," Sunayani cautioned the cat, before shutting the door.

"So what do you want to do today?" Simon asked his wife as they lay in bed. "Our last day of freedom before we have to go back to work."

"Not sure." She gave him a smile and picked a stray hair off his shoulder. "Go food shopping?"

"That would be a good idea. I was looking forward to a fry-up."

Sunayani stretched out under the duvet and emitted a short yawn. "Kitty was looking forward to tuna."

Simon looked around the bedroom. There was a spider crawling along the edge of the wall and heading for the ceiling. Sunayani idly bit at the tips of her fingernails, thinking.

"I wouldn't mind popping to the shopping centre actually," Simon said. "I need a new suit for work."

"A new suit? What's wrong with your old one? Actually you've got a couple, haven't you? I recall taking two to the dry cleaners."

"Yeah. I know. I've got three, one grey and two black. They're just getting old, that's all. That lad, the trainee at work, I swear he buys a new one every month."

"Okay. We can do that. The youth group is meeting on Friday, right?"

The group was where the couple had met whilst doing unpaid work helping local kids achieve something more productive in the evening than hanging about on street corners. Sunayani remembered the first time she saw Simon sheepishly walk in. He'd come after seeing an advert in the local paper for volunteers and felt he should give something back to the community, and the area, he'd recently moved to.

"Yes. I can't believe what a wonderful present the kids got us!"

The children were responsible for getting the pair together, as both had seemingly been unable to overcome their shyness towards one another. For a wedding gift they, and the other helpers, had clubbed together and bought them a bike each. It was something the couple had talked about for some time; long bike rides in the country at the weekend, a big packed lunch, fresh air. But with them both working five days a week, Sunayani as a receptionist at a local glazing firm, and Simon as a call centre manager, plus helping the youth group in their spare time, they had never done anything about their modest dream.

"I know. I can't wait for next weekend!"

"Yeah. We're very lucky." He gave her a kiss on the cheek.

"Come on then." Sunayani climbed out of bed. "I'll just have a quick shower."

Simon yawned. "Okay, well I'll just have a few more minutes then."

"There *is* plenty of milk in the fridge for tea." Sunayani hinted as she meandered out of the room.

Simon smiled to himself and got out of bed.

In the kitchen he dutifully made the drinks, then scrolled through the headlines of the stories automatically downloaded to their electronic newspaper every day, which they'd forgotten to cancel before going away.

"Are you gonna put any clothes on?" Sunayani asked, walking into the kitchen, dressed in jeans and a green t-shirt. She was dragging a brush through her wet hair, which sent droplets of water falling on to the black and white lino.

"I've got me boxers on." Simon looked down at his exposed body and took a sip of coffee.

"Well, I don't mind, but Mrs Pedersen next door might."

Sunayani nodded towards the kitchen window. Simon turned to see Mrs Pedersen in her garden with a pair of shears in her hand. Simon waved frantically at her. She hastily pretended not to have been watching and started pruning her already pruned rose bushes.

Sunayani laughed. "I think she might have *feelings* for you."

"Well, she's only human!" Simon raised his eyebrows. "I wouldn't blame her though. I'm at my physical peak."

Sunayani stepped forward and picked up her tea. "Yeah, right."

"Now I've made your tea, I shall go and cleanse myself."

"Good boy. It is getting late, almost eleven."

"I won't be long."

Sunayani watched him walk away and then turned her attention to the pile of post that Simon had collected off the hallway mat. She found it amusing, as well as deeply annoying, that they still got junk mail even after Simon had sellotaped a laminated message above their letter box saying 'No Junk Mail Please!' It had been there a while and the rain had got beneath the plastic and made the ink run. It now read 'o unk ma l ease!', which was no doubt why they were still getting the superfluous mail. Perhaps the postman thought it was a Nordic greeting or something.

After tearing the unwanted leaflets up and putting them in the recycling she checked through the regular post. A few wedding cards and a letter from the hospital. She, they, had been expecting it and had avoided talking about it on their honeymoon.

"Simon! It's here." There was no reply. "Simon!" She moved to the entrance of the kitchen and directed her voice upwards.

"I heard you. Be there in a minute."

Sunayani stared at the envelope while she waited. She held it up to the light to see if she could see what it said.

Simon appeared, dripping wet and hurriedly dressed in jeans and a checked shirt. "What is it?"

"*The* letter. It's here."

Simon scratched his chin. "Oh."

"Oh?"

"A bit nervous that's all."

"Shall I?"

"I guess." Sunayani began to tear at the paper. "Here." Simon opened a kitchen drawer. "Use a knife."

Sunayani took the blade, hooked it into the envelope and slid it along the edge. "Right." She sighed, produced and unfolded the contents. Simon leant over her shoulder so he could read it.

After a few moments of their eyes darting across the page, both reading and re-reading, they looked at each other.

"Well, that confirms my home fertility tests." Simon walked over to the kettle.

"It doesn't matter, we can try other things."

Simon snorted. "Can we?" He clicked the appliance on.

"Of course."

"We can't afford it."

"I know, but."

"Why can't I just, you know, why can't it just work?" Simon made himself another cup of coffee. Sunayani didn't reply. She reread the correspondence.

"We should go to the doctors to talk through the options," she suggested optimistically, trying to hide her disappointment. Simon grunted an unenthusiastic 'yes', although it could have easily have been a 'no', or perhaps even a 'don't care'.

"Do you still want to go shopping?" he asked, changing the subject.

"What?"

"Do you still want to go shopping?"

She held the letter in the air. "Simon, we should talk about this."

"What is there to talk about?"

"Us, the baby."

"But there isn't a baby! I don't know why we're bothering anyway...."

"We've been trying for ages. We can't just give up."

The couple stared at each other and the same look of disappointment swept across both their faces. They embraced.

"Let's just let this news sink in before we do anything rash," Simon whispered into Sunayani's ear.

"Yeah, I guess you're right." She pulled away from him and looked him in the eyes. "It's just been so perfect the last two weeks."

"I know, I know, it has."

The videophone in the hallway leapt into life.

"That will be your mother." Simon released Sunayani and picked up his coffee.

"I guess I'll have to tell her the news."

The shopping centre was packed. Simon undid another button of his shirt and took a swig of mineral water. Above, through the glass roof, the sun's rays were a flare across the blue sky. He waited patiently for Sunayani who was inside yet another store. Retail therapy to take her mind off the news, searching for the perfect pair of shoes to go with a dress she'd never worn, because she'd never found the right footwear.

Sunayani finally appeared empty handed. Back out on the concourse she noticed that every other shopper seemed to be a woman with a pushchair or a couple carrying a child. Simon could see Sunayani watching them as they passed.

"So, where now?"

"Huh, what?" Sunayani was watching a woman feeding a baby on a bench.

"I said where do you want to go now?"

"Oh, didn't you want to get a suit?"

"Yeah, did you want to come with me? Might be a bit boring."

"I don't mind. I'd better make sure you don't get something hideous."

"Okay, but I've got great fashion sense."

"It's typical though, don't you think?"

They began to walk.

"What's typical?"

"That we're seeing so many mothers."

"Oh, yeah. I did think that. Yeah, it is typical. But it's like when you get what you think is a rare coloured car, then suddenly as you're driving home from the garage you see hundreds of them."

"I suppose."

"This will do." Simon walked through the electronic barriers of a clothes store. "Let's see what they've got." He began scouting around the brightly lit space.

"Good luck." Simon looked at her as she waved him goodbye. "Off you go then. Shout if you need help."

"What are you going to do?"

"I'll mooch."

"Right, you mooch, moocher. I'll let you know when I find something. Which shouldn't take too long. 'Smart and cheap' is the title of today's mission."

Simon wandered off. Sunayani stood by the exit looking at the shoes displayed opposite the door. After a few moments, she couldn't help but stare out of the window at yet more buggies and prams being pushed by women younger than her thirty-two years. She watched them and every move they made, and the way that families smiled at each other as they passed. Two women stopped and talked, each proudly showing the other their child. They chatted for some minutes. Sunayani imagined they were discussing their pregnancies and the births.

She thought back to the day, the evening when they first tried. She had wanted a baby for a year or so before she had plucked up the courage to talk to Simon about it. She felt sure that he would be against the idea, but working with the kids in the youth group had made them both think about it.

"What do you think of this number?"

Sunayani turned to look at what Simon was holding. "Oh." She examined the single-breasted grey suit. "That's quite nice, actually."

"See, told you I didn't need your help."

She felt the fabric of the jacket. "Yep, got to admit it. I was wrong. At thirty-three years young you're perfectly capable of buying your own clothes. I shall phone your mother tonight and tell her the good news."

"Thanks."

"How much is it?"

"Sixty. Cheaper than the online price apparently." He pulled his wallet out of his back pocket and headed for the self-service checkout.

"Aren't you going to try it on?"

"Nah. I know my size. Can't believe we were in Spain this time yesterday!"

Leaving the complex, they made their way home to have some lunch and relax in the garden. As they sauntered along, arm in arm, they almost collided with a dishevelled figure as it stumbled out the doorway of a boarded up house.

"Sorry," the vagrant garbled. He coughed and pulled his threadbare jacket to his chest.

"Hey, it's okay," Simon assured the man. "Here." He pulled out a ten euro note from his pocket. "Get something to eat."

"Oh, ta."

As they walked off, Sunayani's eyes widened as they locked with the tramp's. She saw something behind them, a circling fog of darkness. It was enough to make her gasp in horror. Then she coughed hard, struggling to catch her breath. The tramp limped away with the money gripped tightly in his hand.

"Are you okay?" Simon asked.

"Yeah…."

"Poor guy."

"*Scum,*" Sunayani said, under her breath.

"Sorry hun?" Simon asked, unable to hear her hushed comment.

She shook her head. "Nothing. Sorry, don't know what came over me. Did you notice his eyes?"

"Nope. But yours are gorgeous."

"Huh?" She turned back but the drifter had gone.

"Your eyes."

"Oh, yes, so are yours, lovely."

"You've lost it. She's lost it everybody!" Simon said, pointing his wife out to bemused passers by.

"Shut up." Sunayani playfully gave him a soft punch to the ribs.

"Come on, let's get home. I'm starving."

Two months later Simon sat rigid on the sofa. He swept a hand through his unkempt hair. He could hear her banging around in the kitchen, making dinner, although it sounded like she was hammering dents out of car doors.

He turned on the television, raising the volume to drown out the clamour. The horrors of the day were being recounted on the news.

"Oh," Simon called through, in a desperate attempt to open a line of dialogue with his wife. "Did you hear about that Presidential candidate being stabbed? It's all over the news."

He received no answer.

He looked up at a picture of himself and Sunayani on the wall. The image was one he now barely recognised, the happy couple on honeymoon, their faces lit by their love for each other.

"Can I help you with anything?" He started to get up.

"Don't bother." Sunayani walked into the living room, carrying two dinner plates, one of which she dropped into his lap along with two pieces cutlery.

"Argh, it's hot."

"Of course it's hot." She sat down in an armchair and turned her attention to the television. She began to eat, shoving the spaghetti bolognaise into her mouth.

Simon stared at her for a second and looked down at the meal. "Looks nice," he lied. Sunayani grunted. He passed a fork-full of pasta and sauce over his lips and instantly recoiled. "Salty."

"What?" Sunayani asked through a mouthful of food.

Simon sighed. "I said it's a bit salty."

"Well, cook your own…" She cursed, before finishing her sentence, "dinner next time."

Simon threw the dish on the coffee table and held his head in his hands.

"What?" Sunayani whined.

"You! Why are you like this?"

She flung her plate down on the coffee table. "Like what?"

"Being a complete…."

"What? Go on, say it."

Simon sighed again. He thought about the months of moaning, criticising and sniping. Every day was a battle and he dreaded coming home from work. The child they had desired was now forgotten. There had been no intimacy since returning from holiday and she had also stopped going to the youth group. He was running out of excuses for her, as she favoured the lure of a bottle of wine, or two, every evening instead.

"Well?" Her voice was shrill, resembling fingernails running down a chalkboard.

"It doesn't matter." He sighed and picked up his dinner and forked the food.

And then it began, her invective tongue, each word stabbing into Simon's mind and body. On and on she ranted, and then in the split second between her final words leaving her lips and reaching his ears, something in Simon snapped. It was almost audible and the change was immediate. Days and weeks of mild mannered responses were overcome by a previously hidden anger. He threw the plate down; it smashed on the wooden flooring, sending the contents flying in every direction.

He rolled off the sofa, on to his knees and started punching the floor; a tirade of hate and obscenities spewed from his mouth, his rage consuming him as months of built up frustration flowed out. Sunayani's pupils dilated, her body violently convulsed and a dark formless cloud emerged. It had managed to attach itself to her by feeding on her suppressed insecurities. Now drawn out from her body it circled the dimly lit room before flying at Simon, disappearing into him. His fury increased as from around the terraced house, through the letterbox, similar sinister vapours seized the opportunity and rushed in, forcing him flat on his back, where he lay pulsating, before finally becoming still.

"Simon?" Sunayani said, coming round, only semi-conscious of the preceding events. She appeared instantly different, her voice lighter, her face softer, the deep lines that had been set on her face now gone, and her eyes back to their previous clarity.

Seeing her husband lifeless on the floor she pulled herself out of the armchair she had collapsed back into, and rushed to his side. She lifted Simon's head and rested it on her bended knees. Sunayani stroked his hair and looked at him in way that she hadn't done for many months. But that look of adoration was quickly replaced by fear as Simon opened his eyes and his face became contorted with wrath.

6

Heavy, tired footsteps hauled Dan through the rear entrance of the abandoned house. He slammed the door shut behind him, dropped his backpack and collapsed, letting his whole exhausted body stretch out on the dirty wooden floorboards.

He lay there, his clothes soaked to the skin, for some time. He half slept and dreamt, recalling, in a swirling montage, the journey he'd just made, the months of travelling. The faces of Lowell and Keller, their humanity enticed to evil, haunted him. They had pursued him halfway across the globe, before he was finally rid of them.

Eventually he pushed himself up from the floor and surveyed his surroundings. It didn't look like the place had been broken into. From the fleeting glance he'd given the property before staggering in, it appeared all the metal boards were still fixed tightly against the windows and the front door.

Dan secured the door, positioning a flat iron bar widthways on the two deep hooks at either side. He then picked up his rucksack and made his way into the dark house and up the stairs.

In the main bedroom he stared through the perforated steel sheet that was screwed across the window. The unadopted road was quiet, which was how he liked it. He'd moved in just prior to leaving for Thailand. The area consisted mainly of boarded up terraces, with only a handful actually still inhabited. Somehow the regeneration of Liverpool around the time it was the European Capital of Culture for the third time had overlooked vast estates, with numerous properties that were just left to rot. No doubt their time in front of the wrecking ball would come, but, for the time being, it was the perfect place to hide, to disappear into.

He went into to the back bedroom and proceeded to the far corner by the rear window. Kneeling down he dug a hand into a crack in the floorboards, slowly lifted a plank and shuffled back as another, followed by another, concertinaed up, exposing clothes, bedding, food, toiletries, a book and a laptop, all protected by a thick plastic sheet. He uncovered one other item, a photograph. It was slightly discoloured with one corner missing, torn off. There were three people in the picture: a woman, a man and seated between them on a bench, a boy.

Dan immediately sought fresh garments. He grabbed a pair of jeans and a sweater and made his way to the bathroom. He stripped naked, dumped his sodden clothes into the mildew-stained bathtub and ran a sink full of cold water. He rubbed a disintegrating bar of soap over his body. It was his first wash since arriving in the country.

Refreshed and dressed he returned to the back room and pulled out the laptop and a large packet of crisps. He slid down the damp wall and sat crossed legged on the floor. It was getting cold, the erratic weather bringing as much rain as it did searing hot sun. He dragged a duvet out of the hole and wrapped it around himself. As the laptop powered up he scoffed down handfuls of the salty potato snack. He was relieved that the computer was still working. His power supply came via a hidden cable, threaded through nine abandoned houses, and eventually reaching an occupied property from where he'd siphoned off a spur of electricity. Aside from his laptop, he also had a microwave oven and a lamp. The devices didn't draw too much energy, so he was pretty confident the bill payer wouldn't notice.

With the laptop on, he connected wirelessly to the Internet, hacking into that same neighbour's account.

As soon as he was online he headed straight for the 'The Truth Will Stop The World' website. It was the web's number one conspiracy website, a community dedicated to everything *they*, the eponymous *they*, didn't want you to know – the fake moon and Mars landings, aliens, werewolves, the Loch Ness monster and the rest. Dan knew most of it was rubbish. But there was one section, one niche chatroom that was of interest to him. It was full of stories about biblical artefacts being hunted for or supposedly found. Nothing ever came of them.

Dan logged straight in and scrolled down the subject headings, until he found what he was looking for: the topic titled Thai Giant Search Disaster. He clicked on the heading and read the first post, dated two months ago. It reported that the archaeological dig had suffered a raging, yet isolated, forest fire that had killed the archaeologists and workers hired to excavate the site. The tragedy was made even more distressing as it appeared that the dig had been a hoax. Dan closed his eyes and was about to log off, the memory of his recent experience too raw to confront, when a blue flashing box popped up on the screen.

Devil4Eva wanted to talk to him. 'Hey', it read. Devil4Eva was the screen name of a girl in Canada that Dan occasionally spoke to. He typed back.

"Hi."

"It's been like months. Where have you been?" she wrote, adding a round-faced icon that had its arms folded and was tapping a foot.

Dan smiled. "Away."

"Did you go to Thailand? Have you read about it?"

"No, I didn't and yes I have. I knew it would be a load of rubbish," he typed, wishing that he really hadn't gone.

"Oh. Glad you're safe. Where are you now?"

"In a late night café."

"In the UK?"

"Maybe."

"Are you doing this on purpose?"

"No. Yes, in the UK."

"Still travelling? Still moving around?"

"Trying to settle down actually."

"Found a new place?"

"Maybe."

"When you've settled and got an address I'll send you those out of print books you were interested in."

"That would be great."

"Ok. I have to go. I'm very busy these days."

"You're always busy."

"I know. Speak soon?"

"Yeah."

"Byeeeee."

She had logged off before Dan could reply. Instead he looked at her profile. All her interests, film, music, books, revolved around the satanic. Her picture, however, showed her to be a rather normal looking girl. She had long red hair, green eyes and a slim figure. They had flirted with each other in the past. He actually didn't know her real name, although she knew his. She had posted the original topic about the secret archaeological dig for the 'giants from the Bible' after finding out about it from one of her contacts. If only she knew the truth, thought Dan, that would really stop the world.

It was pitch black when Dan was awoken by a scream, his eyes blinking as he tried to focus in the dark. He heard desperate cries and two hushed male voices. Rising to his feet he tried to look through the

40

pierced metal sheet that covered the window. He could just make out the image of a woman being dragged, mouth covered by one man, as another guided them into the rear garden of the house.

Dan put on a pair of trainers and rushed downstairs into the kitchen. He put an ear to the back door. He could hear the woman's muffled pleas for help. Dan gently removed the iron bar, stood back, and then flung the door wide open.

The two men were shocked; they immediately ran away across the garden, disappearing into the night. Dan felt his adrenaline rise and he was about to chase after them when the moans of the woman distracted him.

"Are you okay?" he asked, helping her to her feet.

"Oh sure," she mumbled, with a soft American inflection. "I'm fine."

The woman was about his age; she had a pale complexion, an oval face, wide blue eyes and full lips. Her hair was dark, in a bob style that was growing out of its cut. She wore a black and white shirt, dark jeans with black boots and a green jacket. She bent down, picked up a red handbag and retied the belt of the jacket around her waist.

"That will teach me for walking around on my own."

"What happened? Are you sure you're all right?"

"Yeah, I'm fine, honestly, thanks to you anyway." She paused, brushing her hair back into place, shaking slightly. "I was on my way to a friend's house. My fault." She raised her hands. "I insisted on finding my own way here. Didn't get a cab, got a bus, got lost." She giggled. "I'm a little bit stubborn. I was about to use the GPS on my PDA, which I'm loathed to do as I'm a bit of a technophobe, when I got...."

"Well, this really isn't a part of the city that you want to be walking around alone," Dan said, concerned for the woman's safety.

"And didn't I find that out! I should really call the police." She looked through her bag for her PDA. "It's broken." The woman exhaled heavily. "This really isn't a good day."

"Listen, let me walk you to your friend's house."

"I don't know."

"You'll be safe."

The woman glanced Dan up and down. She gave a brief grin. "Would you?"

"Of course. I would invite you in." Dan pulled the back door to behind him. "But as you can see...."

She looked up at the barred windows. "You live here?"

"Just drawing plans to renovate the place," Dan lied.

"Oh, I see." The woman again looked up at the dilapidated property and gave a nod.

"So, can I walk you?"

"I guess. Sorry, yes please. Do you know where, erm, Slater Street is?"

"I use to play on Slater Street."

She beamed. "Great! I'm Catherine by the way." She thrust her hand out.

Dan tentatively took it. "Dan."

"Pleased to meet you."

For a split second they just stood staring at each other.

"Right."

"Yes, lead the way. Oh, my suitcase!"

Dan watched on as Catherine disappeared into the dark of the garden and returned dragging a case behind her.

"Let me." Dan took the handle. Their hands touched.

"Thank you!"

Dan escorted her back on to the road and under a full moon they began their walk.

"I knew I must have been getting lost when the roads stopped having names," Catherine said, glancing around at the neglected neighbourhood she'd found herself in.

"Yeah, they call them unadopted roads."

"Sorry?"

"They're private roads that the council aren't required to look after, so subsequently they don't get maintained, a bit like this whole area really."

"It looks like, well, like…." She tried to find the words to describe the rows and rows of graffiti-covered, boarded-up houses.

"Not very attractive is it?"

"Oh, I'm sorry. You're a Liverpudlian?"

"Kind of."

"You don't sound like a local."

"You're right. I don't."

Catherine smiled at him and Dan smiled back. They walked on in an awkward silence.

"Here we are, Slater Street, hasn't changed a bit. What number does your friend live at?"

She took a piece of paper out of her handbag and checked the address. "Erm, forty-seven. He's just moved. He used to live in a nice apartment right next to the train station."

"How selfish of him."

She laughed. "I know!"

"Well, it must be the one with the guy standing anxiously at the door."

"Pardon?"

Dan pointed. "There."

Catherine looked up to see a grey-haired man waving at her. "Markus!" She ran up the road, her heels scraping on the pavement, to greet him.

"Catherine, great to see you again."

"And you."

The pair embraced.

"What kept you?"

She clenched her teeth. "Oh, I, erm, I got a bit lost."

"I said I'd pick you up from the station."

"You should have," Dan said, joining Catherine on the doorstep. "She was attacked."

"What?" Markus said.

Catherine gave Dan a disapproving look. "It was nothing."

"Are you okay?"

"I'm a O K, thanks to Dan."

"Next time, Markus, insist."

"I will, thank you."

"Well, I'd better go. Here." Dan handed her the suitcase.

"Thanks."

"Won't you stay?" Markus asked.

"Yes do," Catherine said.

"No, really, I'm fine." Dan's eyes met Catherine's. "Look after yourself."

She replied with a warm smile, lent forward and kissed him on the cheek. Turning, she followed Markus into the house. Dan watched the door close behind them.

He could hear sirens as he approached his road. Rounding the corner Dan stopped in his tracks as he saw the row of houses, including his, on fire. He stood, unable to move through shock. He watched flames lick out from around the metal boards and black smoke climb into the night sky.

Inside the house Dan's few possessions were smouldering and the one item he cared about, the photo, curled up as the inferno consumed the property. There was nothing he could do except watch the place burn, and as he did, he had a sudden, unnerving thought. He pressed himself back against a wall and observed the drama unfolding in front of him. The few residents were out in the street; they like him could do nothing as firemen tackled the blaze. Dan wondered if he'd been traced. That girl, Devil4Eva, if indeed she was a girl, she could be anyone. Perhaps too evident a moniker. She was always asking where he was, and it was her information that sent him to Thailand, and now, possibly, via his neighbour's Internet IP address, he had been found again. His eyes shifted over the people in front of him; one of them could be…. He slowly backed away.

7

A cubicle door was pushed open; the sound of the toilet flushing echoed around the unisex restrooms. A man walked across the brown stone floor towards the washbasins. He squeezed out a handful of soap from the dispenser and ran some water, hot mixed with cold, into the porcelain bowl. He washed his hands, scooped up some water and splashed it on to his face. It had been a long stressful day, every day was, and that's what life was like as department manager for the world's largest banking institution. He sighed heavily and shook the excess water from his hands. Staring into the mirror on the beech panelled wall he ran his fingers through his soft blonde hair. He was about to leave when an unusual, deep and unassailable voice spoke his name.

"Alec Lars-Coe."

Alec shot around and looked at the person who had addressed him. "Where did you come from? Who are you?"

"You don't know me? Everyone knows me, especially in a place like this. You know me."

Alec backed away. "I've never seen you before."

The stranger laughed. "My, let's call it, my organisation has an unexpected vacancy, which urgently needs filling. My sources tell me that out of twelve billion humans, sorry, people, you're the next best person for the job, and having viewed your résumé, I have to say, I agree."

"Who…."

"I knew your father, actually. We often spoke about you. His soul was in the right place, and…." The man moved closer to Alec. "He told me yours was as well." He took a deep breath. "And that's always good to hear." He placed a pale hand on his chest. "Warms the heart."

44

The restroom door opened and a woman wearing a short skirt, high heels and a tight blouse walked in. Seeing the two men, she appeared immediately uncomfortable, gave them a brief smile and went out again. The stranger's eyes studied her figure as she went.

"Hmm, hmm. Nice." His thoughts lingered on her a while.

"I don't understand."

"Ah, Alec. I have a proposition for you." He paused, considered his words and smirked. "As I said... it's a job opportunity, and let me tell you, there are some great perks, really, really great perks." He laughed again. Alec looked puzzled. "So many candidates, but, like I said, you're perfect. Ambitious, ruthless, greedy, aggressive. I could go on." He stared into the depths of Alec's eyes. "I know you."

"What?"

The visitor raised a hand; the door of the restroom locked. "Listen...."

8

He wasn't going to beg. He was going to steal. He was lost, his will gone. Since the fire two weeks previously, he'd found another property (there had been plenty to choose from) only for the council, fearing a string of arson acts, to employ the services of a private security company to patrol the rows and rows of boarded up houses. Dan had had a couple of close scrapes with guard dogs chasing him and so decided to move on. He was also paranoid, unable to sleep. They were still after him. They would always be after him.

With the loss of the photo, his one link to the past, the realisation of his situation had sunk in. He had nothing, he was no one; he didn't exist. He was down and out with little to his name but the clothes he was wearing, which were as filthy as he was. He was exhausted. Tired of life.

He'd been eating out of rubbish bins and trying to sleep on park benches, in doorways and under railway arches. It felt like it hadn't stopped raining since the fire. During daylight hours, as the precipitation fell, he watched the public going about their daily business. He'd seen kindness, frustration, anger, happiness and a myriad of other emotions displayed on the streets.

He'd also spent hours staring into the murky waters of the river Mersey, watching the waves crash against the flood barriers, half contemplating throwing himself in and hoping that his body's ability to recover would fail.

It was whilst standing on the Albert Dock that he gazed up at the Liver building, one of the city's most recognisable landmarks. It had recently been refurbished and a large financial organization had moved in. Dan had watched the workers coming and going, wondering what a normal life would be like.

One guy in particular caught his eye. He was in his late thirties, had short blonde hair with a strong rugged face and was always flawlessly dressed. Everyone seemed to love him. He was an alpha male: the sort of person whose hair, if the winds were blowing a gale, and they usually were, would stay neatly coiffured, not a strand would come out of place. He seemed to be in a position of authority; others nodded and greeted him, rather than the other way round. He carried a briefcase, arriving at nine am and not leaving the building until six pm.

Dan immediately loathed him. Their positions in life were completely opposite. There was something about the air of affluence that followed this man around and his cool, ambivalent and effortless existence that bothered Dan. His irritation was irrational and he knew it, but he also knew he had the power to take it all away. That thought was consuming him.

Every evening Dan waited outside the grand building. When the man emerged, he followed. In his trailing of the man he overheard someone call him Alec. His routine was always the same. He walked through the city, into a store, bought food and then on to a large municipal car park, where his silver Jaguar, a sleek ultra-modern vehicle, was parked. Knowing Alec's name made it personal. Dan became obsessed, anxious if Alec was a few minutes late pulling into the car park in the morning, on edge when he occasionally worked a little later than usual.

Dan sought a new life, Alec's life. He was tired of living under the radar. He wanted to drink in the best bars, eat wonderful foods, and date beautiful women. To forget who he was, forget the past, live in the present and deny his future. Following Alec gave Dan a sense of purpose. It gave him a routine. It was almost like having a job.

Every day Alec took a short cut down one of the city's dark alleyways, which would give Dan the ideal opportunity to strike. There would still be hundreds of people about of course, but he hoped that a swift hit would mean that even if he were seen, he'd be able to get away.

Dan didn't have the best night's rest, just snatches of sleep in various shop doorways. During the night a drunken youth had just missed urinating on him, and the constant police patrols, and his own fears, meant he had to keep moving on.

He made an effort that morning, visiting a shopping centre's toilets to wash. He made himself look as normal as possible, brushing his tousled hair and beard and putting his sweater on inside out to hide the stains. He went through the perfume section of a store, liberally spraying several different scents on himself. Dan ignored the worried looks from the overly made-up staff, who must have thought he was a deranged tramp. He left before they called for security.

Dan sipped on a cup of coffee that he'd seen someone discard into a bin in front of him. The woman looked disgusted as she dropped the beverage, as if the coffee were burnt, or the milk off. Dan had hurriedly swooped on it and gulped down a mouthful. It tasted fine to him, maybe a little bitter, but a cup of milky white coffee was practically a meal. He couldn't believe how much weight he'd lost in just a few weeks. His face was gaunt and his muscles, once so prominent, were now losing bulk.

Alec's Jaguar pulled into the car park at twenty-four minutes to nine, just as usual, like clockwork.

Dan watched him get out, produce his briefcase from the boot and lock the vehicle. Alec adjusted his suit and tie and proceeded to work. Dan followed as they walked in the accustomed direction towards the Liver building. As customary Alec stopped to buy two cans of energy drink, briefly staying, as he did each morning, to flirt with the shop girl, until he checked his watch, gave her a wink and left. He next went to a cash point to withdraw the money that would be used to pay for the sandwiches which he and his colleagues sent out for at lunchtime. Dan had noted his pin number the previous day; he'd casually looked over his shoulder. They then carried on, down the hill and across the busy road. Dan eased off his pace as Alec power-greeted one of his subordinates. They went into the building deep in discussion. Dan wiped his mouth, the last dregs of coffee dribbling over the rim and down his chin, and threw the paper cup on the ground. He stood back against a railing and waited.

The nine hours passed slowly. The sun had come out, it rained, the wind had blown, the sun had come out again, cloud had come over, and it had once again started raining.

Alec was late. Dan looked up at the Liver building clock. Twenty past six. He was never this late out on a Friday. He paced up and down; he saw a few of Alec's colleagues' leave, but no sign of Alec.

47

At twenty to seven Dan made his way up to the entrance. He tried to act nonchalant as he strolled by, squinting to get a glimpse inside beyond the glass frontage.

Moving back to the railings he saw the clock light flicker on and then, fifty minutes late, Alec finally appeared. He seemed happy, ecstatic, like he'd just landed or closed a big deal. He looked so self-satisfied that he could have been floating.

Dan waited for him to get to a safe distance in front before he followed. With it being a little later and rain falling, there were slightly fewer people around, which suited Dan fine.

They made their way into town. But Alec didn't go into the store as was normal; he just carried on walking.

Dan was perturbed by Alec's break of routine. It gave him less time to focus on what he was going to do. The fifteen minutes Alec usually spent in the shop would have given Dan that extra time to psyche himself up for the robbery, and beating, he was planning to give him.

As they proceeded through the empty city streets Dan got closer and closer, matching Alec stride for stride, their footsteps splashing in the same puddles, until he was just a few feet behind. Dan felt his adrenaline rising. They were coming up to the alleyway. Dan saw some people handing out leaflets ahead. He ignored them; he kept his focus on Alec. They were getting nearer. Dan opened and closed his fists, stretching, feeling the power in his hands. He took a deep breath as Alec rounded the corner.

9

The boy ran as fast as he could. His lungs burned at each breath, as if he were inhaling too little oxygen. Pedestrians on the frost-covered pavement parted as they encountered the lad flying past, chased by a portly, wheezing gentleman, who was shouting for someone to stop the child.

Glancing back to view his persistent pursuer, the boy failed to notice the policeman he was about to collide with. Sure enough he found himself on the cold ground as he rebounded off the officer's stern frame. The boy looked up, gave the bearded PC a mischievous smile and then handed him the bag of sweets that he produced from underneath his sweater.

"Hello, Daniel," the policeman said.

The store manager, from whose outlet the sweets had been stolen, was trying to catch his breath. "This, this little...."

"I think I get the picture, Sir."

"I want him charged. Get him tagged." He was now bent over, hands on thighs.

"Yes, Sir. Come on, lad." The officer held his hand out to the boy and heaved him to his feet. "I'll take care of everything." He handed the sweets back.

The pair began to walk away and the distracted shoppers went back to their business, as did the store manager.

"So, what are we going to do with you, young man?"

The boy thought about running, but the PC had a firm hold on the collar of his coat. "If I took you down the station, the social services could take you away from your parents, and they're very good people. Come on. Let's take you home."

"Thank you, Abdalla," Zaylie said. She ushered Dan into the house.

"I won't be able to keep...."

"I know, I know. I, we, really appreciate it."

"There's something about that boy." Abdalla sighed and turned down the volume on his police radio.

Zaylie didn't vocalise her agreement. She changed the subject. "Are you coming on Saturday?"

"Preaching in the park?"

Zaylie laughed. "Yes, 'preaching in the park'. Ellie calls them guerrilla sermons."

"I like that."

"Everybody welcome!"

"That's the only way. Aren't some people from other religious communities coming?"

"Yes. It should be a good day."

"Let's just pray that the weather is kind."

"I think we'll be all right."

Abdalla tipped his ear to his radio as he heard a call for assistance. "Right, well, sounds like I should be somewhere else."

"Okay. Well, thanks again, Abdalla."

"No thanks necessary. See you Saturday."

"You will."

Zaylie watched him hurry down the road. She closed the front door of their end of terrace house and went through to the living room where Dan was playing on his computer. Picking up the television's remote control she switched it off.

"Oi."

"What are we going to do with you?" Dan shrugged his shoulders. "Why do you keep misbehaving? Stealing, breaking windows, causing trouble and they're just the things we know about, and you're only seven years old!" Dan again shrugged his shoulders. "I think it's time you became better acquainted with the book." Zaylie picked up her contemporary translated and footnoted Bible and flicked through it. Dan rolled his eyes. "There, the Gospels. That's all you need. You can't go wrong." She handed him the tome.

10

"It's Daniel, isn't it? Daniel Ramsey?" the man said in disbelief, when he recognised who he'd collided with.

Dan stared glassy eyed, rainwater dripping from his face. He had been so focused on Alec that he'd failed to notice anyone else in his proximity.

"Oh, my boy." Dan collapsed into the man's arms.

The faint smell of rich Indian cooking was the first thing Dan sensed as he slowly came round. He then became aware that he was lying on something soft, a bed. It was an unusual feeling; he was warm, comfortable. He began to move; every single atom of his being ached. Opening his eyes, he saw that he was under a blue duvet that had been wrapped around him. The room was dark, except for a sliver of light entering from the gap between the unclosed bedroom door and its frame.

He tried to sit up, but couldn't. The bedding had been tucked firmly in and he was too weak to break free. He rested his head back on the pillow. He thought he could see elephants roaming across the dark walls, their trunks elevated to the sky as their babies held their tails.

Dan heard his named repeated over and over. He unlocked his heavy eyelids and in front of him, sitting on the bed, was Abdalla.

Dan gave him a feeble smile, his eyes darting across Abdalla's face. "Your beard is grey."

"It is." Abdalla gave it a rub. "I guess it's been a while."

Dan coughed. "Yeah. It has."

"You've been out for a few hours. Are you hungry?"

Dan raised his eyebrows. "Yeah, I'm hungry." His stomach, at the mere mention of food, and remembering the earlier fragrance, started to rumble and groan.

"Great. Can you get up?" Abdalla folded back the duvet.

"I think so," Dan replied, manoeuvring himself up and on to his elbows.

"Are you sure you're okay?"

"I'll make it." Dan unwrapped himself from the sheets and found that he was naked.

"You'll need this." Abdalla tossed him a dressing gown. "Your clothes. They had to be burnt." Dan responded with a smile. "I managed to get the worst of the dirt off you with a flannel, but I expect you'd like a proper shower at some point."

"I will, thanks." Dan tied the gown around him, and with Abdalla's help, got to his feet.

"Bit wobbly?"

"A little."

"Come on then, I'll help you."

Abdalla guided Dan down the steep stairs. From what Dan could remember the house looked exactly the same as it had done many years ago. The stairway and landing still had green and ivory coloured wallpaper, the carpet was a dark burgundy, and the ornament on the stairway window ledge, a dark wooden boat with a man standing poised with a metal-cast fishing net in his hands, was still there.

Dan's hand slid down the handrail, keeping him steady. The aroma of the food was now stronger. The heat of the house hit him as they reached the ground floor. Abdalla placed his arm around Dan's waist and they went through to the kitchen. There laid out on the table was a huge meal. Dan's eyes widened.

Abdalla pulled out a chair for Dan. "Don't get the chance to cook that regularly."

Dan sat down. "Thanks." His ravenous eyes focused on the dishes before him. "I'm going to have to come round more often."

"Everyone likes curry, right?"

"I know I do." He viewed the agreeable task ahead of him.

Abdalla passed him a plate. "Tuck in, son. Veg is home grown."

Dan grabbed a piece of peshawari naan bread, tore off a large chunk and stuffed it into his mouth.

"But take it slowly, lad. Looks like you haven't eaten properly for a while." Abdalla poured him a glass of water.

"No." Dan thought back to the months of travelling and his weeks on the city's street. "You're right there." He piled rice, vegetables and sauce on to his plate, broke a poppadom in two and dipped half of it in a bowl of chutney.

"Home-made that," Abdalla pointed out.

Dan smiled. "Lovely."

They both ate, with only the low volume of a digital radio, tuned to a local station, breaking the silence. Some time passed before Dan looked up. Abdalla was sitting back, his plate cleared some time ago.

"Sorry," Dan said, noticing that he was being watched. "Absolutely starved."

"You looked it, and I seem to remember you always did have a healthy appetite."

Dan heaved a sigh, observing the now empty serving dishes. "You didn't marry again?"

"How did you guess?"

"Oh, I wasn't being rude," Dan replied, thinking back to the unaltered furnishings. "Just that someone has missed out on some fine cooking."

Abdalla stood and started to collect the plates and dishes together. "Well, it's a little too late for that. Spent too long in the police force, I guess."

"Do you want some help?"

"No, no, relax. I'll wash this lot up in the morning. I want to hear about you. What happened to you?"

11

Dan settled back on to the sofa. He couldn't help but glance around; he never thought he'd be sitting in this living room again. The décor was reassuringly familiar: faded patterned wallpaper, light green carpet worn by years of footfall. He noticed what he assumed to be the leaflets Abdalla had been handing out on the coffee table: 'God is Love – everyone is welcome', black text on white, with a scribbled red heart alongside. Dan shook his head and smiled. The word 'Beacon' was emblazoned in the top right-hand corner, and underneath the wording, the image of a white stone, emitting light. He was about to pick one up when Abdalla walked into the room.

"Don't you have a telly?" Dan asked, sitting back and looking around the room.

"Telly? No. Got rid of mine years ago."

"Oh?"

"So you were saying?" Abdalla sat down in his armchair, keen to move the conversation away from idle chitchat.

Dan sighed. He loathed talking about himself. "That day…." He couldn't bring himself to say any more.

"Yes, that was the last time I saw you. It was a sad, sad day. The, erm, official cause of death for your parents…."

"Heart attacks."

"Oh…."

"I read it in a paper." Dan's face fell. "They were literally scared to death."

Abdalla sighed, thinking back. "Yes. I'm so sorry, Daniel. They were good people, very good people." Dan didn't reply. "But surely you were just fifteen?"

"Sixteen."

"Oh yes, of course, how could I forget? It was your birthday. Where did you go? I was so worried."

"I…." Dan thought for a moment. "I just walked and walked and before I knew it, it was dark. I rested somewhere, a shed maybe, yes, in between shovels and spades, I cried my heart out." He paused and thought. "The days blurred into each other. I eventually got work on a construction site. Then I found myself in London. After that, well, it all blurs again."

"So you're…?"

"Thirty."

"Thirty?"

"Yeah. I've just tried to keep out of the way. So I don't get found. Because if I do, those around me will get hurt."

"Should I be worried then?" Dan didn't respond. "Why did you come back?"

Dan again thought for a second. "I'm not sure. I guess, I guess, I just wanted to come home."

"You look very tired."

Dan rubbed his face. "Yeah, I am."

"Why don't you turn in? There are some people I want you to meet tomorrow."

"People?"

"Friends. Nothing to worry about."

"I don't know about that. I should really…."

53

"Daniel, it's nothing to worry about. You can aspire to have a future."

Dan rolled his eyes. "I've heard that before." He lifted himself off the sofa. "Abdalla, I really appreciate you helping me, but...."

"No buts," Abdalla raised his hand in the air. "You get a good night's sleep. We'll see how you feel in the morning."

"Okay, okay." Dan walked towards the living room door.

"Goodnight," Abdalla said, settling back and closing his eyes.

Dan replied with a faint smile and made his way upstairs. He collapsed on to the bed, the heavy meal taking its toll on him. In a few seconds he was asleep.

∞

I had time in between our days in the bar to research, in one of the few remaining public libraries, a little of Daniel's story. I found several news articles about the death of Sunayani. From what I recall they, the media, called the property at which she was found 'The House of Horror'. From memory I report the following facts: A woman bludgeoned to death, the details so horrific that they were deemed almost unprintable (not that it stopped many sections of the press who salivated and printed every grisly piece of information, including leaked pictures). They also reported that no reason had been found to explain why the police's only suspect, a man who had vanished into thin air, and was reportedly easy-going and heavily involved with his local community, would kill his wife. After her death the closing of the youth group was inevitable. According to the journalists, rumours (probably started by themselves to sell their copy in a declining market) soon circulated about how the couple spent their time with the local youths, and that maybe she, his wife, had found out about some abuse of his position of authority. It did emerge that she had apparently stopped attending the group in the last few months, fuelling speculation that maybe she knew his intentions. No one had a bad word to say about the man, but the bloodstained walls told a different story.

This was the beginning. The press, with their pessimism and anti-theist remit, would go on to paint a bleak picture of a blessed movement that had, up to that point, been growing in strength.

12

"Baby, turn the TV off. We've got to get you to school," Erica, the boy's mother, said as she came downstairs, a toothbrush hanging from her mouth, and walked through the living room into the kitchen. "Harry, did you hear what I said?" She appeared at the doorway between the two rooms.

"Yes, mummy." Harry got up from his cross-legged position on the wooden floor and switched off the television.

In the kitchen Erica swilled water around her mouth. She spat out into the stainless steel sink and placed her toothbrush alongside last night's unwashed cutlery.

She went back into the living room and put on her coat. "Have you packed?"

"Yes."

"Are you sure? Let's have a look." She picked up her eight year old son's school bag and looked through it. "Okay, all seems to be in order; PDA, lunch, juice. No apple?"

"I don't like them."

"What do you mean don't like them?" Erica handed him the bag and picked an apple out of the fruit bowl on the table. "Here you go." The boy reluctantly took it. "Come on, get your coat on, it's quarter past eight. It's getting late and you know what the traffic is like in the morning."

"Yes, mummy."

"Here you go." She passed him his jacket and helped him pull it on. "Are we there?" Her eyes scanned around the room. It was a little cluttered, a little disorganised, but everything had its place. "Right, let's go." Erica picked up her work bag and headed towards the front door of the two-story maisonette.

"Keycodes, mummy." Harry scooped them up from the table.

"Oh, thank you, honey."

Erica opened the door, they stepped out on to the concrete footpath and she closed it behind them.

It was a cold autumn morning and Erica helped Harry put on his woolly hat, stretching the elastic to make it fit over his ears. The narrow street was always lined with cars, half on the pavement and half on the road. The previous evening Erica had got home late, as she always did on Wednesdays, after chairing a meeting at the local village hall. This meant that her usual parking space, outside her house, had gone, and she had to park wherever she could find a space. Last night it had been a few streets away, and by morning she'd forgotten. She held her tongue from cursing when she realised that they were going to be even later.

"Come on." She took her son's hand and half dragged him along as she took long strides in an attempt to make up some time.

"Slow down, mummy," Harry said, struggling to keep up.

"Oh sorry, sweetie." She stopped. "Mummy forgot that she parked around the corner and it's getting late."

"Okay. I'll try to walk faster."

"Good boy." Erica let go of his hand so she wouldn't be hauling him along and they both quickened their pace.

They eventually made it to her yellow three-door car. She unlocked the vehicle and helped Harry into the back seat, fastening him in with the seat belt and putting his school bag in the foot well. She made her way to the driver's side, threw her work bag on to the passenger seat and got in. Glancing at the time on the dashboard Erica saw that it was almost half past eight. She had to get to work by nine, but it would take fifteen minutes to get to Harry's school and drop him off, and then it usually took twenty-five minutes to get from there to work. She started the car, turned the radio on and pulled away from the kerb, hoping she'd get lucky with the traffic.

Erica drove through the back streets and turned on to the main road. They had only travelled a few metres when she saw a procession of red break lights ahead. She sighed. "Oh no, road works. Typical!"

The car slowed and joined the queue. There was a traffic signal in place only allowing one side to pass at a time.

"Are we going to be late?"

"Yes. I think we are."

"Sorry, I didn't walk faster."

"It's not your fault. I should have got us up earlier."

With the traffic at a standstill Erica turned and reached for her work bag. She managed to get a finger hooked under the loop of the strap and dragged it towards her just far enough to get her PDA out of the side pocket. She heard the toot of a horn, and facing forward, saw that the cars in front were moving. Erica raised a hand in apology to the driver behind her, released the handbrake and drove on.

Just as she was about to switch her PDA to its hands free mode, Erica noticed the vehicles in front taking a side street to the right, which was quickly becoming available to her as the queue shortened. She realised they could take that turning and head to Harry's school cross-country. It was a longer route, but she'd get him to school on time, or at least just after nine. Erica indicated, and as soon as she could she crossed the lane and headed down the road. They were soon speeding through a built up housing estate, which eventually gave way to countryside. She was starting to feel confident that they'd reach the school before nine, but she would still be at least twenty minutes late getting to work. With one hand firmly on the wheel she said 'work' into the PDA. It automatically found the number and dialled it. She switched it to hands free, voice only mode; the ringing echoed through the car.

Up ahead a large white transit was parked in a lay-by and just as the call connected the van pulled out. Erica slammed on the breaks. The PDA flew out of her hand, landing somewhere on the floor; the line went dead. Harry's seatbelt saved him from being thrown forward. Erica's seatbelt also tightened around her. Her immediate reaction was to punch the horn. The transit casually reversed back.

"Are you okay?" she asked Harry.

"Yes," he mumbled.

Sighing with exasperation Erica drove tentatively forward. She stared out of the window at the white van. The side windows were tinted just enough so that all she could see was the outline of the driver. As they moved further she saw a man, his head bowed, behind the wheel. Passing the vehicle Erica slowly began to pick up speed again. In the rear-view mirror she saw the van pull out and follow her.

"Almost there, sweetie."

As they approached the turning that would eventually become the road that the school was on, Erica was shocked to see an abandoned tractor blocked it.

"I don't believe this." She glanced around to see if she could see the owner.

"What is it?"

"Some idiot has blocked the road."

"What are we going to do?"

Erica let out a tiny, frustrated groan. She thought about reversing, going back and just admitting defeat. She looked around for her PDA. As she searched she saw the transit driving up behind her. She tutted and had no choice but to continue down the road, which was rapidly becoming a dirt track. The van followed and she hoped there would be somewhere to turn in up ahead. As the gradient dipped they gathered speed. Erica could see the transit getting closer and closer. Its headlights were on full, even though it was light. She squinted and tried to get sight of the driver, but the car was bumping up and down on the muddy trail, and the glare from the lights made it hard for her to focus.

"Slow down, mummy."

"Sorry, this guy is right up my… " She stopped herself from saying any more, but she was right. The white van was inches away from the car. "What does he think he's doing?"

"Slow down, mummy."

The transit made contact with Erica's car, shunting it forward. Erica screamed and Harry started to cry. It hit again. Erica began to lose control. The vehicle started to slide. She tried to steer but the force from behind finally toppled them sideways. They were now being pushed down the track. Erica finally got a look at the driver, her eyes widened in disbelief. The car smashed into the wall of a building. The windows shattered, spraying glass over Erica and Harry. The transit reversed. Erica was stunned, unable to move and unable to speak. She glanced up to see the van speeding towards them. She unbuckled her belt, leaned into the back seat and attempted to unbuckle Harry's, but it was stuck. Over Harry's frightened cries Erica heard the roar of the approaching engine. She desperately tried to free her son. Her brown eyes caught the insane glower of her pursuer's. The transit made contact for the final time.

The rear doors were kicked open and the driver jumped out. The front of the van was crushed into Erica's car. The man surveyed the wreckage. Returning to the back of his vehicle he produced a can of liquid accelerant, which he splashed across the two wrecks. He lit a match and watched the flame, as if he'd never seen one, before letting it burn down to his finger and thumb. He then threw it on to a stream of the fluid, which was forming a puddle on the soil. A blaze ensued, engulfing the wrecks. His job was done. He walked away across a barren field.

13

Dan's eyes slowly opened. They came to rest on the wall clock. It was nine thirty. He was hot. He tried to move but found himself twisted up in the duvet and Abdalla's dressing gown. As he unravelled himself, his eyes smarting from the morning sunlight streaming through the thin curtains, he heard voices coming from downstairs. Sitting up, he felt like he'd been drinking the night before. Despite his apprehension, he pulled the gown to him, rose, and with a sense of trepidation, left the room.

Descending the stairs, he hovered outside the door in the hallway for a few seconds, unsure of what he was going to encounter.

"Ah, here he is," Abdalla said, catching sight of Dan and ushering him.

Inside, four people stared intently at Dan, their faces a mixture of awe, wonder and bewilderment.

"Hello again," the surprised voice of one of the guests said. Dan turned to see a familiar face, although for a moment he couldn't place it.

"Markus, remember?" The man had stood up and had his hand outstretched. "Catherine's friend?"

"You two know each other?" Abdalla asked.

"Yes," Markus said, "he's the one I told you about, the guy who helped Catherine out when she got attacked two weeks ago."

Abdalla beamed. "Is that right?"

"Yes," Dan said, shaking Markus's hand.

"Well, that's a coincidence," an old woman said from the corner of the living room.

"Yes, it is," Dan replied.

"No such things as coincidences when you're in our business, Lian, you know that." Abdalla gave her a wink.

Lian shook her head and smiled. "It's nice to meet you, Daniel. We've heard a lot about you."

"Really?"

"Yes, of course," Markus said. "Oh, Catherine tried to find you, but she said the house you were renovating had burned down?"

"Burnt down house?" Abdalla asked. "I read something about arson attacks in the local paper."

"Yeah," Dan replied. "Long story."

"Yes, she wanted to thank you again for helping her."

"Oh, right." Dan took another look around at the faces in the room. "So, does anyone want to tell me what's going on?"

"First," Abdalla said, "looks like you need a drink. Fresh tea?" Everyone agreed.

"Actually, I think I'm going to take a shower." Dan collected up some empty mugs and followed Abdalla out to the kitchen. "Who are those people?"

"You don't know? I thought you'd met Catherine and Markus?"

"Only briefly. Who are they?"

"I think I should let...." Three sharp taps on the glass-panelled front door interrupted Abdalla. He gave Dan a flash of a smile.

"Right, I'm going to get clean." Dan trailed him down the hallway and as Abdalla went to answer the door, Dan leapt up the stairs, wondering what he had got himself into. Reaching the landing, he instantly recognised the East Atlantic American accent that drifted up the stairs.

"I found a few things," he heard her say.

He closed his eyes, sighed, stepped into the bathroom and turned on the shower.

Dan stood beneath the hot flowing water. The smooth spray and fragrant soap washed away several weeks' worth of ingrained dirt. There was a knock on the door.

"Hello?" Dan said, over the hum of the electric shower.

"Oh, hello." It was Catherine. "I hope you don't mind, but I really, really need the bathroom. I'm bursting!"

"Oh, erm, I'll get out," Dan replied, from behind the curtain.

"No, you're okay, just stay there. I won't be a moment."

Dan tried not to listen; he heard Catherine's footsteps cross the white lino and then the toilet seat bang against the cistern.

"So, Abdalla just told me," she said, breaking the awkward silence.

Dan continued to wash. "Oh, right."

The toilet flushed. Dan exhaled a breath of relief and relaxed a little. He heard Catherine wash her hands.

"Funny, I thought there was something different about you."

"Did you?"

"Yeah." She pulled back the shower curtain and stared him in the eyes. As soon as he saw her face an unexpected sensation swept into his heart. "It's really good to see you again. I was so worried when I saw what happened to your home." Despite the situation Dan was pleased, and somewhat amused, at Catherine's forthright move. "You won't be long will you?"

"Nearly done," he replied, continuing to wash in an attempt not to appear perturbed.

"I think you missed a bit." She pointed at Dan's body.

"What?" Dan looked down to where she had indicated.

Catherine let the curtain go and left the bathroom giggling to herself.

Dan shook his head at her candour and thrust himself under the full power of the water.

When Dan returned to his room he found clothes laid out for him on the bed. There was a pair of socks and underpants, both new and still in their packaging, along with a pair of dark blue jeans, a white t-shirt, a shirt and a pair of tan boots, all of which looked like they might have come from a charity shop. Dan towelled himself dry and dressed. He swept a hand through his damp hair and looked at his reflection in the mirror on the wall. After just one night in a proper bed and a decent meal he looked and felt so much better. He arched his back, stretched his arms and as he did so he heard raised voices echoing up from the front room. He grimaced to his reflection, not out of spite, but because he didn't want to be the centre of attention. He appreciated Abdalla's hospitality, but didn't want to get involved. He wanted to be left alone. Dan edged towards the door and opened it. He could hear the chatter downstairs. Closing his eyes, he sighed once again, then glanced towards the window, wondering if he could make an unnoticed exit.

"Daniel?" Abdalla called up from the bottom of the stairs.

Dan scowled. "Yeah." Taking one final look at the window, he headed downstairs.

Abdalla greeted him in the hallway with a big grin and a pat on the shoulder. "You're looking good."

"Do I?"

"Come on then, son. Lots to discuss."

Abdalla led the way through into the sitting room. Dan gritted his teeth, took a deep breath and followed him.

"Here he is," Abdalla said.

Dan was immediately drawn to Catherine's smiling face. She was sitting on the floor, legs folded under her body, resting against the side of the sofa. He gave a cautious smile back and sat down in the wooden chair that Markus was offering him.

"Those clothes don't look too bad," Catherine commented.

"Thanks." Dan glanced down at what he was wearing, feeling uncomfortable that someone had gone out of their way to dress him.

"Tea?" Abdalla asked.

"No, thanks."

"Right, so you know Catherine and Markus." Dan nodded his head. "This is Lian."

"Yes, we said hello earlier," Lian replied.

"Of course, I'm just making a formal introduction."

"Okay, okay."

"You've got to watch her, Daniel."

"Oh, shoosh you."

Dan politely smiled.

"And this young man here," Abdalla indicated to an elderly gentlemen sitting behind the door. "Is Jean-Paul."

"Pleased to meet you."

Dan responded courteously. The introductions were followed by an uncomfortable silence.

After a few seconds Dan bit the bullet. "So, what's the deal?"

"Ah, well," Abdalla mumbled.

Catherine beamed. "We're followers of Jesus."

Dan laughed. "I guessed that."

"We're all Today Christians," Abdalla said, "like your parents were."

"I remember."

"Of course, of course. But our community has grown since then."

"Right..."

"You sound hesitant, Daniel. Don't let these humble surroundings fool you. What began with proclaiming God's message of love to all: you know, love thy neighbour, love thy enemies; one John four, seven to twenty-one - an unequivocal statement that God doesn't discriminate, has rapidly grown." He closed the sitting room door and perched himself on the edge of the armchair Jean-Paul was sitting in.

"We call ourselves Beacon," Catherine said.

"Ah, yes. I saw a leaflet. Catchy."

"We like to think we cut through the darkness with our light."

"Nice, nice. I get it, good marketing."

"It's more than just marketing, son. Have you felt anything?" Abdalla asked.

Dan took a side-glance at Catherine who was staring at him. "Not yet," he replied, glimpsing the curve of Catherine's bended leg.

"Nothing in the...?"

"No," he firmly replied, centring his attention back on Abdalla's words.

"Ah, well, then I hope you won't mind us relating our shared experiences with you?"

Dan thought about it for a moment. "No, my diary is pretty empty at the moment."

"Right, well, years ago, before I met your parents, Jean-Paul, Lian and I used to go to a local church. It was very.... What would you say, Lian?"

"Boring."

The others laughed at her frank reply.

"Well," Abdalla said, "you could say that. I was more thinking along the lines of uninspiring. You see, Daniel, there was no movement within the church. This is what happened; as individual faith communities got smaller, they got very insular, very protective of their own dogma, creeds and policies. As they got more narrow-minded, they stopped interacting with the world. They saw a world that disagreed, as attacking their beliefs. Subsequently, of course, they ceased to offer anything to humanity and, in effect, did the enemy's job for him. What we, and other like-minded people, have tried to do is reach out and engage with people, as well as other faiths. Generally the church and indeed faith, in all its forms, has, over the past century, experienced a falling away, an accidie. People have stopped believing. Even if they don't want to attend a church, they don't realise that you can connect, on your own terms, without a middleman. Subsequently, no one listens to church or faith leaders any more, in fact I'd go so far as to say most people in this day and age would consider religion a joke."

"True," Jean-Paul mumbled.

"Yeah," Catherine said. "Faiths didn't do themselves any favours when they stopped evolving, stopped changing with the world around them." She paused. "It wouldn't be unreasonable to say that these days if you have a belief, a belief that taps into the universal truth, which is love, then you're in for a really rough time." Dan tried not to laugh. "What?" Catherine queried. "You know it's true! Love is the universal truth."

"You can see we sometimes get very passionate," Abdalla said.

Dan shot Catherine a wry smirk. "I can."

"However, we are now seeing a great influx of people. That's why our outreach work is so crucial. Part of our work is to re-examine scripture for our time and be open to other religious voices." Abdalla stopped, hoping Dan would comment on what he'd just heard, but he kept silent. "The people involved with Beacon come an eclectic range of backgrounds. Many had never even contemplated religion, but whatever their stories, they all had the same ending, or beginning. With us they've found sanctuary in a disbelieving world."

"Disbelieving world," Dan half-heartedly repeated, "got it. I do recall most of this stuff."

"I'm sure you do. It's just been a long time for you. We are all regional co-ordinators; there are seven teams in total. We chair meetings with our cell leaders twice a month, and the cell leaders then engage with their groups in weekly meetings. The simple task of Beacon is to help new believers nurture faith in a world that has a mistrust of religion. The onus on us is to strip off the pageantry, be contemporary with our teachings, and encourage new believers to go forth and tell others."

"It's like a call to arms," Markus said.

Catherine smiled. "Yes. I like that."

"You've read Revelation haven't you?" Adballa asked, making it sound like an offhand comment.

"Yeah," Dan sighed, wishing he'd exited via the bedroom window.

"Not too long ago, I never even thought about whether there was a higher power or not," Markus said.

"Me neither," Catherine said. "Well I did, maybe, for a few seconds, now and again, you know. But I wasn't really interested."

"Oh?"

Catherine rolled her eyes. "It's a long story."

"What about you?" Dan asked Markus.

"Another time-consuming story, but let's just say it involved prison."

"Right."

"I'm sure they'll share their stories with you sooner or later," Abdalla said.

"Oh, well, actually I was hoping to get going." Dan lifted the curtain and checked the weather conditions outside. It was overcast, but not raining.

"Go? Go where?" Abdalla asked, shocked.

"You know I can't stay."

"But...."

"No buts." Dan stood up.

"Dan, you're wearing the only clothes you have. It's autumn, it's cold."

"I'll find something."

"Steal something? You have no money. How have you supported yourself all these years?"

Dan thought back to all the jobs he'd undertaken, and to some of his more dubious activities. "I'll be fine."

"It's really important you stay," Catherine said. "We have so much to talk about."

"Do we?"

"Yes," Abdalla replied. "We may need your help."

"My help?"

64

"Yes," Lian said.

"Look, I need to get some air." Dan walked past Abdalla and out into the hallway.

"Dan." Abdalla followed him out. "Look, take this coat." He handed him a woollen, hooded garment. "It's cold out there."

"Thanks."

"You will return won't you?"

Dan paused, thinking of his options. "Yeah."

"Good, good. That's good."

Dan opened the door and left. Abdalla rejoined his friends.

"Shall I go after him?" Catherine asked.

"No, he'll be okay."

"Do you think he'll help?"

"I don't know, Jean-Paul. He's been through a lot, more than we'll ever know."

"I think he will," Catherine said, giving everyone a nod.

"We need to tell him about this," Jean-Paul said, flinging an electronic paper on the coffee table. The story, dated two weeks previously, read: 'House of Horror'.

"Yes. But maybe we're wrong about that?" Lian replied.

"But what if we're not?" Abdalla sighed. He looked out of the window. "What if we're not?"

14

DCI Anchel sat at his desk. It had been two weeks and he had no leads, no sightings and no motive. Simon Moulson had disappeared into thin air. He tilted his head back and yawned. In his twenty years as a police officer he had never seen such a brutal crime scene. He'd scrolled through statements from Simon's friends, work colleagues and family. He'd read and reread them. There was nothing on this man. He was a saint. Not so much as a speeding ticket or a caution for a childhood misdemeanour. They'd found nothing incriminating on his computer hard drive. No evidence of affairs.

He ran a hand over his bloated stomach and rubbed his forehead. The media interest was intense. They wanted news, something to print, but he had nothing. He lifted up his videophone's receiver and rang down to his colleagues who were watching endless CCTV footage from the area in an attempt to find Simon driving away in his car.

"Got anything?" he asked, when PC Hanman's face appeared on the screen.

"No, I'm afraid not, Sir. We're checking fuel station forecourts."

"Okay. Let me know."

He put the receiver down and exhaled. Standing, he picked up his cup and went over to the kitchenette in the large open plan office. Opening the fridge he bent down to retrieve his lunch.

"Sir," came a voice from behind him.

He turned to see a young female detective walking towards him. "Yes, Natasha?"

"We've got something," she told him, twisting her long red hair into a bun and fixing it with pins as she spoke.

"What?"

"His car. It's turned up."

It took just over two hours to leave London and reach Beachy Head, just outside Eastbourne. The area, and Simon's car, had been cordoned off, and local police detectives were already investigating the scene.

"DCI Anchel?" asked a fresh-faced man, seeing the two officers flash the badges to a PC.

"Yes."

"Will Phillips, C.I.D. Bit cold today."

"Hello." They shook hands. "Yes, it is. This is DC Natasha Garilad. So, what have we got?" Anchel said.

"This way, Sir," Phillips replied, but Anchel was already a stride ahead of him.

They followed the detective through the cordon and the assembly of ramblers and reporters, over to the vehicle.

"Well," Anchel said, "it's definitely his car." He looked towards the cliff tops. "So we think he went over?"

"It appears so," Phillips said.

"Have you found a body?" Natasha asked, shivering. She tightened the scarf around her neck and faced the once popular seaside resort.

"No, but if he jumped when the tide was in, and it was last night…"

"Right," she replied, focusing her attending back on Phillips.

"He could have been carried out to sea," Anchel said, finishing Phillips' sentence.

"Yes, Sir," Phillips replied.

"And another psycho escapes justice."

"But the body might get washed up," Natasha said.

"It may do," Phillips replied.

"Or it may not," Anchel said. "Okay, well, there's nothing much more to see here, and it's freezing. Keep us updated. I want your report, plus photos, e-mailed over as soon as. And get this," he pointed at the vehicle, "towed to forensics."

"Yes, Sir. Of course," Phillips said.

Anchel pulled his jacket to him and walked back to the black 4x4 they'd arrived in. He sat down in the back, and Natasha settled behind the steering wheel.

"Is that it then, Sir?"

"Pretty conclusive to me."

"But he could just have left the car here."

"Maybe, but here's how I see it," Anchel leaned forward and rested his arms on the front seats. "Ordinary guy loses it, kills his wife, full of remorse, drives up to well known suicide spot and throws himself over."

"Seems plausible. What about Beacon? That cult?"

"No connection," Anchel said.

"Are you sure?"

His reply was stern. "Yes."

"So case closed?"

"It is for me. Let's go home."

Natasha put her thumb on the ignition panel and the engine purred to life. She put the car into reverse, and as it moved off, she caught Anchel's eyes in the rear-view mirror. For a split second, she thought she saw his iris cloud over, black, like his pupil, before returning to its usual brown.

15

Dan wasn't sure how long he'd been walking for. Abdalla's coat was a snug fit, and was doing a good job of keeping him warm as he made his way along the dirty, litter strewn city streets. He considered his dubious assurance of returning. He was torn. Half of him yearned for a stable environment. The other half knew he shouldn't get involved with anyone – it would, more than likely, end badly. Then there was Catherine. She was vivacious, intelligent, attractive.... Dan shook his head. He couldn't let himself get concerned with them. Not after Anya, not after what had happened in Thailand. After fifteen years they were still after him. And they would find him again; they'd come so close already. It was only a matter of time and he didn't know if he had the strength to resist them again. Despite his outward ambivalence, inside he struggling to control his emotions. If he didn't, he would be theirs, and the consequences were…. He knew he should get out of the city. It had been unwise to return in the first place. He recalled the day after the fire, when he'd revisited his childhood home: the whole street, which he'd left in a hurried panic all those years ago, was now one huge block of flats. He'd also wandered through the municipal cemeteries, in the pouring rain, until he finally found his parents' shared remembrance marker, the rusted plaque containing a simple engraved epitaph: 'In His Care'.

There were hundreds of towns and cities to be anonymous in, but he'd chosen to come back to Liverpool. Was it that he had unfinished business? Or just that after being away for so long it would be the last place they'd look? The city was big enough to get lost in; if you kept yourself to yourself you could go ignored. He'd worked on construction sites throughout the North West of England, making just enough money for a room, food and clothes. There had been occasions when he'd stolen. He was quick, he could get away with it; he could be almost invisible. It was easy; it was addictive, but he couldn't exploit his abilities. He knew that they could consume him and he couldn't risk drawing attention to himself. One slip and he'd show up on their radar.

His hands clasped the cold railings that overlooked the river Mersey. Grey waves bobbed up and down. This was a place he'd come to when he was younger. It helped him think. To his left some tourists were having their picture taken. To his right a young couple walked arm in arm.

"Hey you," said a voice behind him. It was Catherine.

He turned around, surprised to see her. "How did you find me?"

"Well, we were praying and I, well, Abdalla said you used to like coming here as a kid."

"I could have been anywhere."

"But here you are."

"Yeah. Here I am."

"Oh, it's freezing. I can't get used to this weather. It gets cold in the States, but not this horrid wet-cold combination you guys have got going on."

"You get used to it."

"Listen, do you want to get a cup of coffee?"

Dan looked down at the woman by his side. Her bright blue eyes met his. He took a deep breath. "Yeah, okay, but you'll have to pay. I have no money."

"Sure. But not one of those chains, somewhere independent."

"Right. There aren't many of those left, but I know just the place."

It had started raining heavily by the time the pair reached the café. There were only a few people inside and they sat down at a booth in the window.

"Now this is what I call independent," Catherine said, looking around. The interior decoration was simple; white walls adorned with cheap reprints, red tiled floor, bolted down tables and chairs. Dan picked up a laminated menu.

"Yes, it is."

A waiter approached the table. "Hello, how are you, my friend?"

"Hi," Dan said.

"I haven't seen you for a while."

"No, I've been away."

"Right, right. So what can I get you?"

"I'll just have a tea."

"Okay, and for you?" the waiter asked Catherine.

"Do you do a primo, decaf, fairtrade, soya latte?"

"Erm?"

"She'll have a milky coffee."

The waiter smiled. "Will you be ordering food?"

"Maybe, but just the drinks for now."

"Okay." He turned to his colleague, who was behind the counter at the rear, and shouted the order to him in their native Iranian.

"Did you want to eat?" Dan asked, handing Catherine a menu.

"Oh, I'm not sure. I'm on a diet. What girl isn't?"

"I had the all-day breakfast last time."

"Bit late for breakfast. Sounds like you come here often."

"Actually I've only been here once." Dan looked towards the waiter. "They're very friendly, aren't they?"

"I think it's great." Catherine studied the menu and found the picture and description of the breakfast. "That's more than I eat in a day! Besides I'm vegetarian. I tried being a fruitarian once, but that didn't work out for me."

Dan kept his eyes on the menu. "Right."

"Hey! Plus it's important to think about where our food comes from, you know? Especially these days."

"I guess. Well, how about beans on toast?"

"That's the sort of thing Markus makes for me."

"Not much of a chef then?"

"No. I do the cooking when I'm in town."

"How did you meet? Oh, let me guess, long story?"

Catherine laughed. "Yes, yes, yes." Her enthusiasm almost overcame her. "So, do you want to hear my testimony?"

"What?"

"My testimony."

"Yeah, erm, sure."

"Really?"

Dan paused.

"Dan!"

"Yes, of course I do. Sorry."

"Okay, but I want to hear yours too."

"I don't have a testimony."

"I mean your story. Abdalla told us a bit," she continued, without drawing breath, "but he said you should tell us, you know, when you're ready."

"That's good of him."

"Hey. He's a good man."

Dan sighed. "Yes, he is and he's a good cook."

"Is that right?"

"Uh huh."

Two mugs were placed in front of them. "Here you go, my friends."

"Thank you," Catherine and Dan said in unison.

"Any food?"

Dan and Catherine looked at each other.

"You order something for me. I'm going to use the little girls' room. Excuse me." She shuffled off the plastic chair. "Where is the bathroom?"

"Straight down, past the counter, on the right."

"Thank you."

"A nice lady."

Dan nodded and watched Catherine walk away. "Yeah. Anyway, could we have…." Dan's eyes flicked over the colourful menu. "Oh, just make it two all-day breakfasts, but make one of them vegetarian."

"Okay, thank you."

The waiter once again turned and shouted the order at his colleague.

Dan stared out of the window. The rain had stopped and a few people meandered by. He glanced around at the others in the café, all absorbed in their own worlds. He returned to the view and in his head he practised what he was going to say to Catherine. Where was he

70

going to start? Where was the beginning? There was so much to tell and he hated talking about himself.

"You look like you're miles away." Catherine sat back down and took off her coat.

"I must have been, didn't even see you, or hear those heels."

She looked down at her shoes. "They're not too bad as heels go."

"I'll take your word for it."

"What did you order?"

"The breakfast."

She looked at the picture on the menu and then held her stomach. "Oh, no. I'll never eat it all. You did get the veggie one?"

"Yes, and just eat as much as you can."

"I hate wasting food."

"Whilst there's so many people starving in the world, right?"

"Yeah." Her thoughts seemed to linger on the subject as she sipped on her coffee.

"Is it all right?"

"Yes, it's fine. Okay, so do you want to hear it?"

"I do."

"Okay. Oh, you'll have to excuse me if this sounds rehearsed. I relate it quite a bit."

"I will." Dan sipped at his tea.

"Right. Well, I grew up in Boston, Massachusetts." Catherine took a deep breath. "My father was a mechanic and my mother was a house mom, looking after my two younger brothers and me. Neither of my parents was religious. There were no religious studies at school, so I never got the opportunity to hear about any faiths. I was just a typical girl I guess, loved playing with dolls and helping mom in the kitchen, but when I reached my teenage years I started to, well, I stopped eating. Got into a really negative place. Wore dark clothes, thought the world hated me. I was cutting myself." She stretched out her arm and pulled up the sleeve of her red sweater. Dan held her wrist and examined the scars.

"There's quite a few there."

"Yeah, I know! On my legs too, but it's too cold to get them out."

"Oh, shame."

"Hey!" She took her arm back and covered up. "Anyway. It, I call it *it*, was a part of my life for years, and then there were the relationships, always the wrong guys."

"Oh?"

"I don't usually go into that."

71

"Why not?"

"Because it doesn't matter now."

"I thought this was a testimony?"

"Dan!"

"Okay."

"Here we are," the waiter said, putting a plate in front of each of them. "I take it you're the vegetarian?"

"Yes, thank you." Catherine examined the food in front of her. "Wow, I might be here some time."

"Looks great," Dan said, unwrapping a knife and fork from a paper napkin.

"Enjoy your meals."

"Thanks."

"Thank you," Catherine replied.

Dan sprinkled salt and pepper over his food and added a large pool of tomato ketchup to the plate. "So you still haven't got a big appetite?"

"Not this big. I'm only small. I do a lot of exercise. Circuits and weights, helps burn the calories."

"Right." She was small, about five feet, slim, probably weighing seven stone, if that. The food passed over her full lips. Her wide eyes darted around the café. She pushed strands of her jet-black hair behind her ears to stop them falling in front of her face as she ate.

"Shall I continue?"

Dan stopped chewing. "Yes, of course. Why not?"

"Table manners?"

"Nah, carry on, we're friends."

She smiled. "Okay. So I went off to university a bit of a mess."

"What did you study?"

"Law, would you believe."

"I believe it."

"I was quite a horrible person, really bitchy. I wanted to be the centre of attention all the time. Get my girlfriends' guys, all that stuff. I was pig headed and rude."

"You would have made a good lawyer."

"Probably. I wanted fame and money. And then there were the drink and drugs."

"Drugs?"

"Coke mainly. It's what everyone did. I couldn't leave my apartment without doing lines and having a bottle of wine. I never ate. Just lived off coke and red wine."

"Really?"

"Yeah."

"So, how did that all change?"

"Okay, well, I'm getting to that part. So, I'm like a walking wreck. My friends, and I didn't have many, were trying to help me, but I wasn't interested. Oh, it's embarrassing to look back on it. Then." Her voice wavered. "Then my family was killed in a car crash, mom, dad and my two brothers."

Dan stopped eating and looked up at her. "I'm sorry."

"Thanks." She stared out of the window.

"How did it happen?"

"A freak accident, so they said. A tyre blew out on the car. Unfortunately they were vacationing in Utah. It's very mountainous in Utah."

"Oh, I see."

"Yeah, they went over."

"I'm really sorry, Catherine."

"It's okay. We've both lost our parents."

Dan sighed. "Yeah. We have. So, is that when you...?"

"Found God?" she said, waving her hands in front of her face.

Dan grinned. "Yes." He resumed his meal.

"No, I got worse."

"Worse?"

"Yeah. I lost it completely."

"That's not surprising. What happened?"

"I dropped out of law school, got into heroin." The expression on her face changed; she seemed to be reliving that time. "Got into heroin big time."

"Heroin? Nasty."

"It was. I ended up living with other addicts in this horrible apartment in Inwood, which is in Manhattan, New York. I blew all my inheritance. I've got nothing to show for it, I blew it on drugs and drink."

"I can't imagine you like that."

"I was, truly."

"I believe you."

"I know." She smiled at him. "I know you do."

"So how low did you go?"

"What do you mean?"

"When the money ran out? How did you get your fix?"

"Oh, I see what you're saying. No, that's when it happened."

Dan stopped between mouthfuls. "I did go out on the streets. The guy I was seeing, well, just with, when my money ran out, he made me go out."

"Did he hit you?"

"Oh yes, we were always fighting, when we weren't passed out or high."

"What a charmer."

"I was no angel, I gave as good as I got."

"That I do believe!"

"Hey!"

"Sorry. Carry on."

"Okay, I'm getting there, I'm getting there. Right, and I can't believe I did this, seems like a lifetime ago, like I'm talking about a different person."

"I have that feeling a lot."

"Great, well, not great, I mean in some ways it's great. Anyway. So, yeah I went out after dark, wearing a belt of a skirt, low cut top, heels, bigger than these ones before you ask, make-up. I looked like a child who'd raided her mother's wardrobe."

"Some guys like that look."

"Yeah, I know. I was sick to the stomach with nerves. It was cold, oh… it seems like a dream, a bad dream, a nightmare."

Dan wiped his plate clean with a piece of buttered bread. "Then what?"

Catherine had a faraway look in her eyes. "Well, I waited to get picked up and do what I had to do to get some money. A few cars passed. Some slowed, men eyeing me, looking me up and down." Once again she appeared to be reliving the experience. "I could see their souls etched on to their faces…." She trailed off, but after a few seconds she continued. "Anyway, one stopped." Dan watched her face as she spoke. "I approached really slowly. I was terrified, but I just tried to think of the fix I'd get, that that would make it all right."

"Have you finished, my friends?" the waiter asked.

"Oh, yes," Catherine said, sitting back and giving him a wide smile. "Thank you."

"Everything okay for you?"

"Yeah, cheers." Dan slid his plate to the edge of the table.

"Lovely," Catherine said, passing across her half eaten breakfast. "Sorry, too much for me, but it was lovely."

"Would you like anything else?"

"I'm okay," Dan said.

74

"Yeah, me too."

"Maybe another drink?"

"Yeah sure."

"Two teas?" the waiter said.

"Yes, thanks."

The waiter took the plates and their empty mugs and returned to the counter.

"So," Dan said, returning to the conversation. "You were picking up your first punter."

"Don't put it like that!"

"But that's what you were doing."

"Yeah, I know, I guess. Sounds so seedy now." She sighed. "Okay, so I approached the car, the driver's window rolled down and it was Markus."

"Markus?"

"Yes."

"Right."

"He explained to me who he was."

"A follower?"

"Yes, and he had been for a while. It was his first night out on the streets of Manhattan."

"What was he doing in America?"

"He was on an exchange with his non-denominational church. I think he was living in Borrow?"

"Barrow?"

"Yeah, that's right, Barrow in Lan-caster-shire."

"Lancashire."

"Yeah, that sounds right."

"But what was he doing trawling the streets?"

"Well, before he became a follower, he was heavily into pornography, using prostitutes and escorts, and all kinds of dark stuff. This was his way of giving something back, turning his old lustful life into a positive, helping the kind of women who he'd once used for his own gratification."

"I see."

"I thought you might."

"You thought I might?"

"Sure."

Dan raised his eyebrows.

They were interrupted as the waiter brought over their drinks. "There you are my friends."

75

"Cheers."

"Thank you," Catherine said.

"Any desserts? We have delicious homemade cakes?"

"I think we're okay."

Catherine nodded in agreement.

"Well, let me know," the waiter said. The door opened and two people walked in. "Hello, my friends. A table for two?"

"This is a nice place. It reminds me of this lovely little deli in Boston," Catherine said.

"Is that where you are living now?"

"No, New York, but I travel quite a bit."

"With Beacon?"

"Yeah, it's great meeting new people. Wonderful."

"What's your role? If that's the right word?"

"Development."

"Development?"

"Yes."

"Sounds strange."

"Does it?"

"A little."

She took a sip of tea. "Shall I continue?"

"Yeah, sorry."

"No, it's okay. Right, where was I?"

"Markus was explaining what he was doing?"

"Oh, yeah. Well, I was just annoyed as he talked, because cars were passing and I might have been missing chances to make some cash. I think he realised that, so he offered to buy me a cup of coffee and give me some money."

"He paid you to have a cup of coffee with him?"

"Yeah, he paid for my time. It was bizarre. He gave me a hundred bucks and we, well, he talked all night."

"Where did he take you?"

"Just an all night coffee shop. He bought me a donut too."

"What did he talk about?"

"Himself mainly, and, as you can imagine, a little bit about some guy called Jesus , as well other less traditional prophets, and about another way, about the light." Dan laughed. "What?"

"Sounds very cheesy, Catherine."

"Yeah," she said. "I know it does. Sometimes that can be a problem."

"I can believe that."

"But that's the truth. Anyway, I was just pleased to be somewhere warm and to be getting some money to buy drugs."

"I bet."

"At about five am he dropped me back at my apartment."

"Did you tell your boyfriend?"

"Are you serious? No way. I gave him the money and he called our dealer. He never asked what happened, he wasn't interested."

"Oh."

"The next night, Markus was there again."

"How did you feel about that?"

"I thought it was very strange, but I liked getting something, the money, for nothing, so I went along with it. We talked more and more. I started to open up. It was the same again the next night and then the next."

"He was spending a fortune on you!"

"I know! It was crazy."

"You must have thought he was a sucker."

"I did a bit, yes, but it was sinking in, what he was talking about."

"How do you mean?"

"It was making sense. I don't know. It gave me hope more than anything. Maybe there was more to life, etcetera, etcetera."

"I see."

"Then, I think it was the seventh night, after I got home, my boyfriend called the dealer but he couldn't get hold of him. He went to try and find him and the guy had been arrested."

"So, no gear?"

"No. We both started to get really sick."

"How bad?"

"Very. We were withdrawing involuntarily, going cold turkey. We smoked a huge amount of pot to try and get something, but it couldn't match the hit we got off heroin."

Dan thought about reaching out his hand and touching hers. Her face looked pained as she recalled the past. "Are you okay?"

"I'm fine." She shook her head. "It was a long time ago."

"How long?"

"About four years. Look, do you want to get some fresh air? It's brightened up a bit."

Dan glanced out of the window. The sun had emerged from behind the clouds. "Yeah, why not."

"Great. I'll just pay the bill." Catherine stood up and walked to the counter. She paid and returned. "Ready?"

"Yes." Dan had put his coat on. He passed Catherine hers.

She smiled. "Thanks." Dan held it for her to slip into.

"Goodbye, my friends," the waiter said, waving as he served another customer.

"Thanks."

"Bye," Catherine said.

Dan held the door open for Catherine and they went outside. "Thanks for the meal." They began to stroll into the city centre.

"Oh, my pleasure. Sorry it wasn't the Ritz."

"Maybe next time?"

"Of course!"

They grinned at each other and walked on in silence.

After about ten minutes they found themselves passing a church. It was a grand sixteenth century gothic building.

"I bet not many people go in there any more."

"I think you might be right." Dan nodded to a sign indicating that the structure was scheduled for demolition.

She looked up at the basilica, breathing in the past. "A beautiful building though." Catherine pointed to a bench in the graveyard. "Shall we sit over there?"

"Okay."

They walked through the rusting steel gates and sat on the semi-rotten wooden bench. From their position they could see cars and people passing.

"Are you warm enough?" Dan asked.

"I'm okay. Why, are you cold?"

"No, just checking."

"Okay, where was I? Withdrawing?"

"Yep." Dan leant back on the bench and crossed his legs. He studied Catherine's face as she spoke. They were sitting close enough for him to smell her perfume, a sweet honey fragrance. He liked being close to her.

"Right, okay, well, let me think. Oh, yes. I couldn't sleep, I felt so ill. I mean you can't imagine, just so sick and in so much pain. So there I was in the middle of the night, and then I started thinking about what Markus had said, about asking for forgiveness and how Jesus wanted to have a personal relationship with me, to be my friend, and all that he'd said just kept going round and round in my head. Then I remembered a piece of paper he'd given me."

"Not a Bible or anything?"

"Oh, no, he said I wasn't ready for that. Anyway, this piece of paper, I crawled, literally crawled over to my coat pocket and found this piece of paper."

"What did it say?"

"It was a repentance prayer. I still remember it now. Well, we use it quite a lot actually: 'God of Love, I know I have sinned in my thoughts, words and actions. There are so many good things I have not done. There are so many sinful things I have done. I am truly sorry for my sins and turn from everything I know to be wrong. Gratefully I give my life back to you. Now I ask you to come into my life. Come in to cleanse me. Come in as a friend to be with me, and I will serve you, the light and love, for all the remaining years of my life. Amen.' I like the friend part, but of course, it's all good."

"Of course."

"Hey!"

"Sorry, so you said all that?"

"Yeah, well, mumbled, through the pangs of pain. I think that was the lowest point I could have gotten to. I could have ended my life quite easily. I had had enough."

"And it worked?"

"No. Nothing happened."

"Oh."

"I think I passed out. *But* I awoke the next morning and sunlight bathed the room and I felt totally clean. 'Come in to cleanse me'. I looked around and it was like a veil had been lifted from my eyes and I felt like I was on fire! All through my body I had this tingling sensation. It was amazing. I was repulsed with my surroundings; I could hardly look at my boyfriend who was asleep on our filthy mattress in the corner of the room. I just dressed and left. I called Markus from a payphone and he collected me."

"And that was it?"

"What do you mean?"

"No more withdrawal?"

"No, my addiction had gone, or should I say addictions were gone. I was so happy. I couldn't wait to start learning more. Markus was quite shocked too. But it wasn't just the words, Dan. I'd reconnected with the light, the light that is within us all, which dulls when the world, the world we've created for ourselves, grips its fingers around us and…."

"And?"

79

"And we forget. We forget about the light, we forget about the truth. We forget about universal love, a love that doesn't show prejudice. Everybody is a precious child of God, no matter what. But that's not to say that people can't live good, charitable lives without a faith, because they can."

"Of course."

Catherine smiled, leaned in to him and whispered. "However, you and I both know what good people are tapping into, whether they know it themselves or not." She giggled.

"Sure."

Catherine sat back. "Two sides to the same coin."

"What?"

"Two sides to the same coin. You can live a progressive and optimistic life in awe of human potential, embracing nature, rationalism, science, philosophy, without acknowledging...." She pointed upwards with a finger. "We cherish those things too, indeed anything that enriches life, but...." Catherine paused. "I guess we're a little more open with our hearts."

"That's a nice way to put it."

"Thanks! I should write it down. Another Halston gem!" Dan grinned. "Although...."

"What?"

"Nothing."

"Go on."

"It's just that in the times we're now living in, people might have to choose what side they're on. If they're brave enough, that is...." Catherine continued before Dan could reply. "I've learned so much since leaving that filthy room, Dan. It was like waking up. I've learnt that God's light, God's love, shines through the other ancient religions and other prophets too, other people throughout history who have tried to show us the way." She sighed. "Hmm. I guess that's pretty obvious though, if you're smart enough to look. Anyway...."

"Well, I don't know what to say. That's quite a story."

"It is I suppose. Oh, Markus told me later that he'd meant to go to another part of town that first night, but a water main had burst on the street he needed to take, so he went down the one I was standing on."

"So if the water main hadn't burst, you wouldn't have met?"

"No."

"I know what Abdalla would say to that."

"Yes, I know, and he did! My story isn't unique you know."

"So I hear."

"Thousands of people who you wouldn't expect...." Catherine sensed that that conversation wasn't for now. "That was the start. Markus and the church looked after me. I read and read. Studying original biblical translations, as well as other progressive texts, and applying them to our lives now, and realising how it all connects and still speaks to us today. It's beautiful."

"Yes, my parents did the same."

"Of course, yes, sorry. Well, that's my story. What about yours?"

Dan glanced around. "It's getting dark."

"It is. I suppose we should get going." She was disappointed that Dan wasn't going to talk.

"What are you doing tonight?"

16

"A bar?"

"Or pub. You do drink, don't you?" Dan asked.

"Of course. Just a little though. Not as much as I used to."

"Well, will you buy me a beer?"

Catherine shrugged her shoulders. "Okay. But I'd better let Abdalla know I've found you."

"That makes me sound like a lost child."

Catherine laughed as she searched for her PDA in her handbag. "It does, doesn't it?" Catherine dialled the number and waited for it to be answered. "Hello Abdalla. Yes, yes. He's all right. We're just going to have a drink. Tell Markus not to wait up for me. Okay. Yes, I will. Bye. Bye."

"All right?"

"Yep. So, where are you taking me then?"

"There's a pub just around the corner."

"A quaint old English pub?"

"If you like."

"Great. Lead the way."

Catherine held her arm up and Dan responded by letting her slip it through his. They walked away from the church and into the city.

They soon found themselves sitting on red leather in a booth in a pub. Catherine had got herself a glass of red wine and Dan a pint of lager. It was quiet, with only a few regulars propping up the bar.

"It's nice in here," Catherine said.

"Is this what you thought a quaint English pub would look like?"

"Sure. It's an old building. Kinda Victorian?"

"Yeah I think so. My mother used to send me down here to get my father."

Catherine laughed. "Really?"

"Yeah. He liked a drink."

"Speaking of your parents, are you going to tell me any more? Not that you've told me much anyway."

"You don't give up do you?"

"I'm tenacious."

Dan smiled. "You certainly are." Catherine grinned back at him. "Well, seeing as you've bought me two cups of tea, a very late lunch, and a beer, I guess I should."

"Now I know your price!"

"Not too high is it?"

"Quite reasonable I'd say."

Dan tried to think of something else to say that would delay having to talk about himself. His eyes focused on a silver chain around Catherine's neck. The interlinked segments held a crucifix; it rested on her chest. Catherine noticed Dan's line of vision.

"Oh, you like my cross?" She held it in her hand.

"What?"

"You were looking at my necklace weren't you?"

"Oh yes, of course. What else?"

"A friend gave it to me. I switch between the cross and the fish."

"Oh, right."

"Come on then."

"What?"

"Dan, you're impossible."

"I'm sorry. Okay, look I'm not too good talking about myself."

"I really hadn't noticed, Daniel." She took a sip of her drink.

"How about you ask me some questions?"

"Questions? What, a Q and A?"

Dan laughed. "Yeah, a Q and A."

"You're not a holo-rock star, you know."

"I'm not anyone." He took a swig of beer. He seemed distant as he remembered his circumstances.

Catherine slapped her hands down on the table to get his attention. "Okay, question number one."

"Hang on. Something has been bothering me."

"What? What now?"

"What exactly has Abdalla told you about me?"

She shook her head in a matter of fact way. "I know what you are, Dan."

"You know what I am?"

"Sorry, I...."

"And that doesn't frighten you?"

"Why should it? Abdalla says you're one of us and that's good enough for me."

"I'm not one of you."

"Then if you're not one us, you're one of them."

"I'm not one of them either. I'm no one. That's the only way I can be. That's the way I like it."

"I don't believe you. Tell me about your mother, your real mother. What happened?"

Dan sighed. "You can guess that for yourself."

"Well, kind of, but what was she like as a person? Where was she from? What did she do?"

"I don't know. I'm going to the toilet." Dan stood up and headed towards the bathrooms.

"Dan!" Catherine watched him disappear from view. Twisting back, she faced the empty seat in front of her and chastised herself. "What am I like?"

Catherine sat for a few minutes by herself getting unwanted glances from the men at the bar. It occurred to her that Dan might not be coming back. She could picture him forcing his way out of the toilet window. With that thought in her mind she started to stand up, with the intention of finding him, but as she did she saw him walking back.

"Oh, hi...."

Dan had seen her about to get up. "Did you think I wasn't coming back?"

She gave a coy, embarrassed smile. "Perhaps."

"I don't think I could get away from you if I tried." He sat down.

"Hey! Look I'm sorry for firing questions at you, but as you can imagine I'm really interested in you."

Dan met her eyes and smiled. "I don't know."

"What?"

"The answer to your question about my mother, my real mother. I don't know."

"Oh."

"All I know is that something terrible happened, something really, really terrible. And I was the result." Catherine nodded her head, not wanting to interrupt now that he was talking. "I was adopted. I know nothing about her."

"Is she still alive? Do you know her name?"

Dan ran his hands through his hair. "No, I don't."

"Sorry, I go on a bit, once I get something between my teeth."

"I've noticed. I'm sorry for snapping at you."

"It's okay."

"Well, how did you know you were different?"

"I didn't notice, other people did. I was a handful, I think it would be fair to say."

"A handful?"

"Yeah, I was badly behaved, a tearaway. Stealing, swearing, fighting, even from a very young age. I was strong too. I could run much faster than the other kids, and I never got ill. It wasn't until my sixteenth birthday that…. Anyway, my adopted parents were really good people. As I grew up though, I just, I, had, have, a bad nature. I was always getting into trouble, for loads of different reasons. Abdalla caught me just after I stole something. He knew my parents from church."

"I see."

"Anyway, that day, after Abdalla brought me home, my mother made me read the Gospels, and a lot of other texts after that."

"But did you believe?"

"Sort of. A part of me didn't want to, but looking back, I think, that even at that young age I knew what I was." Dan's tone of voice changed; it became grave. "I knew there was darkness in me."

Catherine instantly dismissed the possibility. "There isn't."

"You don't know me."

"I…."

"If it wasn't for what my parents did." He paused.

"What?"

"I don't know. Maybe I'd be with…."

"The enemy?"

"If you like. That's why I have to stay hidden. They are still looking for me."

"How do you know?"

Dan took a deep breath. "They found me. Two months ago."

"They found you?"

"Yes. I played right into their hands. There was an archaeological dig. They were looking for the remains of the 'giants from the Bible'." Dan's eyes shifted left as he recalled those events.

84

"Your ancestors?"

"In a manner of speaking, I guess."

"And did they find anything?"

"No. It was a hoax to lure me there. I guess they thought I'd be interested. I found the info on the Internet. I screwed up. They killed everyone. Including...." Dan stopped.

"Including?"

"I met someone."

"Oh. I'm sorry. What happened?"

Dan looked directly into Catherine's eyes. "She got a bullet in the head."

Catherine gulped. "Oh."

"I got away, just."

"And what did they want?"

"Something about me fulfilling my destiny. That is why I have to stay hidden. I don't want any part of it. If I stay, I endanger you all. I don't want anyone suffering because of me."

"What if it's not about you, and what you want?"

"But that's what is best."

"We all know what we're getting into. Beacon is so vital. We're at the beginning of the last days, Dan." Catherine leaned forward as her passion once again ignited.

Dan looked surprised. "How do you know?"

"It's obvious. The empowerment we have for starters. And, as we know, the end begins with the sequential opening of the seven seals, trumpets and bowls. One each for every year, and we're two and a half years in!"

"I thought the book of Revelation was a coded message to the first century church?"

"We all did, until...." Catherine paused, thinking about how Beacon came into being. "It was, but it's also a more literal prophecy for us now."

"Maybe."

"Maybe? Just turn on your telly. Oh, you haven't got one, have you?"

"No."

"Okay, scroll through a newspaper. You'll read about military aggression, global pollution of the sea and land, disease.... We've ruined this world. The beginning of the end has started."

"So, four and a half years to go?"

She sighed. "I'm afraid so, I'm afraid so. Perhaps that's why they want you?" Dan gave her a reticent stare and thought back to their increased pursuit of him. "Well, you're important, aren't you? And, besides, we know who wins, right?"

"Right." Dan ignored Catherine's remarks about him.

"How about, what if, *they* still think, despite what is written, that *they* can still win?"

"You think *they*...." Dan emphasised the 'they' even stronger than Catherine was doing.

"Oi!" She crossed her arms and slouched back into her seat.

"Sorry. So, you think they'll make sure that the end, as it is written, doesn't come to pass?"

"Yes. They aren't going to play by the rules are they?" She sat forward again, putting her elbows on the table.

"I don't know, Catherine."

"Well, they're winning at the moment. All religions, well, all those which are, or have tried to be, connected with the light and love, are pretty much dead and despised. People with faith are seen as insular and exclusive, part of a cult even. The enemy has made sure of that. As I said, he, they have done a great job. Hats off to them."

"You really think it's happening?"

"Yes, I, we do. Can't you see it? Everything that is happening in the world?"

"I can, but it's happened before."

"Not like this. It's been magnified tenfold. That's why Beacon has come into being."

"Right."

"We're in the end times...."

"Okay, okay," Dan replied, unconvinced.

"I'm pleased you're a good guy." Catherine placed a hand on his and smiled. Dan slid his hand out from under hers. Her face looked puzzled and a little hurt. "What is it?"

"I'm not a good guy, Catherine. I struggle to stay in the...." He tried to think of the right word. "Light."

Catherine's eyes moved away from him as she thought. "You've finished your drink," she finally said, changing the subject.

"What?"

"Your drink. Do you want another?"

"I don't want you spending all your money on me."

"Oh, don't worry, the exchange rate is very good. I'm getting plenty of euro for my dollar."

"Same again then."

"Right, you got it." Catherine picked up their empty glasses and went up to the bar.

Dan examined her svelte figure as she stood waiting to be served. He closed his eyes and tried not to think the thoughts he was thinking. His lust for women was something he hadn't been able to lose. He tried to compact those urges down, but they still remained. He was at least able to control himself, though he wished he didn't have to. He didn't want to be constantly yearning.

"Here you go." Catherine handed him his drink and sat down.

"Thanks. Another glass of wine?"

"What's wrong with that?"

"I hope you're not slipping back into your old ways."

"No, no, no. Just a taster."

"Fair enough."

"It's only when you let something like alcohol, drugs or shopping, or whatever, fill that Love-shaped hole that it becomes a problem. But when that's already filled you can enjoy a drink!" She raised her glass. Dan lifted his and they clinked them together. "But this will be my last one."

Catherine clung to Dan as they stumbled forward. Her head was spinning. The two glasses of wine had quadrupled as the evening wore on.

"Oh, I think I'm going to be sick." Bending over, she retched.

"Feel better?" Dan asked, when she'd finished.

"Much." She wiped her mouth. "I'm so stupid."

"No one is perfect, Catherine."

"But I should be."

"You're only human. Come on, we're almost there."

Dan put his arm around her and continued to support her as they walked along the empty streets.

Outside Markus's terrace, Dan searched through Catherine's handbag. It was late; there were no lights on, apart from the one illuminating the hallway. Dan found the keycode he was looking for and led Catherine up to the porch.

"Thanks for looking after me," she mumbled. Dan went to unlock the door.

"That's okay."

Impulsively, as if a switch had been flicked, Dan pushed Catherine back against the wall of the covered entrance. He kissed her and ran his hands through her hair. He couldn't resist.

"What are you doing?"

"I want you," he told her. "I want to...." Catherine started to cry, as the next two words left his mouth. It was his voice, his emotion, yet it wasn't from his heart, but from his clouded mind.

"Dan, stop it, please." He began to lift the hem of her dress. "Dan." She attempted to push him away and managed to shove him, and as he stepped back, she slapped him hard across the face. Catherine snatched the keycode from his hand, unlocked the door and went in. She slammed the door shut. Inside, she fell against the hallway wall, shaking. Her red lipstick was smudged around her mouth. She stood for a few moments in shock and then staggered towards the stairs, turning the light off as she went.

Dan was left in the dark. His mind began to clear and he was appalled at his actions. He punched his forehead with a clenched fist and swore. As he stepped off the porch, it began to rain heavily, and a distant rumble of thunder echoed. He pulled Abdalla's coat to him and looked up at the night sky. A torrent of water poured down on him.

17

Bubbling hot milk frothed into a stainless steel jug, almost overflowing.

"Thank you," the young girl said.

Chika handed her a latte to go. The girl glanced to Jake, Chika's colleague. "That's okay, honey. You take care now." Chika turned to Jake after they'd watched her leave. "All you have to do is stand there!"

"What do you mean?"

"Didn't you see the way she was looking at you?"

"No."

"Yeah, right."

"I didn't."

"Hmm, it's those boyish good looks and that floppy dark hair. How do you get it to go like that?

"The hair?"

"Yeah."

"I don't do anything."

"Do you know how long it takes me to fix my hair?"

Jake looked at Chika's bouffant afro. "I can't imagine."

"Ages. That's how long. I have to get up at four to do it, so I get here looking good by six."

"Wow."

"You bet wow. Anyway, when do you go back?"

"Next week." Jake went over to the sink and washed out the milk jug.

"You've got a few more shifts then?"

"Yeah, need the money. There are a lot of books I need to buy and I need to be concentrating on my studies and not working here! I've got lots on my plate."

"Sure, and the rest."

The door opened and one of the regular customers walked in.

Jake brushed back his wavy hair. "Hello, mate."

"All right, boy, usual please," the man said in an Essex accent. "How's it going all right? Bit early isn't it?"

"Yeah, it is. I'm fine, you?"

"Not bad, not bad." The man bent down and looked at the pastries on display in the glass cabinet. "I always like the look of your cakes, but the wife says I'm on a diet." He tapped his paunch.

"What's he drinking?" Chika asked, standing by the coffee grinder.

"Americano," Jake replied. "That's four-eighty please, mate. Sure you don't want something? It's all fresh."

"Better not. The wife will know. You'll find that out one day. They have their ways."

"Hey!" Chika gave him smile.

"Ha ha. Should've kept me mouth shut. How are you, love?"

"Fine, fine." Chika added hot water to his drink.

"There you go, boy," the man said, handing Jake five grubby coins from his fluorescent orange work trousers.

"Cheers."

"Looks like you were out last night."

"Yes, going back to uni soon, so just seeing some mates. Stayed over with one of them – talked all night!"

"Oh, right."

"Good laugh though."

"Yeah. My clubbin' days are done and dusted. Hard to do when you've got kids and a naggin' missus."

"I see." Jake leaned on the till waiting for Chika to finish making the coffee.

"Had many in?"

"A few, including the guy over there." They both looked towards a man seated in the corner, he appeared worse for wear, as if he hadn't slept for a week. "I think six in morning is a little early to open. Maybe seven, at a push." Jake took the coffee handed to him by Chika and passed it on to the man.

"Cheers."

"But I suppose everyone's on their way to work."

"Yeah, like me." He took a sip of his drink. "Okay, I'll see you later, boy, take it easy. Thanks, love."

"Okay, bye."

"Have a good day," Chika said.

As the man swaggered out, a harassed looking woman walked in. She glanced around and headed for the man in the corner.

"Doug?" she said, her voice full of concern and worry.

"Oh, Jane."

"How are you? I came as soon as I could. Your phone call really frightened me."

"I had a bad night, sorry." He rubbed his unshaven face.

"Can I get you anything?" Chika asked, approaching the table.

"What?" Jane replied, reaching forward to hold Doug's hand.

"Sorry." Chika sensed that she'd interrupted something. "Um, can I get you anything?"

"Oh, I'll just have a coffee, no, a small black tea."

"Small black tea. No problem." Chika wandered back to the counter and began preparing the drink.

Jane gripped Doug's hands tighter. "Do you want to talk about it?" Her brother shook his head. "Okay, you don't have to."

She remembered back to when Doug had come out of hospital and how she had hoped that his mania, which alternated with severe depression, and from which he'd suffered for most of his life, had been treated successfully. But here they were again. Jane had wanted to call the hospital straight away, hoping that his deranged phone call had just been a slip; after all he'd been managing well up until now: his own flat and working as a volunteer in a charity shop. He had independence and was settling back into the community. She stared at her brother; his eyes were wide with fear.

"Here you go." Chika put the drink on the table.

"Thank you. How much is it?" Jane let go of Doug's hand and opened her handbag.

Realising something more important was happening, Chika replied, "Just pay on the way out."

"If you're sure."

"That's fine. I'll leave you two in peace."

"Thanks."

Chika raised her eyebrows at Jake as she crossed the floor back to the counter.

"What's going on there?" Jake asked.

"Not sure, but he looks really terrible."

The café door opened and a procession of people walked in. The morning bus had dropped off the first wave of town workers eager for caffeine.

Jane took a sip of tea, still staring at Doug. She tried to smile. Putting the cup down, she once again took his hands.

"So, you can't tell me what happened?"

"Not sure I can." Doug's voice, although clearly upset, appeared controlled.

"Well, just try to start at the beginning. I can't help if I don't know what the problem is."

"I'll try, I'll try." He coughed and cleared his throat. His eyes remained wide as he began his story. "Last night. I was on my way home from the pub."

"You're drinking again?" Jane's first thought was this might all be alcohol induced.

"No, no. I just had a few pints before I got my dinner from the chippie. It was only about seven o'clock."

"Okay," she cautiously replied. "So you got your dinner and you're on your way home?"

"Yes, yes, on my way home. I go the back way to the flats. It's quicker and quieter."

"And what happened?"

"Nothing, but I thought I was being followed as I walked down the alleyway, or at least watched."

"Did you see anyone?"

"Yeah, a few people. But it wasn't them."

"Okay, so you got home safely?"

"Yes. It wasn't until later. I...."

"What?"

"I may have been drinking from a bottle of something."

"Doug!" Jane let go of her brother's hands.

"It was only whiskey!"

Jane sighed and shook her head in frustration.

The morning rush hour had well and truly started. Chika was taking the orders as Jake made the drinks. It was busier than usual. The town's new shopping centre was opening today and there was an extra influx of new employees and eager shoppers.

"Five twenty please, dear," Chika said. The lady passed Chika a note without interrupting her conversation with her friend. "Well, excuse me," Chika whispered under her breath, but loud enough for Jake to hear. He stifled a laugh and handed a waiting customer their drink.

"Is Rani in at nine?"

"She'd better be."

"You got that right. What time are you working until?"

"I'm not sure, baby. You'll have to check the rota. Eleven, I think."

"Me too. A grande mocha?" He passed the drink to the woman who nodded. "Thanks, have a good day. You know I think we might be running out of milk."

"Running out of milk? Six sixty, my love." She took the customer's money and returned their change in seconds, shoving the till drawer shut with her stomach.

"I can only see half a pint of each left in the fridge. Primo latte? Thanks."

"Pandesh should have stocked up last night. I'll have words with that boy when I see him," Chika said, helping Jake make the beverages.

"I know. He must have forgotten."

"We'll send Rani out to get some when she gets here."

"Good idea."

"What did you see?"

"I'm not sure," Doug replied, visibly trembling. "But it scared me to death. I've never seen anything like it."

"What?"

"I went out to see what the dog next door was barking at. As I got closer, I heard a whimper. It just stopped barking. Then I peered round the corner and I saw it."

"It? The dog?"

"No. It. It was holding the dog, a doberman, up as easy as I can hold up this cup. It was biting into it, eating it like, like a sandwich." Jane stared at her brother. She didn't know what to say. "Then it kinda snarled at me, blood foaming from its mouth. I was so scared."

92

"It's okay now." She touched his arm and thought about phoning the hospital.

"You... didn't... see... it... it... was straight, straight... from hell."

"Okay, okay." She was alarmed at her brother's distress. "What happened then?"

Doug took a deep breath. "It flung the dog aside and started coming towards me!"

"And after that?"

Doug's eyes focused on Jane's concerned, but unbelieving, face. "I ran. And didn't stop running, until I phoned you."

The last drops of milk from the penultimate bottle rolled into the jug.

"That's almost it, down to the last one," Jake said, putting the empty container into the recycling bin.

"Oh, I don't believe it. What time is it?" Chika glanced up at the clock. "Ten to eight. All right, my dear, you'll have to pop out."

"Will you be okay by yourself?"

"Of course. Be as quick as you can. Oh, here's the company credit card."

"Thanks."

"Okay, won't be long. I can cut through the new shopping centre. I should only be five minutes."

"Did it follow you?"

"No," Doug replied, who was still trembling. "I didn't see it again." He leaned forwards; his eyes had remained unchanged during the exchange, still wide and fearful. He lowered his voice. "It was a demon! A demon!"

"Look." Jane tapped his arm gently, trying to placate him. "Why don't we get you home? Did you sleep at all?"

"Sleep?! I had to keep my eyes open!"

Everyone in the coffee shop turned to see Doug standing, having pushed his chair back against the wall.

Jake and Chika watched the drama unfolding. "Are you sure you'll be all right?"

"Oh, yeah. I can handle anybody."

"You know, I believe you."

"You bettcha."

Jake put on his coat. "Funny. I think I recognise that guy."

"Oh?"

93

"Yeah. I think he might live near me, a few blocks down."

"Well, you'll be carrying him home if he makes another scene."

"Right, well, see you in a minute."

"Okay, sweetie."

Jake left and peered through the café window as he passed. He saw the man storming out, followed by the woman, who flung some money at Chika. He turned and watched the guy rush away in the opposite direction. The woman went after him, trying to catch up.

The entrance to the new shopping centre was only metres away. Inside stores were open and some were already displaying banners declaring sales. There were also a number of units empty, some boarded up and plastered with 'to let' signs, others still being fitted out by workmen.

In a split second, he was pulled backwards, grabbed by his coat collar, into one of the vacant stores. The wooden door slammed shut behind him as he was thrown to the dusty floor. It was dark, except for a few shards of daylight coming through the gaps in the temporary timber frontage. There was just enough light for Jake to see a figure towering over him.

"What do you want?" Jake managed to utter, as panic descended upon him. The second the words left his lips, and before he could cry for help, he felt a steel-strong arm wrap around his neck and a filthy cloth was shoved in his mouth. His subsequent cries were muffled.

He watched the man pick something up from the floor. It looked like a drill, but no, he heard a click, which echoed around the empty space. Something shot out of the object and embedded itself in the floor. It was a nail. The figure lifted Jake up with one hand and held him against an internal wall. A shaft of light hit the side of his attacker's face. Jake's eyes expanded with shocked surprise. The first tack embedded itself. Many more followed.

18

"No, he didn't come home, Markus," Abdalla said. "His bed hasn't been slept in. Does Catherine know where he is? What? Hungover? Really? Is she all right? Okay. Good. Look, I need you all to get here asap. I've phoned the others. I'm afraid I've got some very bad news. No. I'll tell you when you get here. Okay. Ten is fine. Bye." Abdalla ended the call. He felt sick to the bottom of his stomach. A tear escaped from the corner of his eye.

Dan had hung around all night. He was cold and tired. While he waited, he replayed what had happened with Catherine over and over in his mind. Dan had never loved anyone apart from his adoptive parents, and that was a different love, a caring love, a love that came from familiarity and fondness. He knew lust, which he had felt for Anya, and others. He became blinded and fogged by it. With Catherine he felt something else, he felt an immediate kinship; he was drawn to her and it wasn't just sexual. Last night he had got the two, lust and love, confused. He had acted like an animal. He despised what he was but, ironically, that only increased the dark potential within, and the feelings that could consume him. He was only a blink away from wrath. He knew it was what they wanted. Dan closed his eyes and took a deep breath. He thought back to his childhood, to his parents. He exhaled an apology.

Abdalla ushered Markus and Catherine through to the living room where Jean-Paul was already sitting waiting for them.

"How are you feeling?" Jean-Paul asked Catherine. She dropped herself down into an armchair.

"Like an elephant has sat on my head. Where's Lian?"

"She's not feeling very well. She ate in China Town last night with relatives. I suppose it couldn't compete with her home-made Scottish-Chinese cooking. What happened to Dan?"

Catherine looked at Markus. "They had a little...."

"He tried it on with me!"

"Oh." Abdalla lowered his head. "That is a shame."

"A shame? I'd say. It was horrible. I slapped him, hard. I don't know where he went."

Abdalla sighed. "I'm afraid that's may be something he can't help."

"I know. I just thought he was...."

"Normal?" Markus said.

"Yeah. Why not?"

"You know why not, Catherine," Abdalla replied.

"I guess. We were having such a nice time. He had told me a bit about himself. Perhaps I shouldn't have slapped him."

"Well, at least he came to his senses."

"Hmm."

"So, what's going on?" Markus asked.

"You'd better sit down."

Markus glanced at Jean-Paul who shrugged his shoulders; Markus joined him on the sofa.

"I'm afraid...." Abdalla's voice started to break. He bit his lip, clasped his hands, but couldn't stop the tears from forming in his eyes.

"What is it?" Catherine asked, seeing his distress.

"A detective from the Dorset police force phoned first thing. Erica and her son Harry were killed yesterday morning."

Markus leapt to his feet. "What?"

"What happened?" Jean-Paul asked.

Catherine began to cry. Markus placed a consolatory hand on her shoulder. "I can't believe it. First Sunayani and now Erica."

"I don't know; he was a little sketchy on the details." Abdalla sat down, wiping his face with a handkerchief. "Also...."

"What?" Catherine said.

"After you all left yesterday a detective from London phoned, Anchel was his name."

"About Simon?" Markus asked.

"Yes. They found his car near a well-known suicide spot. They didn't find a body, but said it might have been washed out to sea."

"He did it then." Catherine put her head in her hands and tried to make sense of it all.

"I don't believe it," Jean-Paul said. "I just don't believe it."

"Did they say if Erica and Harry had been murdered?" Markus asked.

"No. They just said they'd been killed. They didn't seem to have made the connection between Sunayani. I mentioned it, but they weren't interested."

"Maybe it's just a tragic coincidence?"

"Yes, they can't be linked." Catherine wiped her eyes and sniffed. "For some reason Simon, I don't know, lost his mind, or something, and killed Sunayani, then two weeks later killed himself. And Erica's death must have been an accident."

"They said they haven't found Simon's body," Abdalla said firmly.

"But he wouldn't harm anybody, he was so full of light and love," Jean-Paul replied.

"But from his actions it's obvious that he murdered Sunayani," Catherine said. "Isn't it?"

Jean-Paul shook his head. "How well do we know this Daniel?"

"What?" Catherine said. Her eye-liner was smudged and running down her face.

"This all start around the time he reappeared. And he tried it on with you...."

"He didn't mean it...."

"I personally vouch for Daniel," Abdalla said.

Jean-Paul sighed. "Okay."

"Have you spoken to Jake and Lisette?" Markus asked.

"I spoken to Lisette yesterday, she's fine. She's gone to a meditation retreat today. I phoned Jake's landline and PDA earlier this morning, left messages, but, so far, I haven't got hold of him."

"They are the only other two who aren't here."

"What are you saying?" Jean-Paul asked.

"You know what I'm saying. I'm saying that Jake and Lisette, along with Erica, Sunayani," Markus took a deep breath, "*and* Simon, should have been with us these last few days, but they couldn't make it."

"And they're all Britain's regional coordinators, like us. Well, apart from Catherine," Abdalla said.

Markus nodded his head. "Exactly."

There was silence as they all thought. Finally Abdalla spoke. "We all know how important Beacon and our commission is."

"I was telling Dan about us and our initial fear, although I decided not to mention Sunayani's death and Simon's disappearance in case he thought I, we, were being paranoid." Catherine took the tissue Jean-Paul was handing her. "Thank you." She dried her eyes. "But now...."

"What did he say?" Abdalla asked.

"He was, well, open minded about it. I think."

Abdalla sighed. "Good. That's good. If you're right, Markus, then we might need him. I hope he returns to us. We should pray for him and, of course, for Erica and Harry and also for Jake and Lisette."

19

Dan's patience had paid off. Alec's Jaguar rolled into the underground car park, and as soon as he was out of the vehicle, Dan was there, knocking him unconscious. He had tried to justify his actions to himself all night, but had eventually given up. There was no way that he could. He had nothing, but he could take. Alec had got away from him before, and although his irrational anger for him had dissipated, he could still use Alec's Jaguar to get out of the city.

Dan took Alec's keycodes and wallet from his jacket pocket and dragged him into the dimly lit corner of the car park where he had been standing, out of sight of the CCTV. The vehicle's main security feature was that it required the owner's fingerprint to gain access and start it. From his trouser pocket Dan produced a penknife, stolen from a store earlier, and flicked up the blade. He hesitated, then proceeded to sever Alec's forefinger from his hand.

Dan opened the car door and placed the bloodied digit on the ignition screen. The engine turned over. Dan slid into the driver's seat. It was soft, the black leather smooth. He flicked through the tunes on the digital music player and chose some twentieth century rock 'n' roll. Then he noticed Alec's sunglasses on the passenger seat. He put them on, cranked the music up and drove away at speed.

Outside, the sun was shining. The car's electric powered engine purred as Dan put his foot down on the accelerator.

A camera flashed. Chief Inspector Jenna Fabris nodded and her colleagues moved forwards to try to get Jake unpinned from the wall.

"What do we know about Mr Taylor?" she asked Emile Corvisiero, her Detective Inspector.

"He worked around the corner in a coffee shop. He went out for milk just before eight am and didn't return."

"When was the body found?"

Emile looked at his watch. "Forty minutes ago. A workman found him."

"Right. Who would do this?" she asked, more rhetorically than as an open question.

"Some lunatic?"

"Hmm. Any witnesses?"

"Not so far."

"There must have been people around. This place only opened today, didn't it?"

"Yes, even though half the units are empty and yes, there were loads of people around."

"CCTV?"

"Ah, yes and no."

"Yes and no?"

"The shopping centre cameras, for some reason, only recorded static."

"Static?"

"Yes. We're not sure why yet."

"Great. So anyone could have walked in."

"It would seem so."

"But this isn't random, Emile. This seems personal. Someone went to a lot of trouble to do this."

"I know. I've never seen anything like it. Ritualistic?"

"I have no idea. Did you find anything else on him?"

"No, just his wallet and PDA, which was switched off."

"Anything in the wallet?"

"Bank cards, I.D. card, which we identified him by, and this." Emile passed Jenna a card with the image of a white stone on it.

"Beacon. Jake Taylor, Eastern Coordinator. Why does that ring a bell?"

"Oh yes. That 'House of Horror' story from a few weeks ago, didn't the news reports mention them, this Beacon?"

"Yes, I think they were both members. They said the husband had killed the wife and then disappeared."

"That's right. Are they some kind of cult then?"

"I don't know, but I think we should find out."

Dan had driven out to Alec's home, which had been helpfully programmed into the Jaguar's satellite navigation system. Alec's house was situated on the edge of the city in a leafy, affluent suburb. He drove into the driveway, stepped out and admired the three storey Georgian-inspired building in front of him. He walked up to the door, opened it and went in. It was immaculate inside, light with minimalist furnishings. Alec was clearly single. Nothing stood out as remotely feminine. Dan headed up the winding metal staircase. He wanted new clothes.

The bedroom was opulent in its refined decoration. Sliding open the wardrobe doors, Dan started rifling through Alec's garments. They were roughly his size. He chose a pair of designer jeans, a dark shirt, some socks, underwear and a pair of still boxed and unworn trainers. He began to get undressed and then thought he could, and should, take a shower.

Dan went out into the hallway and pushed open the doors until he found the bathroom, a luxurious tiled wet room. He stripped off and washed, making sure he used all of Alec's scented shower gel. He also shaved, smothering his face with plenty of cream. When he'd finished, he dried himself, threw the towels to the floor and walked back into the bedroom. Dan dressed, sprayed himself with expensive eau de toilette, swept back his hair, working in some pomade, and then checked his reflection in a full-length mirror. Not bad, he thought. He then squeezed out a handful of moisturiser from its bottle and rubbed it into his face.

Back downstairs, he headed for the kitchen. It was a custom made room, dark wood standing out against shining white terrazzo. It appeared to have hardly been used. In one corner, by a huge set of French windows, stood a refrigerator so big that Dan could quite easily step inside. It was filled with every imaginable type of food and drink. Dan took a pre-cooked chicken and a four pack of low calorie beer. He walked through to the living room, flopped down on the couch and, via its remote control, turned on the seventy-inch 3D screen that hung in the middle of a swirling patterned wall. He channel hopped as he ate and drank.

It didn't take him long to demolish the chicken and beer. He stretched out and yawned, deciding that he'd better make a move before he fell asleep. Alec would be found. Heading out, he saw a light orange leather jacket on the antique coat stand. It was a perfect fit.

Leaving the house, he felt like a different person. He was clean, fed and looking good. All he had left to do was to empty Alec's bank account and settle down somewhere quiet. Maybe move abroad; he was sick of the British weather. He'd spent some time in Portugal during the fifteen years that he had wandered and thought that might be a good place to revisit.

He slipped back into the Jaguar, and placed Alec's finger on the ignition screen. The car started. Looking up, Dan was shocked to see two police vehicles appear from nowhere and block the driveway. The car must have been traced via its satellite positioning system. Dan grinned and revved the engine. He spotted a gap in the trees surrounding Alec's house. Releasing the handbrake, the vehicle shot forwards and Dan steered it through the fissure. The Jaguar bounced up and down as it went over the rough ground, crossing a front garden, before hitting the pavement and ending up on the road. Dan increased speed and was, in seconds, up to one hundred miles an hour. Some way behind him he could see the blue flashing lights of the police cars. Dan weaved along the city streets, in and out of the traffic. It wasn't long before a plethora of police vehicles were trailing him. He glanced up through the sunroof and could see a helicopter above. Dan turned the music up and made for the motorway.

He was soon pushing the convertible to its limits. The speedometer bar was brushing two hundred miles per hour. As he flew past the other traffic he spotted a break in the central reservation. He decided to turn around and go back the way he had come, and then take the exit he'd just passed. As he approached the opening he hit the breaks, pulled up the handbrake, and twisted the steering wheel around. The car violently spun, sending up smoke as the tyres burned on the asphalt. Now facing in the opposite direction he put his foot down and kept it there. The police were astonished to see him heading past them in the opposite direction. Dan took the exit he wanted and was soon heading out into the country. For a while there was no one behind him. He slowed and wound down the window, putting his arm on the sill. It was a clear autumn day. For a few moments he felt normal, just a regular guy taking a drive in the countryside. Dan pressed a button and the sunroof glided open. Turning down the rock 'n' roll for a moment, he heard the helicopter above, and wasn't surprised to see the return of the familiar azure illumination in the rear-view mirror.

Dan increased speed and cranked the volume up again. Through the winding country roads he drove, almost losing control on a few tight, hidden bends. He felt sure there would be cops waiting somewhere for him. He thought about ditching the car and making a run for it. Even with the helicopter above and its thermal imaging, he knew he could easily make an escape. He glanced over his shoulder; they were closing in on him. With his eyes back on the road, he caught a glimpse of a police car up ahead on the right, trying to stay hidden in a bend. A stinger, a blanket of detachable hollow nails, that would embed in and deflate tyres, shot out across the road. Dan's immediate reaction was to swerve, and he did, but at over one hundred miles an hour. The vehicle lifted as Dan pulled hard on the wheel. The Jaguar came off the road, flipped into a field, and rolled and continued to roll, turning over twenty times, with parts flying off in all directions. When it finally came to rest in wet pasture it was flattened and crushed. A few police 4x4s pulled up and officers rushed over to the smouldering wreck. They were startled to see what remained of the door being kicked open. Dan stepped out. He cranked his neck, arched his back, took off the shades and threw them into the vehicle.

"Hey fellas." The approaching men surrounded him, some drawing collapsible batons, others aiming automatic weapons.

"Get down on the floor!"

"There's no need for that, I don't want to get these clothes dirty." He held out his wrists for handcuffs. "I'm coming quietly."

Two PCs grabbed him and another officer slapped a pair on him. "You must have nine lives to survive that," he said, tightening the shackles, which dug into Dan's skin.

"I guess I'm lucky."

"Well, your luck's run out. I'm arresting you for theft of a motor vehicle, and well, that's just for starters." The policeman read him his rights. "Anything you want to say?"

"I'm a little tense. I could use a massage."

"You won't like the hard beds in the cells then. Come on."

Dan was led to a police van and was shoved inside. He sat in a reinforced cage that smelt as if an alcoholic skunk had slept in it the night before. With the door slammed shut, he was again in darkness. Dan could hear the officers outside discussing the chase. The vehicle started and he settled back. He would soon be back in the city.

20

"Is there any more information you can give me?" Chief Inspector Jenna Fabris asked.

"None, I'm afraid," DCI Anchel replied. "As far as we're concerned, case closed."

"But you didn't find a body?"

"No, but it's only a matter of time."

"Right. Well, I'll let you know if I need...." The line went dead.

"Any luck?" Emile asked.

"No." Jenna put her PDA in her pocket. "Utterly unhelpful. What have you got there?" She indicated to the PDA in her colleague's hand.

"A mother and child where killed in Devon yesterday. I've just spoken to the investigating officer."

She took the device. "Oh?"

"Yes, and you'll never guess."

"Beacon. Erica Michaeli, South West Regional Coordinator. So that makes three."

"Apparently so."

"Right. I'll have a word with our Superintendent. I think we need to get jurisdiction on this."

"That's what we do."

"And I think we'd better contact these people. Do we have a number for them?"

"They have a website. I'll pull it up for you."

"Right, get me a contact number and an address. I think we need to find out what they are all about."

"Yes, ma'am."

Dan was led into the custody suite. He stood and listened as the charges against him were read out. It was a long list. An officer went through his pockets, producing Alec's snakeskin wallet.

"That's not mine."

The custody sergeant took a look at it. "Hmm. Alec Lars-Coe."

"That was the man he assaulted and stole the vehicle off, Sarge."

"Right, well that's evidence now. Okay, name?" the burly sergeant asked.

"Dan."

"And the rest."

"Dan-iel."

"He's got a sense of humour," the arresting officer said.

"Has he? Surname?"

"Just Dan."

"Look, we can do this the easy way or the hard way."

"Well, I don't mean to make your life difficult. I appreciate that you've got a job to do, but I'm afraid Dan is all you're getting."

"Right. No chance of an address then?"

"Well, I can tell you that."

"Good. Go on."

"I haven't got one."

The sergeant sighed. "Fine." He saved the document on the computer. "Put him in cell two, Boender. We'll take his DNA."

"This way."

Dan was led down a magnolia corridor. They stopped outside a cell and Dan was told to take his shoes and belt off. With them removed he stepped into the enclosed room.

"Any chance of a tea?"

"Yeah, okay." Boender slammed the steel door shut and locked it.

Dan studied his new surroundings: white walls, single mattress and a stainless steel toilet. He shuffled over to the bed and sat down. It was hard, very uncomfortable. He'd never been in a police cell before, but he'd certainly been in worse places. Maybe prison would be the best solution. Dan wondered if he could get convicted without having a name.

The cell door opened and Boender walked in with a plastic cup containing tea.

"Thanks," Dan said.

"No one can work out how you survived that crash. I've never seen anything like it. Do you need to see a doctor?"

"No. I'm fine."

"Really?"

"Yeah."

"I'll have one come in anyway, we need to take your DNA."

"I'll be here. I'm not going anywhere."

"You're quite right there."

"Cheers for the drink."

Boender walked out and locked the door. Dan sipped the tea. It was white hot and tasteless. He figured he'd have to get used to it if he was going to stay at His Majesty's Pleasure for some time to come.

"Who was that?" Markus asked.

Abdalla walked slowly back into the living room, replaced the phone back in its hub and sat down. His face was expressionless. "The police. Again."

"What's wrong?" Catherine's voice carried trepidation; it was obvious something else had happened.

"More bad news." The group was silent. He took a deep breath. "It's Jake...."

Catherine held her hands to her mouth. "Oh no."

"He was murdered this morning."

"I don't believe it," Markus said.

"I'm afraid so."

"That's it then. This is no coincidence. There's no doubt now. We're being targeted."

"It would seem so," Abdalla said. "It really does seem so."

"What else did the police say?" Jean-Paul asked.

"It was a different detective, a Chief Inspector. She said she'd been assigned the case, and that they are now linking the deaths to each other and... to us. She will be paying me, us, a visit."

"A visit?" Catherine asked, wiping her eyes as Markus comforted her.

"Yes, they think we may be in danger too. They're trying to keep it, the connection, out of the papers, for now."

"Do you think we need to warn everyone?" Markus asked.

"Our communities?"

"Yes."

"It just seems to be those in a position of authority."

"But why?" Catherine sobbed.

"Like I said before, to destabilise our commission!" Markus replied. "Us here in the UK, nurturing local communities, gathering people in."

"I agree, Markus, I agree," Abdalla said.

"What about the rest?" Jean-Paul asked.

"Around the world?"

"Yes."

"This is where it started, Jean-Paul. We're the foundation. We're the rocks. Take us away and it's sand, and the tide will wash it all away."

"You'd better phone Lisette," Markus said.

"I can't. She's at a meditation retreat, remember?"

"Oh, yes, sorry, you said earlier."

"The retreat doesn't have a phone and she said she wasn't taking her PDA. I'm not even sure where it is. Somewhere in the middle of nowhere. She'll be back tomorrow as she's got a cell leader meeting. I think she'll be fine, there will be plenty of people around."

Catherine was trying not to break down. "Maybe. When is the detective coming?"

"The Chief Inspector, who said her name was Jenna Fabris, is driving up today with a colleague. They said they would call by tomorrow."

"Right." Catherine sniffed and thought of Jake and how he used to make her laugh. "I hope Dan is back by then. Perhaps I'd better go out and look for him?"

"I can't imagine you'll get lucky again."

She stood. "Probably not, but I really need some fresh air."

"I don't think that's a very good idea. Not with all that's going on," Markus said.

Abdalla nodded his head. "I agree. We don't know…."

"I'll be fine." She headed towards the door. Abdalla and Markus glanced at each other.

"Catherine…." Markus said.

"I'll be fine."

Markus sighed. "Okay, Catherine."

"Let me give you a lift?" Jean-Paul said.

"No, it's fine, thanks. I'll catch the bus." She put on her coat and picked up her handbag. "It will be really busy. I'll be safe."

Abdalla placed his hands on her arms and stared into her eyes. "Catherine, take no chances. I mean it, no chances. Be very, *very* careful."

Catherine nodded her head. "I will, I promise."

Abdalla closed the door behind her and faced his friends.

Markus dug his hands into his pockets. "She's always been like that."

"I know, I know," Abdalla replied, moving over to the front room window and watching Catherine walk down the street. "I just hope I don't live to regret letting her go."

Catherine raised her eyes from the pavement and viewed her surroundings; a quiet suburban street, like thousands across the country, normal people and normal lives. As she walked, tears rolled down her face. She was struggling to understand how what was happening could be happening.

The doctor had checked Dan over; he was fine. He'd also taken Dan's DNA, which had subsequently been fed into the police's database. There was no match.

"Are you a missing person?" the sergeant asked, standing at Dan's cell door, eating a sandwich.

Dan was relaxing as much as he could on the bed. "Not quite."

"The longer you keep this up, the harder they'll go on you in court."

Dan shrugged his shoulders. "I really don't mind."

"You could be looking at ten to twenty."

"Years?"

"It's hardly going to be days, is it?"

Dan smiled. "Doesn't sound so bad."

"Have you ever been to prison?"

"Well, no, otherwise you would have found me on your database."

The sergeant realised his mistake. "Hmm. Well, let me tell you that prison isn't the holiday camp it used to be. Hard labour these days, as it should be. I was so happy when they brought back the death penalty."

"How enlightened," Dan said, under his breath and with more than a hint of sarcasm.

"What?"

"I think I can handle myself."

The sergeant observed Dan's physique and thought he was probably right. "Well, we'll identify you sooner or later."

"Okay, let me know."

The sergeant grimaced and closed the door. Dan looked down at his feet and the floor. He exhaled. He thought about how his life had turned out and what his future was now going to be. He got up, stood on the bed, and peered out of the barred window. Outside he saw a line of high rises, heard the sound of police sirens and smelt noxious fumes emanating from a nearby factory.

Catherine looked out on to the river Mersey. No Dan. He wasn't in the café either. It was a long shot to think that she would find him as easily as she had done before. She tried to think of other places that he might be, but none came to mind as, of course, she didn't know him very well, at all even. Catherine resigned herself to the possibility that he may have vanished, just gone. It was conceivable that she might never see him again. She closed her eyes and wished that she hadn't got drunk. She was sure Dan was important; on paper a threat, but her instincts told her that he had a good heart, and if there was someone after her, and the others, then he could protect them.

Looking back out on to the river, she shivered. It was getting dark and she was starting to feel apprehensive. Although there were plenty of people about, she couldn't help but stare at them, thinking that one of them might be.... She dug her PDA from her pocket and dialled Jean-Paul's number. She wanted that lift now.

∞

My dearest, I feel I am about half way into recounting the tale. I do hope that the unfamiliar scenery, contemporary to the time, hasn't affected your understanding of events. As I mentioned at the beginning of this account, the time I spent living in the first decade of the twenty-first century had a profound effect on me. I quickly became absorbed in the culture and very much felt myself to be a denizen of the time. As I wrote before, politically I saw how those years were shaping the future. But I should say how many tragedies had occurred, and were still taking place. Man's inhumanity towards man would sadden any righteous heart. I refer to wars, famine, disease and global pollution – man-made and without thought for nature and the environment. It was only when it was too late and Mother Nature had struck back, the four Angels standing at the four corners of the earth, that man realised he could be nothing without her, that their relationship was symbiotic.

You would have been horrified to see what I have seen. Pictures of starving men, women and children; children in poorer countries paid a meagre amount to make clothes for richer nations; children holding guns, being forced to fight in barbaric wars that led to genocide; refugees displaced by conflict living beneath plastic sheets; the underprivileged living in unsanitary conditions, drinking from water in which sewage also flowed; wars started purely for profit. The scale of the humanitarian crisis was overshadowed by frivolous news stories about 'celebrities' and the television channels broadcast non-stop programmes that pandered to humans' basest instincts. These shows did nothing to enlighten or bring joy, only to exploit and degrade. Would you believe they called it entertainment? I'm sure the cumulative effect of these horrific scenes would have brought tears to your eyes, like it did to mine.

I should now perhaps explain how I funded myself during those ten years and subsequent trips. Before the capsule developed a fault, I had seen that a substance, widely available in our time, was now banned in the future. It's value, for just a small amount, was unfathomable. The material I am alluding to is cocaine, which you'll recall was found in my study upon my final homecoming, and contributed to my present circumstances. Thus on my second trip into the future, I brought with me a substantial amount of the drug in its pure form which I distributed, for a reasonable cost, to those who wished to buy it, and they came from all walks of life. With what I know now, I cannot express how full of sorrow I am for contributing to an addiction and dependence. I fear this error will catch up with me, if indeed it hasn't already.

I must continue. This is perhaps the most heartbreaking part of his story.

21

The doorbell rang, more than once, the caller pressing intermittently to recreate a popular melody.

"Good morning, Mrs R," Josh said, when the door opened in front of him. His beaming face was all freckles and his hair, a mop of ginger, flopped down.

Zaylie smiled. "Good morning, Joshua. How are you dear?"

"Fine thank you, is he up?"

"Yes, come on in. Glenn and Chock are already here."

Josh followed Zaylie into the living room.

"Happy birthday!" Josh tossed an envelope on to Dan's lap and dumped his rucksack on the floor. He sat himself down on the arm of the sofa.

"Hello mate," Dan replied, tearing the paper open.

"Where have you been?" Glenn asked. His face was covered in adolescent acne.

"Yeah, where have you been?" Chock repeated, who was munching on his fourth chocolate bar of the day.

"I was helping my mum with the shopping."

"Oh, you are a good boy, Joshua," Zaylie replied. The two other boys rolled their eyes. "Can I get you a drink?"

"Beer?" Josh said, under his breath.

Glenn and Chock stifled their giggles. Dan pulled out the card and quickly rammed it back again when he saw the boorish moving image and flashing message.

"Sorry, what was that, dear?" Zaylie asked.

"A can of cola would be nice, Mrs R, thanks."

"Right, oh, let's have a look at your card, Daniel."

Dan shot Josh a glare, and then, inexplicably, Josh was propelled off the arm of the sofa and on to Chock's lap.

"Careful," Chock said.

"You been drinking already?" Glenn asked.

"Erm no." Josh swiftly moved. Dan smiled to himself.

"I'll show you later, Mum."

"Okay. Are you boys okay for drinks?"

"Yes, thank you," Chock and Glenn replied.

"Daniel?"

"I'm fine, thanks."

"Okay, back in a second." She left the room humming an old pop song to herself.

"How did you do that?" Josh immediately asked.

"Do what?"

"I felt something push me off the sofa."

"Another one of your powers, eh Dan?" Glenn asked.

"'Powers'? What does he mean 'powers'?"

"Dan woke up this morning hovering above his bed," Chock said, scrolling through an electronic Liverpool Football Club annual that Dan's father had given him for his birthday.

"Is that so, Chunky?" Josh replied.

"It's true," Dan said. "But I'll tell you about it later." His voice became quieter as his mother walked back in the room with Josh's drink.

"Here you go, Joshua."

"Ta, Mrs R." Josh cracked open the can and took several gulps.

"You boys will be careful won't you?"

"We've been camping before, Mum."

"I know, I know. Well you all look the part," she said, referring to the fact that they were all dressed in army fatigues. "Not that I like warfare."

"They are only clothes, Mrs R," Josh said.

"Yes, I know, but…. Oh, Daniel's father has got you a few beers to take with you seeing as it's Daniel's sixteenth birthday!"

"Thank you very much, Mrs R." Josh saluted the air and gave Glenn, Chock and Dan a wink. "That's very generous. Sixteen, eh Dan, you can legally do a lot of things now that you do anyway."

"What does he mean, Daniel?"

"No idea, Mum, I think he must be tired from 'helping' his Mum with the shopping."

"Yeah, I am actually. So when are we going?"

"Now that you're here we can get going soon, can't we?"

The boys nodded.

"Well, please be careful. You'll be back tomorrow evening?"

"Yep."

"Don't forget we've got people coming around."

"I won't. I'll be here."

Fifteen minutes later they were walking through the streets, heading for the city's railway station.

Josh sniffed and wiped his nose with the sleeve of his coat. "So, what's this 'powers' business then?"

Dan's tone changed. He was reluctant to elaborate, because it was ludicrous. "Oh, erm, yeah, I woke up this morning, and as I told the others, I was floating above the bed."

"Rubbish. You're not funny."

"It's true," Dan replied, in a way that made it sound like he wished it weren't so.

"Drinking your Dad's whiskey again last night? Or your Mum's cider?"

"No."

"Anything else?"

"Yeah. I can move things."

Chock opened a packet of crisps. "Like he did with you."

"Shut up." Josh took the crisps from him and stuffed a handful in his mouth.

"Oi!"

"You don't believe me?"

"No, mate, no. I can only believe what I see with my own eyes. I can see Chock is fat and that girl over there is pretty. Is that Menna from 7c?" They all turned to see who he was pointing at.

"That's not Menna," Glenn replied.

"Oh yeah, you *love* her." Josh puckered up his lips.

"I think she likes me," Chock said, opening another packet of crisps.

"Maybe if she was blind, Chunky." Josh tipped the crisp packet up and the remaining contents slid into his mouth.

"Anyway, I'll show you properly when we get to the forest," Dan said.

"Nothing to do with that 'God of love' nonsense is it? Dad says people who believe in, well, anything like that, are nutters."

"Nutters," Chock mumbled.

"Let's not upset Dan on his birthday," Glenn added.

"No, it hasn't." Dan sighed, ignoring their comments. He was used to defending his parents' beliefs.

"Well, I look forward to it," Josh said. "I look forward to it."

A few hours later, after a train journey and walk from the station to the forest, they crunched through woodland until they found an isolated, spacious area amongst the otherwise tightly planted trees.

They set up their tents, and then went about making a fire, piling up dead wood, sticks and branches, building the pyre wide and high.

Dan lit a match and held it between his thumb and forefinger. "Right, take a look at this."

"What?" Josh crossed his arms. He and the others watched on as Dan projected the flame through the air and on to the tinder-dry wood, that had also been generously splashed with petrol. The stack blazed.

"How do you do that?" Chock asked.

"I'm not sure."

"Magic. What do you think, Josh?"

"I agree with Glenn, it's magic. It's a trick. You downloaded a book or something. Maybe you got it for your birthday?"

111

Dan shook his head, unsurprised at his friend's dismissal; he wasn't sure he believed it himself. The notion of what he appeared to be able to do made him feel sick to his stomach. He felt as if he was on the edge of something that he didn't want to embrace.

"I think it's smart," Chock said, taking a biscuit and chewing on it.

"You'll eat all our food!" Josh snatched the packet away from Chock. "Anyway, that is some fire. What if someone sees?"

"There's no one around for miles," Dan said.

"There's always people around, but who cares. Let's have another beer!"

"Good idea!" Chock said.

Dan snorted a lungful of air, irritated at his friend's dismissal.

Glenn dug into his rucksack and pulled out four bottles of cheap beer and handed them around. Chock opened his and the contents sprayed everywhere. The others laughed.

"Oi!"

"Got ya!" Glenn had shaken the contents.

"Hey anyone some deodorant?" Josh asked, watching the flames get higher.

"What?" Dan asked.

"We can throw it in the fire – it'll explode!"

"Great. Here you go." Chock wiped the beer off his jacket and handed over an aerosol from his bag.

"Cool."

Josh shook the can and sprayed some of the contents under the arms of his jacket, before tossing it into the fire. They all ran for cover, apart from Chock who just stood there, gulping down his beer.

"Chock!" Dan said.

"Quiet." Josh held a finger to his mouth. "Let him stand there."

"He could get hurt."

"Yeah, it'll be funny."

"Chock!"

Chock turned, his face filled with horror as he realised his friends had hidden behind a fallen tree. "Bloody hell." He ran to them, his large belly bouncing up and down, but he wasn't quick enough. The can exploded and Chock fell to the ground, taking in a mouthful of dirt.

Josh and Glenn laughed. Dan got up and went to help Chock to his feet. "Are you all right?"

"Yeah, spilt my beer though." Dan smiled and watched Chock brush the dirt from his clothes.

"He's fine," Josh said, walking over swigging on his drink. "Come on, you and Chock, me and Glenn. We'll guard the base and you'll have to try and rescue the Princess. I'll draw out a perimeter and we'll have to stay by our tent, but we might come after you!"

"Okay," Dan agreed.

Glenn passed Josh the 'Princess', one of Glenn's sister's plastic dolls, from his rucksack. Josh placed it on the ground near the fire.

"Not too close," Glenn said. "It will melt."

"You're going down!" Chock said.

"Sure," Josh replied, rejecting the prospect.

Dan got himself and Chock another bottle of beer and they disappeared into the woods with their weapons slung over their shoulders. Josh had managed to get them some paint-ball guns, which they were using without the protective equipment, from his Dad.

"They're always taking the mickey out of me," Chock said, digging out a chocolate bar from his jacket pocket.

"They just think they're funny. We'll take them."

Chock gave a big smile and bit a huge chunk off the bar.

Dusk was beginning to fall. Josh and Glenn warmed themselves by the fire.

"When do you think they'll attack?" Glenn asked.

"Not for a while, and we get to drink the beer and sit by the fire *and* we've got all the food." Josh clapped his hands together.

"Oh, yeah."

"Yeah, let's chill, brother." Josh threw his empty beer bottle into the fire and uncapped another one.

About an hour passed and there was no sign of Dan or Chock.

"I think I'm going to be sick," Glenn said.

"Ha ha, can't handle your beer?" Josh also felt ill from necking too many in a short space of time. Glenn stood and rushed into the forest. Josh heard him being sick. "You big girl." Turning back to the fire he heard the sound of branches snapping. "Hey, Glenn, get back over here. I think I heard something."

Glenn returned holding his stomach. "What?"

"Pick up your gun, you dummy. I heard them."

"Okay, okay."

"Come on, let's take cover behind the tent."

They hid, one at each end.

"What did you hear?" Glenn asked.

"Snapping twigs, probably Chock."

113

"Yeah, his footsteps would wake the dead."

"Did you hear that?"

"No."

"They're out there." Josh checked the position of the Princess. "We need to let them get close and then they get it."

"We'll have to be careful not to hit them in the face." Glenn's eyes flitted around, watching for any movement.

"Hey, these things happen in combat. We've got to take them down, no matter what." Glenn gave Josh a hesitant look.

There was another noise, this time from behind them.

"They must have split up!" Josh said. "Quick, over to that tree, we'll be able to watch from both angles."

They crawled over to the fallen tree that they'd sheltered behind before.

Josh rested the tip of his gun on the log. "If they can't see us they might make a run for the Princess. We have to be ready."

"I am, I am."

"Good, no way I am losing this."

As they waited, the boys heard another sound and as they both raised their weapons, a fawn appeared.

"A deer!" Glenn said.

Josh was annoyed; his adrenaline was pumping and he was ready to defend with force. He fired a shot at the deer. It missed, the paint exploded on the ground, and the animal fled.

"What did you do that for?"

Josh rested against the tree trunk. "Why not?"

Dan and Chock sat down on a felled tree.

"So when are we going to attack?" Chock asked.

"Soon, soon. We want to lull them."

"Lull them?"

"Yes, keep them waiting, send them to sleep."

"Ah, I see. I need the toilet," Chock said, all in one breath.

"You should be able to find a spot." Dan gazed around the vast woodland surrounding them.

"Yeah. See you in a minute."

"Okay."

Chock shambled off. Dan examined his hands. What had happened to him? It hadn't sunk in that he could suddenly move objects, control fire, what else? He had always been stronger and faster than his friends, but he could now feel that power increasing.

"Dan!"

"Shoosh!"

Chock yelled his name again. Dan got up and followed friend's cries until he found him. "Be quiet, they'll hear you."

"Sorry, but look what I've found."

"What?"

Chock wandered down a slope and pointed at an area overgrown with bracken and sheltered in the shadow of a huge oak tree. Dan squinted at where he was pointing to and finally saw a wooden door hidden beneath overgrowth.

"You can get in," Chock told him. Dan walked forward, put a palm against it and pressed. It creaked open. "Wait until you see inside."

Dan stepped down into a sizable space. "Wow. How did you find it?"

"Well, I was...."

Dan cut Chock's story short. "Don't worry."

The room's walls were constructed from planks of wood and the roof was corrugated tin. The area was, surprisingly, furnished: a wooden table with two chairs stood in the middle, wooden shelves held label-less tins and several oil-burning lanterns. Towards the back there was a bed; a pillow, sheets and a thick rug sat folded on top of it. The one other prominent feature was a wood-burning stove with a tin chimney heading into the ceiling. On top of the stove lay cutlery, and next to it stood a heap of desiccated wood, paper, turned yellow by time, and a large box of matches.

"This is amazing," Dan said. "Looks like no one has been here in years."

"I know. Shall I get the others?"

"No. We can hide out here."

"While we lull?"

"Yeah, if you like. Let's see if we can get a fire going!"

"What about the smoke?"

"There's a chimney here, but I didn't see one outside." Dan exited the room and looked over the roof. It had rusted, and the colour, along with the moss and leaves, helped it blend perfectly with the forest façade. Through the dense bracken he saw what looked like a large tin can.

"Well?" Chock asked, when Dan returned.

"The smoke gets dissipated through the bushes."

"Disa-what?"

115

"Erm, dispersed, so no one sees."

"Right. I wonder what's in these tins?" Chock lifted a tin off the shelf and blew the dust off. "Ah."

"What?"

"Spider."

"Oh."

Chock noticed Dan playing with the flue of the chimney. "What are you doing?"

"I thought it might be blocked. Leaves and stuff. Don't want to fill the room with smoke."

"Will this help?" Chock produced a brush with an extendible handle from a corner of the room.

"Ah, yeah, yeah it would. Light one of those lamps will you? It's getting dark." Chock handed the brush to Dan, who set about clearing the shaft, and then pulled a box of matches from his pocket. "Be careful."

"I'm not stupid," Chock replied, spilling a little oil from the lamp down his coat as he spoke. He lit the wick and held it up.

"Thanks. I think it's clear. Let's see if we can get it going!"

It was night when they emerged, the black sky prominent with gleaming white stars and a crescent moon.

"We'll have to come back here soon," Dan said, gazing up. "But remember, don't tell anyone, especially not Josh."

"Okay."

"Right. Let's make our way back. Absolute silence now." Chock was about to reply eagerly, but just managed to stop himself. He nodded in agreement instead.

Between them they had drunk the half bottle of scotch that Chock had liberated from his father's drinks cabinet. Now they gingerly returned, determined to rescue the Princess. Approaching slowly, they saw Glenn and Josh lying by the fire with empty beer cans next to them. Their paint guns were propped up against the tent they were sharing.

Dan gave Chock a military-esque signal to advance. They moved forwards quietly, down into the camp and around the fire. Dan picked up the Princess and put her in the top pocket of his jacket.

Dan loaded his gun. "Wake up."

"What?" Josh mumbled.

Dan fired, and bright orange paint exploded across Josh's chest. Chock fired at Glenn; pink dye covered his chest.

Josh cursed. "That's cheating!"

116

"What is?" Dan asked.

"Where have you been? You've been gone hours."

"A war of attrition."

"What?" Glenn asked

"Yeah, what?" Chock said.

"Wearing you down."

"Lulling!" Chock replied.

"Oh, shut up," Josh said, annoyed. Chock loaded his gun again and faced Josh. "All right, all right. You win. This paint smells of rotten eggs."

"Why don't you two get clean and we'll set up the stove for a fry up," Dan said.

"Great idea," Glenn replied. "Want a beer?"

The next morning, grey smoke drifted up from the dying fire, and beer cans were strewn around, as well as discarded food packaging. They had been up all night and were now lying in their tents, apart from Dan.

The copious amounts of alcohol hadn't had the same effect on him as it had the others. He strolled back to the concealed cabin. It had been just over twenty-four hours since he'd suddenly been able to do unnatural, supernatural, things. Just being up and about so early after what he'd drunk the night before was abnormal.

Uncovering the doorway, he went inside. It was just how they had left it. He had another good look around. On one of the many shelves, behind rusting tins, he found a half empty carton of cigarettes; the packet was emblazoned with warnings about severe consequences to health. He had never smoked before: cigarettes cost a fortune, and only a few stores sold them. He took one out and with a match lit it. The first lungful made him choke and the smell made him nauseous, but he persisted, slowly smoking it down to the butt. When he'd finished, he threw the end into the wood burner and put the packet into his pocket. He lit another match. He watched it burn. He moved his free hand around it. The flame rose and trailed his movement. "Amazing."

A torrential downpour accompanied them on the journey home; it hadn't rained for weeks, months. The parched earth cried out for liquid. This was another fall-out from global pollution – the traditional four seasons were meaningless; it snowed in summer, rained in spring, was warm in winter and very dry in autumn. The monsoon-like conditions slowed their progress. More than once they thought about calling their parents to get a lift, but they had purposely not taken their PDAs. The heavy rain was just another part of the adventure.

Dan, who like his friends was soaked to the skin, waved goodbye to the trio from the porch of his parents' house. It was dark, and he was surprised to find that all the lights were off. The thought of a surprise birthday party crossed his mind. He smiled, searching for his key in his sodden fatigues, and braced himself for a barrage of adulation. But he couldn't find his key. It was gone. His father would be annoyed that he'd lost another one. He rapped on the glass. A loose pane rattled in the door. There was no answer. He berated himself for spoiling their surprise. He tried again. No answer. He placed his face against the glass and tried to see in. Dan could make out his mother's coat and handbag draped over the banister. Dan bent down and lifted the letterbox flap. "Mum?" No answer. "I've forgotten my key, sorry. Mum? Dad?" No answer. He stood and looked down the road. The rain showed no signs of abating. The road resembled a river as water washed along it and the drains overflowed.

Dan decided to try to get in via the garden, where he'd be able to locate the hidden back door key and let himself in. His mind raced with reasons why nobody was home. He considered that something might have happened to a distant relative, or a family friend, and that they were at the new super-hospital that served not only the city, but the entire county. He began to wish that he had taken his PDA with him after all.

To access the garden he had to walk to the end of the road, go down a narrow side alley and then down another one that ran parallel to the rear of the houses. Dan reached their back gate and lifted himself up, peering into the garden. Straight away he saw that the back door was ajar. He vaulted the fence with ease and ran to the house. Approaching, he saw a pair of feet in slippers, a Yuletide present from the previous year, behind the partly open door.

"Mum!" She was lifeless on the kitchen floor. "Mum?" He knelt down beside her. "Mum?" Her body was cold to the touch and her face, set in the moment of death, wore a horrified expression, as if she'd seen something utterly terrifying. Dan wept.

"Get up," a terse voice said.

Dan's eyes shot up towards an unknown face. Above him stood a short, muscular woman. She held out her hand.

"Who are you?" Dan said, through his tears. The stranger responded by grabbing him by the arm and dragging him to his feet.

"Who are you?" Dan struggled to free himself from the woman's tight grip. "You killed her!"

"No, *they* killed her." Her voice carried authority, and her words resonated truth. "Your father's dead too." The woman loosened her hold, but kept a hand on Dan to steady him.

A familiar face appeared from the hallway.

"Abdalla!"

"Oh my boy." He embraced Dan. "Thank heavens we found you in time."

Dan tried to hold back his tears. "What?"

"I know, I know. It's dreadful."

"What, what happened? Who is she?"

"You've come of age. I'm surprised they didn't find you sooner. I guess we got lucky, for once." The woman's eyes were wide, almost mad with their intensity. Suddenly there was the sound of banging on the front door, rampant beating, determined thumping. "They've returned."

"Who are you?" Dan asked, desperately seeking answers.

"She's here to protect you," Abdalla replied. "Her name is…."

"Fereshteh. Demon hunter." The woman's pitch was urgent. "I can hold them off, but not forever." From out of her long coat she produced a silver automatic pistol. It glinted in what little light there was. She loaded it. "Go." She gave Abdalla a glance and a nod, and then rushed to the hallway. Abdalla took Dan's hand and pulled him out into the pouring rain. As they made their escape through the garden they heard gunfire. Dan looked back. The weapon discharging produced flashes that illuminated the dark house. They heard the front door splinter. An irreligious howling followed. The firing continued until they were out of earshot.

22

Dan woke, sweat pouring down his face. He sat up, swung his legs off the hard cell bed on to the floor and rubbed his head. When awake he blocked that day, fifteen years ago, from his mind, but every once in a while it invaded his dreams. That woman's face, Fereshteh, had haunted him for a long time. The vehemence of her expression had been imprinted. Leading Dan away Abdalla had told him all he knew of the woman, which wasn't much. She'd appeared out of nowhere. Abdalla had found her in the Ramsey house, standing over the body of Zaylie Ramsey. The circumstances could not have been more alarming for

119

Abdalla, but Fereshteh had spoken with such exigency and conviction, her eyes burning, that he knew to believe without question. The manifestation of Dan's powers had alerted those who had been looking for him for sixteen years to his whereabouts. Fereshteh knew of Dan's existence. She knew of Dan's mother. It was she who had been employed by the adoption services. She'd placed Dan as far away as possible, covering the tracks; she knew this day would come, and she knew how important Dan was, and he that couldn't fall into the hands of darkness. They had found Dan's father's body in the soundproofed basement where Dan kept his drum kit. Abdalla had listened to Fereshteh explain that Dan wasn't a normal boy, something he had already surmised from observing him. She'd told Abdalla that Dan needed to stay hidden or he would become a part of the enemy's plans.

From that day, until his return to Liverpool, Dan had wandered, learning about who and what he was, and in the years that followed he had faced many things that no one would believe. The only possession he had had to link him to the past was the photo of himself, his mother and father, which Abdalla had snatched off the refrigerator as they left on that ghastly evening.

Dan snapped out of his thoughts with the sound of the keypad lock being pressed. The door creaked open.

The custody sergeant beamed at him. "Good morning, Daniel Ramsey." Dan raised his eyebrows. "One of my PCs recognised your mugshot, remembers your face from fifteen years ago, would you believe. Missing persons. Disappeared after parents died from heart attacks on the same day." He smiled. "What are the chances? Says you haven't changed a bit."

Dan tried to control his anger. "You got me." He was too tired to deny it.

"I told you we'd identify you."

"You did, you did. I'll give you that."

"Now you can be formally charged, but first we need to get those clothes off you. They've been identified as stolen property."

"Such a shame, I really dug these threads." Another officer appeared in the doorway with a clear plastic bag and blue overalls. "Oh great," Dan said, spotting his new attire.

After washing, changing and eating a sparse breakfast, Dan was led out into the custody suite and formally charged with GBH, theft of a motor vehicle, dangerous driving and breaking and entering.

"Right, Mr Ramsey," the sergeant said, after he'd finished reading out the list. "This detective would like to ask you about some other offences. How are you Eddie?"

"Fine, thanks."

"What?" Dan turned to his left to see a young man walking up to him. "I haven't done anything else." Dan thought back to some of his other misdemeanour's. "Are you trying to pin all unsolved cases on me?"

"It's just a little chat," Eddie said. Dan sighed, wondering why they couldn't just leave him alone. "Which interview room is free?"

"Number one," the sergeant said, handing him a keycode.

"Thanks."

Dan shook his head and was led out. In the corridor they stopped outside a door. Up ahead three people emerged through a set of double doors and walked towards them. Dan noticed Eddie straighten his back as he pressed the code into the keypad. The device gave a sharp beep.

"Need some help?" Dan asked.

"No. I think this is the wrong keycode," he replied, more to himself than to Dan.

Dan eyed up the people coming towards them. Two men, one dressed in uniform, clearly a senior officer, the other in a suit, and a woman also dressed in a trouser suit.

"Morning, Sir," Eddie said to man in the uniform. It was his Superintendent.

"Morning," he replied, giving Dan a glance. "Having problems?"

"Erm, yes," Eddie said. "Wrong keycode, I think."

"Well, go and get the right one," the Superintendent said, smiling at his guests. "I'm sure we can handle one prisoner."

"Yes, Sir." Eddie scuttled off.

Dan exhaled and leaned back against the wall. The three carried on talking amongst themselves.

"So you think these people could be in danger?" the Superintendent asked.

"Yes," the woman replied, the other man nodded in agreement. "There have been five suspicious deaths and they all seemed to be linked."

"But the detective in charge of the first case is adamant that the prime suspect in the first murder is dead."

"Yes, Sir, but no body has been found."

Eddie reappeared and jogged back to the group. "Got it." The senior officer gave a weak smile.

"And you think we have a killer targeting this little group. What are they called?"

"Beacon."

Dan's eyes widened, he adjusted his posture, but managed to hold his tongue just as he was about to interrupt them.

"A cult?"

"It depends on your definition of a cult."

The interview room door unlocked. "Thank you, Sir."

"Fine, fine," came the reply.

The group strode on. Dan continued to listen in.

"Okay, well, we'll give you any support you need."

"Thank you, Sir."

"This way," Eddie said, pointing into the room.

Dan watched the trio until they disappeared from sight. His immediate situation now was totally irrelevant. Abdalla and the others were in danger. He wanted to stay out of it. He was going to be incarcerated for his crimes and prison was the best place for him. Then, in his mind's eye, he saw Catherine.

"This way," Eddie repeated, a little louder.

Dan looked at him. "Sure." He walked forwards. The door closed behind him.

23

A trembling finger on Lisette Lecompte's hand ended the call on the videophone. She stood motionless, as the new information Abdalla had learned the day before sunk in. Then she fell back into the armchair behind her; the rest and relaxation she'd achieved from her twenty-four hour stay at the meditation centre had instantly evaporated. First Sunayani, and apparently Simon, then Erica and her son, and now Jake.

She tried to digest it all. Abdalla had suggested that she cancel that day's meeting with her cell leaders, and travel up from her home in Coventry to Liverpool straight away. She hadn't intended to go to their monthly coordinator meeting until later that week. Many of the cell leaders would have already set off on their journeys.

She got to her feet, walked through to the hallway and made sure that her front door was securely locked.

The doorbell rang just as Listette had finished laying the dining table with homemade cakes and sandwiches. She looked at her watch. It was one o'clock. It must be Stefan, she thought, cell leader of the smallest group in her region, numbering just thirty-six people. He was always the first to arrive. Lisette went down the hallway and checked the spy hole. She smiled to herself and unlocked the door to her fourteenth floor flat. Stefan's grinning face greeted her.

"Hello, my dear." He stepped into the flat and placed a kiss on her cheek. "What a drive! How are you? Looking good for an old lady! No more bad news I hope?"

"Watch who you're calling old!" Her voice momentarily lifted. "I've been better, but, erm, no more bad news."

"At least that's something," he said, relieved. "You wouldn't believe the stick I have to put up with at work. They made me peel off a small 'God is Love' sticker from my computer."

"I'm sorry to hear that." She thought about Erica, who had also had problems at work because of her belief.

"And the guy who sits a few booths down from me had his little Buddha figure chucked down the toilet and, well, you know, it didn't flush away, got stuck."

"Really? Someone did that?"

"Yep. So, everything is okay?"

Lisette had debated what she should say. She didn't want to lie, but knew, as Abdalla did, that the news of yet another brutal death could turn people away. It would unnerve them. It was hard enough living with a faith, without it being tested to this degree. She'd heard from some of the other leaders that a few people had already been absent from meetings, and hadn't returned their cell leaders' calls.

"There are just a few things going on at the moment."

"Yes, I know," Stefan said, concerned and thinking back to the recent headlines. "Is there anything I can help with?"

"No, no."

"Wow, a spread." Stefan's eyes rested on the full dining table.

"It's not for now."

"Oh."

"Go through to the living room. I'll put the kettle on. It's a shame the hall was booked today," she added. "I don't know how I'll fit you all in."

There was another knock at the door.

"I'll boil the water, honey. Looks like everyone is turning up."

"Okay, thanks." Lisette headed for the front door, biting her lip and rehearsing what she was going to say. Nothing was forthcoming. She took a deep breath, hoping something would pop into her head and depressed the handle. "Oh my."

"What was that?" Stefan asked from the kitchen, half-hearing her mumbled words.

Before Lisette could say any more, a powerful hand pushed her back into the room behind her. She tried to speak, but was too petrified. She was pushed again and collapsed to the floor. The sliding door to the balcony was opened and Lisette was grabbed by her neck and groin. In one swift movement she was thrown over the railings.

"Lisette? Who is it? Bet it's Raymond, he keeps saying he'll meet me for a drink, but never does. He's a naughty one! Lisette?" Stefan sauntered into the hallway. "Lisette?" He noticed the open door and went in. The wind was blowing the curtains into the room. He tentatively went out on to the balcony and looked down. Below, he saw a crowd gathering around Lisette's body.

24

Abdalla showed Chief Inspector Jenna Fabris and DI Emile Corvisiero into the living room where Jean-Paul, Catherine and Markus were sitting. They exchanged greetings and sat down.

"Cup of tea?" Abdalla indicated to a pot that he'd just brought through from the kitchen.

"Oh yes, thank you," Jenna said. "Just milk, no sugar."

"And you?"

"No, I'm okay, thank you," Emile replied.

"So what is going on?" Catherine had had enough of the pleasantries.

"Catherine!" Abdalla said, handing Jenna her drink.

"What?"

"It's okay. That's what we're here to talk about," Jenna said. "Well, as you know there have been five deaths and I can tell you that we're linking them all."

"Do you think the same person?" Jean-Paul asked.

"Yes, most definitely."

"Simon?" Catherine said.

"We can't eliminate him," Emile replied.

"We were told he committed suicide," Markus said.

"The detective initially in charge...."

"So you're investigating now?" Catherine asked Jenna.

"Yes I am, and as I was saying, the detective initially in charge thought Mr Moulson had killed himself, but as you know we haven't found a body."

"But Simon wouldn't hurt anyone," Jean-Paul said. "What evidence have you got?"

Jenna paused. "None, really. No fingerprints, no DNA, no CCTV, no eyewitnesses, which is very strange." Catherine and Abdalla exchanged glances. "But it's becoming clearer with each death that they're linked, and Mr Moulson remains our number one suspect."

"I see," Jean-Paul replied.

"Tell me, us," Jenna added, turning to her colleague, "about, erm, Beacon."

Abdalla sighed. "Yes, yes, of course. Well, first, it's clear to us that our regional co-ordinators are being targeted."

"Why would that be?"

"It would destabilise the work we do."

"How do you mean?"

"How can I explain...."

"We're fighting the good fight," Catherine said. "There are dark forces in the world. Taking out the regional co-ordinators would provoke an instant negative reaction from those we're nurturing."

"Thank you, Catherine," Abdalla said.

"Right," Emile said, giving Jenna a dubious look. He took out his PDA. "Let me just get that down. Nurturing. Okay, so, how many regional co-ordinators are there?"

"Seven teams," Catherine said, before Abdalla could reply.

"Seven?"

"Yes," Abdalla replied. "I cover Wales, Markus over there covers the North West and Northern Ireland, Lian with the help of her husband Jean-Paul here covers Scotland and Lisette Lecompte, who is not present, covers the Midlands."

"Where's Lian?" Emile asked.

"She's ill. She's back at the hotel," Jean-Paul said.

"Right. Carry on."

"Simon, along with Sunayani, covered London and the South East. Erica covered the South West and Jake the East and North East. Each region has up to one hundred cell leaders, leading groups ranging in membership from ten to one hundred plus people."

Jenna turned to Catherine. "And what do you do?"

"I'm an international development co-ordinator."

"International? This is quite a big organisation then?" Emile asked.

"Yes and no. We're not an organisation. Put simply...." Abdalla hesitated, considering his words. "We help people develop their faith."

"Right. Faith…." He tapped the word into his PDA. "Not many people go in for that anymore do they?"

"We do." Abdalla gave him a brief smile.

"Have you spoken to Mrs Lecompte?"

"Miss," Markus said.

"Sorry, Miss Lecompte?" Jenna asked.

"Yes. This morning. I told her the dreadful news about Jake." Abdalla replied.

"Did she say if she'd seen anything or noticed anything unusual?"

"No, she didn't."

Jenna turned to Emile. "I think under the circumstances we should get her protection."

"Yes, ma'am."

"Do you have Miss Lecompte's details so we can get someone to her?"

"Of course." Abdalla picked up a black diary from beside the videophone and flicked through it until he found Lisette's details. He handed the book to Emile, who stood up and left the room to make the call. "She did say she would come up after the meeting she was having today."

"Meeting?"

"She's having a meeting with the cell leaders in her region. That's why she isn't with us already."

"Okay. So just tell me about these cells again?"

Catherine sighed and rolled her eyes. "Each regional co-ordinator has, well it varies depending which area, but up to one hundred cell group leaders. And there could be up to one hundred members, or more, per group."

"Got it. Thank you. So were the others supposed to be with you?"

"I wish they were," Jean-Paul said.

"Yes. Well, Simon and Sunayani, who had been ill for a few months…." Abdalla said.

"Ill?"

"Yes, Simon wouldn't elaborate. I don't think it was serious. Anyway, they had work commitments, as did Erica and Jake. And Lisette had booked a day in a meditation retreat."

"I see." Jenna nodded and took a sip of tea.

"But we do like to get everyone together when we can. We were planning a gathering at Christmas. Sorry, Yuletide as you call it."

"So how many members does Beacon have?"

126

"Around the world?"

"Yes."

"Just under one hundred thousand."

"That's quite a few."

"It is."

"How do you communicate with them all? Email?"

"Yes, we send out newsletters and such. We have a great deal of teaching resources online that the cells can draw from. I'll need to email those groups affected by the deaths of their regional leaders. But…." Abdalla sighed. "I don't know what to say. They already know about Sunayani, and Simon, of course, it's been all over the news. Sadly, that tragic event, and the way it's being reported, seems to have driven a few people away."

"Well, we have to tell the truth," Markus said.

"I know, but I'm worried about the negative impact," Abdalla replied.

"Catch-22," Jean-Paul said.

Emile re-entered the room. "I'm afraid I've got some more bad news."

Everyone looked at him.

"Lisette?" Jean-Paul asked.

"Yes. I'm sorry. Police are on the scene," he told Jenna.

Catherine burst into tears.

"What happened?" Jenna asked.

"She was attacked in her home just an hour ago."

"In the middle of the day?"

"She was thrown from her balcony, there don't appear to be any clues." No one could believe what they were hearing.

"Someone must have seen someone, or something at least?" Jenna said.

"No one saw anything."

The seriousness of the crimes Dan had committed, and his refusal to give an address, meant that he was to be held in custody and transferred to a prison until his trial. He paced the small room, considering when the best time to leave would be. He was being moved the next day, which would present the perfect opportunity to abscond. However, he wanted to destroy the records they now had on him, and that would mean having to wait until night when it would be quieter.

The day passed slowly. All he could think about was Catherine.

A police officer had been placed on the door outside Abdalla's house. Jean-Paul was escorted back to Lian at the hotel, where there was already an officer guarding her. Catherine and Markus had decided to stay with Abdalla, and had been driven across town by the police to get what they needed from Markus's house.

"Are you okay, Catherine?" Markus asked, once they were heading back. Catherine was staring out of the car window watching the city. It was quite beautiful at night. For a moment all their worries seemed immaterial. She felt normal. There was a small part of her that wished she were, despite all she knew. The people they passed were unaware of the future. "Catherine?"

"What?" she replied, breaking away from her daydream.

"Are you okay?"

"Sure. Fine. Just thinking." She turned back to the window.

"About Dan?"

"No, no, I wasn't actually." Markus's comment brought her thoughts back to him.

The car pulled up outside Abdalla's house. They got themselves and their luggage out and were led inside.

"How are you both?" Abdalla asked, greeting them.

"Fine," Markus said, carrying their suitcases in.

"We find ourselves in a strange place."

"You can say that again." Catherine closed the door on the policeman outside.

"I've made us some supper."

"I'm not really hungry," Markus replied.

"Me neither," Catherine said.

"You've got to eat something. Try a bit?"

"Okay," Markus said.

Catherine nodded. "Are Jean-Paul and Lian all right?"

"Yes, he just called. Lian is feeling better." Abdalla directed them into the living room. "Sit down."

"Thanks. Well, that's good," Markus said.

"They're settling in for the evening. He said they'd be round about ten."

Catherine collapsed into an armchair. "So what are we going to do?"

"You know what we have to do. We start by putting it to prayer."

"I know, but if we die then...."

"That's what they want, isn't it? We're in a war, Catherine. We're on the front line," Markus said.

"I know. We've all faced intense spiritual warfare, psychological, but this is actual physical attack."

"Catherine, we have to stay strong," Abdalla said.

"I guess. I'm just really... scared."

Abdalla knelt by her. "Remember that whatever happens we're not alone. There's nothing to be afraid of."

Catherine gave him a weak smile and placed her hand on his.

The carpeted floor squeaked as feet strode across it. The corridor was light but dull. Unattractive wallpaper clashed with the colour of the heavy fire doors. At the end of the hallway a policeman stood outside a room. He faced the approaching person and smiled, tipping his head as a welcome. The policeman's eyes clouded over. He took a step back to allow the visitor to pass. A hand gripped the handle, and with one shove the door swung open. The policeman pulled it shut.

In the darkness Jean-Paul fumbled for the light. "Who's there?"

"Jean-Paul?" Lian mumbled.

Jean-Paul's fingers found the switch. Just as he was about to press it, he felt another finger alongside his. It switched the light on. Lian and Jean-Paul both leapt in shock.

In the hallway the policeman smashed the fire alarm. It echoed throughout the hotel, covering the noise emanating from the room. He then pushed open the fire escape and fled, followed moments later by startled hotel guests.

Dan placed his palms and fingertips on the cell door. It was still relatively early, approaching midnight, but he was impatient. He couldn't wait any longer. He knew what he was about to do would alert those after him to his whereabouts, like a flare illuminating the sky and the land below, but he wasn't planning on hanging around.

Jenna couldn't believe the news when it was conveyed to her in the hotel she and Emile were staying in. Jean-Paul and Lian had been killed in their beds, and the policeman charged with guarding the room had been found with his neck broken in woodland near the hotel. No one had seen the assailant enter the building and, as before, the CCTV inside and out had only recorded static.

Moments later they were in the car. Emile drove them as fast as he could over to Abdalla's house.

The car screeched to a halt outside. "Where's the officer gone?" Jenna immediately asked, seeing the door unguarded.

"I don't know," Emile replied, looking around.

It had begun to rain heavily. Jenna jumped out, ran up to the door and banged on it. They were soaked to the skin by the time Abdalla answered.

"Where's the PC?" Jenna asked.

"It's a bit late isn't it?" Abdalla said, checking the time on his watch as he let them in. "I'm not sure where our policeman friend is." He looked up and down the road.

"Are you okay?" She and Emile stepped into the house. "We tried to call, but couldn't get a connection."

"Did you? And yes, I think we're okay," he replied quizzically. Catherine and Markus appeared on the landing in their nightwear.

"What's happened?" Catherine asked, as she began to descend the stairs.

"There's been another attack," Emile said.

"Lian?" Abdalla asked.

"I'm afraid so."

"And Jean-Paul?" Markus said.

"Yes, I'm afraid so. They're dead."

"Murdered you mean," Abdalla replied.

"Yes. I'll go and see if I can find the officer who was on your door. Maybe he's sitting in a car or something."

"Okay, Emile. Once you've found him, call for back up."

"Right." Emile went out into the rain and closed the front door behind him.

"What happened?" Catherine was now sitting on the stairs with tears welling up in her eyes.

"They were attacked in the hotel."

"But I thought they were being guarded? I thought we were too."

Jenna ran a hand through her hair. Her eyes were darting backwards and forwards as she tried to comprehend the situation she now found herself in. She exhaled heavily. "I don't know what is happening. But the killer is here in Liverpool and you're all in severe danger."

"What are we going to do?"

"We need to get you to a safe house."

"Do you really think that will help?"

There was a knock on a pane. Abdalla reached around Jenna and released the catch. Emile's body fell through. It had been propped up against the door; his throat had been ripped out.

130

Jenna screamed in horror, as did Catherine. Abdalla and Markus cursed at the drama unfolding in front of them. The moment Emile's body hit the floor all the lights flickered out.

"Close it!" Markus shouted, rushing down.

Jenna reached for her PDA. "There's no signal, no Internet. Why can't I get a signal?"

Abdalla and Markus managed to pull Emile's body into the house and close the door.

"Out the back!" Abdalla yelled as he rushed through the hallway and into the kitchen. The others followed. Abdalla attempted to open the door, but couldn't depress the handle; it had been jammed from the outside.

"Quickly, upstairs," Markus said.

"Upstairs?" Jenna said.

"We'll have to barricade ourselves into a room."

"Right." Abdalla grabbed Catherine's hand and hauled her up with him. Markus and Jenna followed. "Into the back bedroom."

Once inside, Abdalla and Markus set about blocking the entrance with the bed, and they covered the small window with a wardrobe. If it weren't for moonlight entering through a gap between the wardrobe and window, the room would have been in total darkness.

"Now what?" Jenna asked.

"We wait and hope and pray," Abdalla said. "Catherine, are you okay?" He could just make out her silhouette, huddled up with her arms around her knees.

"No," she murmured.

"Come on, get up." Abdalla dragged Catherine to her feet.

"Pray?" Jenna said.

"This could be your last chance," Markus replied.

Dan slowed his breathing and cleared his mind. He could feel himself, every atom of his being, becoming lighter. Stretching out an arm, Dan pressed the tips of his fingers on to the steel cell door. They passed through the surface; he stepped forwards, out into the corridor and looked back at the solid metal. Facing the entrance to the custody suite, he approached slowly and peered out. He saw no one. His eyes focused on the back doorway, which led out into a car park. From there he would be able to disappear. But first, entering the office, Dan casually strolled over to the desk. Behind it sat an officer staring at a computer screen.

"Excuse me."

"Yes?" The officer looked up. "What the?" he said, when he saw Dan in front of him.

Within a blink of an eye, and before the PC could raise the alarm, Dan had leapt over the counter and wrapped a muscular arm around the man's neck, leaving him struggling to breathe.

"I'm sorry about this. Let's cut the idle threats, shall we? Delete my files, now."

The officer nodded, reached forward and began tapping away. The file flashed up on the screen.

"And the back-up." Dan squeezed tighter.

"I can't breathe."

"Hurry."

Just as the constable deleted the back-up file, another policeman burst through into suite. His eyes were clouded. Possessed, he had been alerted to Dan's presence as soon as he had used his powers. Dan let go of the man he had been holding, picked up the computer screen and threw it at the approaching officer, knocking him to the floor. Two further PCs appeared, each with a cup of coffee and a sandwich.

"What's the...." one of them said.

The men dropped their food, drew their batons and proceeded towards Dan, but he was too quick. Vaulting the desk, they watched in amazement as he sprinted through the solid steel back door. Outside, it was pouring with rain. Dan stopped, caught his breath, and got his bearings. He heard the alarm sound behind him. He started to run.

Jenna listened to the group praying. After a few minutes she found herself joining in, her words confused, soft. She thought of her family at home. Her husband, Raj, who she'd known since high school, and her two children, Amelia who was three and Karl who was one. Was she really never going to see them again?

A bang made them all jump. The front door was being kicked open. They heard a primal bellow.

"This is it," Catherine whispered. "It's over."

"This can't be happening," Jenna said. "I wish I had my gun."

"Bullets won't help," Markus replied.

Abdalla stepped forward. "Perhaps with our combined...." He didn't have a chance to finish his sentence. The bedroom door was smashed apart. The bed disintegrated, splinters of wood flying off in all directions. A hefty shard impaled itself in Jenna's stomach. She cried out in pain and fell. A large figure waded into the room. Markus went to help Jenna, but was struck across the back with a bedpost. He crumpled down and was battered again.

"Markus!" Catherine said. He collapsed on to Jenna, who was choking on her own blood.

A flash of lightening illuminated the room. Abdalla caught a glimpse of their attacker. He gasped. "Simon." He stared up at the form approaching him. Simon's physical appearance had changed. He was taller and wider. All his muscles were accentuated. His veins were pushing up under his skin, which was a translucent grey. His face was cast in pure malevolence.

Simon raised his hand and swept Abdalla out of the way. He crashed against the wall, dropping lifeless to the floor. Simon lumbered towards Catherine, who had backed away into a corner. She tried to speak, but no words would come. Simon picked up another broken piece of wood and held it like a spear. He pulled his arm back, preparing to launch it at her. Catherine wanted to scream, but she just screwed her eyes shut and waited.

25

Simon drew a sharp intake of air as he was heaved backwards out of the room. Catherine opened her eyes and her body immediately flooded with relief. It was Dan. The two men faced each other on the landing.

"You!" Simon said. His voice was a mixture of several others; they spoke at the same time. "You're coming with us."

Dan glanced at the devastation. Catherine looked back at him. "I don't think so."

The pair clashed, but they were evenly matched. Both had incredible strength, and the landing walls were soon demolished as they hurled each other against them.

Dan held Simon by the neck. "Catherine, run."

It took Catherine a few moments to register his words. She got to her feet and in the dim light from the hallway she staggered over to Abdalla and turned his body over.

"No...." she murmured. His face was covered in blood. She turned towards Markus. He appeared to be dead. And Jenna was now quiet; her mouth hung open, her screams of pain ended.

"Catherine, get out of here," Dan yelled. She hesitated. She wanted to tend to her friends, but nothing could help them now. "Catherine!" Simon started raining down punches on Dan.

Finally she got to her feet and ran from the room. Dan watched her dash down the stairs, losing her footing and faltering as she went. She leapt over Emile's body and out of the house.

Dan returned his attention to Simon. He could smell his acrid breath. He pushed Simon's head into the wall and then hit him as hard as he could in the face. Simon slumped and Dan took the opportunity to make for the stairs.

The rain was relentless. Catherine's nightwear was quickly soaked through and clung to the curves of her body. She stood on the pavement looking into the house. She was in shock. She couldn't move and had no idea what to do next. Her heart lifted when she saw Dan emerge.

Dan grabbed her trembling hand. "We've got to move."

"What about...?"

"Come on."

They sped down the street, and turned into an alleyway, which sheltered them from the rain.

Dan stopped and looked back to see if they were being followed.

"I, I...."

"It's okay," Dan said.

"Okay? *Okay?*" Catherine screamed. "My friends are dead. It's over."

Dan glanced around, worried about making too much noise. He grabbed her shoulders. "Calm down. Who is that?"

"His, his name." She tried to compose herself. "Is Simon, Simon Moulson. He's been killing Beacon's regional co-ordinators."

"He's possessed?"

"Yes." She wiped away the rainwater from her face. "I didn't think I'd see you again."

"I didn't think you would either."

"Dan, I need to tell you something."

He turned back to her. "What?"

"I've found your mother."

Dan stared at her in disbelief.

Behind them a loud thud echoed down the alley. Out of the shadows Simon emerged.

Catherine got her breath back and straightened her posture. Simon advanced, flexing his muscles, scowling at them. Dan took a few steps backwards, tugging on Catherine's sleeve for her to follow him, but she stood her ground.

"In the name of…." she said, but before she could continue he brushed her aside with a sardonic laugh. Catherine flew into a wall, landing unconscious in a pile of rubbish.

"You're coming with us!" Simon pointed at Dan. "They've been just one step behind you for a while now."

"I know."

"They say you're one of us, but we'd rather kill you."

"You're a charmer aren't you, Simon? It is Simon isn't it?" There was no reply. Dan and Simon began circling each other. "Why Beacon?"

Simon seemed to be wrestling with the demons within. Dan could see them swimming around under his flesh. "You know. The end is nigh."

"So I hear. And?"

"And we're going to stop it from happening. This is our world," he said, indicating to the ground.

"Our world?"

"It's for those who live in darkness."

"Right."

"The human race can't be saved."

"You can't change the future."

"We have. The founders of Beacon are dead." The many voices laughed. "We have a sense of humour. We chose this body, one of their own. Now it won't become what it would have."

"The 144,000?"

"The influential group." Simon spat out a mixture of blood, rainwater and saliva. "Who would have helped nurture so many. Now they'll fall away. It's over. We win."

Simon dived for Dan and they began exchanging blows, strike for strike. The sound of police sirens became audible and two cars flew past the entrance to the passageway. Their presence caused Simon to break off the fight.

"Next time will be the last time." He turned and ran back into the shadows.

Dan watched him disappear. Then he remembered Catherine. "Catherine!"

She stirred. "Dan?"

He hauled her out from among the strewn refuse. "Come on. We've got to get out of here."

"Oh."

"Are you okay?"

"Yeah, a little wobbly. I'm fine. What happened?"

135

"Simon's gone. I guess the police scared him off."

"Police?"

"Yeah." They stumbled to the end of the alley and looked down the road. Outside Abdalla's house there was a vast array of emergency vehicles. "The neighbours must have called them."

"We've got to tell the police," Catherine said, making a move.

"I can't."

"Why?" Dan pointed to what he was wearing. "Where have you been?"

"Jail."

"Jail?"

"It's a long story," He spat blood out of his mouth.

Catherine stared at the man in front of her. She realised how much of a stranger he was. "I have to go." She turned away.

Dan grabbed her arm. "What are you going to tell them?"

"The truth."

"They won't believe you."

"I know, but *I* can't just disappear."

"Okay." He let her go. "I'll find you."

"Good." She turned and started to walk away.

"Catherine?"

She glanced back. "Yes?"

"My mother?"

She flashed a brief half smile. "Yes, she's alive."

Dan couldn't find the words to reply. He watched Catherine run back towards the house.

26

Catherine felt she wasn't treated as a witness but a suspect. She had changed out of her nightwear into jeans and a black top from the suitcase that the police had brought out of the house. She sat in an interview room, holding back her tears, while an officer who looked liked he'd only just left high school, fired questions at her.

"So, tell me again?" Detective Inspector Osuobeni asked, placing his crossed arms on the table and leaning forwards.

"Emile, DI Corvisiero, went out to see if he could find the policeman who was supposed to be guarding the door."

"The officer wasn't there?"

"No."

"Then what happened?"

"Jenna told us about our friends who had been murdered. She said we were all going to be taken somewhere for our own safety. Then there was a knock on the door and when Abdalla opened it, Emile fell in."

"Right. How could a dead man knock on the door?"

"Well, obviously he didn't."

"It was Simon you say, who is," Osuobeni looked at his PDA, "possessed?"

"Yes, by a demon, or demons. He was toying with us. Sorry, I didn't have time to take a picture."

"That would have been useful. Right, let me get that down, demons...." He entered the information into the device. "Then what?"

"Jenna tried to ring for help, but couldn't get a signal."

Osuobeni looked at her in disbelief. "Couldn't get a signal?"

"Yes."

"Why not?"

"Simon's presence." Osuobeni didn't reply, but Catherine continued. "We tried to get out of the back, but we couldn't open the door. So we went upstairs into a bedroom, and barricaded ourselves in. A few minutes later, which only felt like seconds, Simon burst into the room." She paused. "I'm not sure what happened after that. I was so scared."

"Right. Why did Simon wait two weeks until he continued his killing spree?"

"I don't know. He must have been watching us, studying our routines, and he would have known we were meeting this week. He was probably waiting until we were all together."

"Only you weren't."

"No, but we were supposed to be. Obviously he picked us off one by one."

"Obviously," Osuobeni said, under his breath. There was a knock on the door. "Come in."

"Can I have a word, Sir?" a female officer asked.

The detective left the room, leaving Catherine to stare into space and replay the evening in her head.

A few moments passed and the detective re-entered the room. "Well, you'll be pleased to know Abdalla Miller is going to be all right and he is confirming your story."

Her spirits instantly lifted. "He is? He's not dead?"

"Yes and no he isn't."

"Oh, thank God." She was relieved and couldn't quite believe it. She realised he'd not mentioned Dan's involvement. "So, he's really going to be okay?"

"Yes." Catherine ran her a hand through her hair and exhaled. "But tell me more about this cult."

"It's not a cult."

"Whatever it is then."

Catherine took a deep breath. "Beacon nurtures new believers. We're two and bit years into the end times."

The officer didn't respond for a few seconds. "Two and a bit years into the end times?" he eventually repeated, with a raised eyebrow.

"Yes, four and a bit to go." Catherine leaned forward and stared him straight in the eyes. "Have you ever thought about…?"

"No," he replied quickly.

"Oh." She sat back in the hard plastic chair.

"So, why has this Simon started killing?"

"He's possessed, working for the enemy, who wants Beacon destroyed. That way we won't be around to support believers and direct people towards the light when the darkness fully descends."

"The enemy, darkness," he repeated, tapping away.

"You wanted the truth. That's the truth."

"And where's this Simon now?"

"How should I know? He ran when he heard the sirens, but he'll be back."

"Because you and Mr Miller aren't dead yet?"

"Yes."

"That's a very interesting story."

"It's the truth. Didn't Jenna have all this in her PDA?"

"Yes, we're going through it at the moment, but I know she wasn't sold on the idea. Right. Let's go over this one more time, so I'm absolutely clear on what you are saying."

Catherine sighed, rolled her eyes and once again retold her story, omitting Dan's participation.

"I have to be honest with you, Ms Halston. I can't believe what you are telling me about possessions and your cult."

"It's not a cult," she replied, annoyed.

"Right. All I know is that I've got a deranged killer on my hands."

"You've got a killer on your hands, yes."

"Chief Inspector Fabris thought you should all be taken into police protection, and I'm inclined to agree."

"Nothing is going to stop Simon."

"We'll see about that."

"I think I'd feel safer looking after myself."

"Do you now?"

"Yes."

"Why's that?"

"Because he'll know where to find me, if I go with you. Is Abdalla being protected?"

"Yes. We have an officer at the hospital."

"Good. Which one?"

"Hospital?"

"Yes."

"There's only one." Catherine seemed puzzled. "The super-hospital in Aintree."

"Oh, right."

"I really think you should be moved to a safe house."

"No way."

"I have to take the public's safety into consideration, Ms Halston."

"I appreciate that."

The detective sighed. "Well, I can't make you do anything."

"Can I leave now? I'm not a suspect am I?"

Osuobeni studied the woman in front of him. "Of course not. Look, where will you be going?"

"Straight to the hospital."

"And from there?"

"I'd rather not say."

"Why is that?" he asked.

"For my own protection."

"Okay, okay. Have it your way. I can't force you."

The detective stood, as did Catherine. "I'm afraid the story has made the news."

"What are they saying?" But she already knew the answer.

"Erm, 'Cult of Death' seems to be a popular headline."

Catherine groaned.

The detective held the door open for her and they stepped out into the corridor. Catherine collected her belongings, made a quick phone call and left the building. Outside she looked around for Dan. She couldn't see him. It was a busy main road. Traffic zoomed past and people went about their day. Catherine couldn't help but wonder if Simon was watching her.

"Halston? Aintree hospital?" The taxi she'd ordered slid to a stop by her.

"Yes."

The driver stepped out of the car, took her suitcase and placed it in the boot. Catherine got in and settled back. She wasn't in the mood for idle chitchat, but the driver spoke at her, giving his commentary on the killings that had been carried out in the city. A copy of that day's local newspaper had been left on the back seat. She examined the headlines and scrolled through a story. She fought to hold back her tears as she read the egregious reports about her departed friends and Beacon.

Entering the grounds of the hospital, Catherine was amazed at the size of the site before her. The main building, white painted steel and glittering glass, seemed to stretch on and up forever.

The car stopped outside the huge revolving doors that led into the reception area. Hundreds of people were milling about. Catherine rolled the electronic paper up and shoved it in her handbag. She paid the fare and the driver got her suitcase out, placing it on the pavement next to her. She took a deep breath and went in.

"Hi," she said, to a grey-haired, stern looking woman behind the information desk.

The lady looked up over the rim of her silver-framed glasses. "Can I, erm, help?" she asked, having apparently forgotten what her job was.

"Yes. I'm looking for Abdalla Miller."

"Aba-dal-a."

"No, Abdalla. A b d a l l a."

"Right." She typed his name into her computer. "Oh yes. Are you family?"

"Kind of."

The lady frowned. "I'll have to call the ward and see if he can take visitors." She leant into her videophone.

"Okay, thank you." Catherine brushed back her hair. It needed washing. She had hardly slept that night: after being taken to the police station, she had been kept, for her own protection they told her, in a cell.

The woman ended the call and looked up at Catherine. "You can go up, but visiting time is almost over for this morning."

"Okay, where is he?"

140

"St John ward."

"St John ward? You're joking?"

"No? Why?"

"Oh, nothing."

"The first director of the hospital was…." The receptionist cleared her throat. "One of *them*." Catherine nodded her head, surprised at what she was hearing. "He was sacked after, well, inappropriate behaviour, shall we say, with children."

Catherine gulped. "Oh."

"He denied it, of course. Said he'd been set up." Her mood lightened. "He killed himself before he got to prison." She smiled. "At least you and I don't have to pay to keep him in there now. I don't know why he insisted on naming the wards after such fairy tales. We live in enlightened times now, don't we? I've started a petition to have them changed to more normal names. I mean, just numbers would do, don't you think? Will you sign it?" The woman presented a PDA with a form on the screen, and a plastic scriber for Catherine to take, which she did. She scribbled on to the screen. "Almost nine thousand signatures!" the woman proudly stated. "The board said they'll change them if we get ten thousand!"

"Right," Catherine said sadly, handing the PDA back. "Where is, erm, St John ward?"

The receptionist huffed, shaking her head at the mere mention of the name. "Down to the end of the corridor. Take the stairs, or lift, on the left to level two. Then turn left, go right to the bottom and it is on the right."

"Wonderful," Catherine replied. "Thank you very much."

She turned and trotted down the corridor, dragging her suitcase behind her. The sound of her heels clipping on the polished floor accompanied her.

The woman looked down at the form on the PDA and was horrified to see what Catherine had written: 'I will sing to the Lord all my life; I will sing praise to my God as long as I live. Psalm 104 33'.

Outside the ward, Catherine spotted a police officer chatting up one of the nurses. She slipped past them and spotted Abdalla in bed, talking to someone who was half obscured by a curtain, drawn round to divide up the bay.

"Catherine," Abdalla said.

She smiled at him. The visitor turned as she got near. "Dan!" she said, surprised to see him.

He held a finger to his lips, directing her to be quiet. Catherine drew up a chair next to them. Dan pulled off the woolly hat he had been wearing.

"How are you?" she asked Abdalla.

"Fractured ribs, bump on the head. I was very lucky and so were you."

"Wasn't luck, it was Dan."

"So I hear."

Catherine looked at Dan. "Where did you get those clothes?" She gawked at the yellow trousers, green corduroy shirt, blue anorak and filthy trainers he was wearing.

"I got these, borrowed these, from a washing line and found these in a bin." He pointed to his shoes.

"Right. You mean stole, by the way."

"You told him then," Abdalla interrupted, slightly concerned.

"Yes." Catherine looked at Dan for his reaction.

"What's her name?"

"Kristina," she said, touching Dan's hand, "Kristina Blake. We could...."

"Don't. Don't say anything."

Catherine was about to protest, but caught Abdalla's eye; he gave a quick shake of his head.

With Dan staring into space, his thoughts solely on the revelation, Catherine changed the subject.

"Have you seen this?" said asked, retrieving the paper from her bag and laying it on the bed.

"Yes," Abdalla sighed, taking it.

"Our commission destroyed! They're calling us a cult, a nutty fundamentalist sect!"

"Of course they are, Catherine."

"So, you really thought you were going to be the 144,000, an elite band of believers?" Dan said, breaking his silence.

"Oh yes," Abdalla said, with all seriousness. He reread the front page of the paper.

"Right."

"Our job was to raise people up during the coming tribulation, when darkness falls. This world, that God made good, has, over a great deal of time, been eroded. Light to dark." He paused. "I believe in a God of love, a God of second chances. You can't force belief on anyone. That's been tried. It doesn't work."

"Why should people care?"

142

"Dan!" Catherine took a deep breath. "Look, imagine if you took all that's good from the world. Nature, beauty, creativity, love - what would you have left?" Dan shrugged his shoulders. "You'd have a very grey world," she told him, like a schoolteacher addressing a pupil. "Hell is being separated in that way from God. All you knew and were grateful for, but didn't appreciate who you should be grateful to, would be gone. Some might like it that way. For most though, they create their own hell by surrounding themselves with unhealthy things."

"Eschatology has always fascinated me," Abdalla said. "This is the deal: heaven, with nature, beauty and love, will always be waiting, if you wish to see it, if you wish to reconnect with the light. As Catherine said, people create their own hell, but they hold the key to the gate that will liberate them. With Beacon we endeavour to cut through the darkness with our light and be there for new believers when they reconnect. What we are seeing is a deliberate counter-attack, an attempt to pervert Revelation, the prophesy of John, that cryptic unveiling of the final confrontation between the forces of good and evil, light and darkness. A portent that I never thought was literal."

"I said that the other day."

"And it's working, the counter-attack?"

"You've seen it with your own eyes," Catherine replied. "No one will want to be involved with Beacon. Have you read this…." She had to stop herself from swearing as she tossed the paper at Dan.

He read the headline and the report.

"If you take a look around the world you'll see war, global pollution, disease, famine earthquakes, volcanic eruptions. And it's accelerating; the first two sets of seals, trumpets and bowls," Abdalla said.

"I know, I know, Catherine has said. Four and a half years to go."

"Glad you were listening. In a few years, this will all be gone."

Abdalla adjusted his position in the bed and looked Dan in the eyes. "We're in the end times, and it might be too late to recover from this." He paused. "The press are like vipers."

"I see."

"Why don't you believe?" Catherine asked. "Even with all that has happened?"

"I do…."

"But?"

"It doesn't matter. Right now we should be more worried about Simon. He's still out there and he isn't done yet."

Catherine and Abdalla took another fleeting look at each other.

"You have to take Catherine away from here, out of the city,"
Abdalla told Dan.

"Hey, I'm not leaving you!"

"I'll be fine." He shot a look to Dan, and then fixed his eyes on
Catherine. "You must salvage our commission. Start with the website.
Post a message about the aggression towards us."

"Yes, of course, but I'm not leaving!"

"Okay," Dan said to Abdalla.

Catherine shook her head. "I'm not losing you as well."

"We're all hurting." Abdalla reached for Catherine's hand.

"I know they're in a better place now." A tear ran down her
cheek. "But they had so much good work to do." She started to cry.
"And Markus, I wouldn't be here without him."

"They did their work and we must continue to do ours."
Catherine nodded and wiped her face with a tissue.

A bell rang, echoing around the ward.

"Time's up," Dan said. The other visitors started to leave.

"You both know what to do," Abdalla told Catherine and Dan as
they stood up.

"Yeah."

"I'll look after her. I promise." Dan picked up Catherine's
suitcase.

"You'd better, son."

Catherine leant over and kissed Abdalla on the cheek.

"We'll be together again soon," he told her.

Catherine began to well up again. She felt Dan's hand take hers.
"I'll meet you outside."

"Why?"

"I've got to avoid the policeman guarding the ward. He was one
of the ones who arrested me."

Catherine tutted and Abdalla shook his head. They looked back
to Dan, but he was gone.

Under a grey sky Dan waited by the service lift that he'd taken to avoid
being seen by the officer.

Catherine emerged from the reception doors pulling her suitcase
behind her. "There you are."

"Sorry."

"So what were you arrested for and how did you escape?"

"A few things, and," he paused, "and...."

"Special powers?"

144

"Something like that."

"Something like that? I see. You're a man of mystery, Dan."

He smiled. "Thanks." He turned and started to walk.

"Hang on. Where are we going?" She tried to catch up with him. She was tempted to mention his mother again, but resisted.

"Abdalla gave me his keys, including the key to his car. So we're getting out of here."

"I was just pretending to agree with him. I'm not going anywhere."

"You either come with me or I stick you on a plane."

"You can't do that to me! Besides there's that dense cloud of volcanic ash across the States, so I can't get home anyway. There are no flights."

"True, but Abdalla said I have to protect you. They want you dead."

"Okay. But where are we going?"

"I know somewhere."

"Can't you slow down? Where's that?"

Dan stopped. "Sorry."

"It's okay, just slow down. Where are we going?"

"Just a little spot I know. And I'm sorry."

"I know, you just said that."

"No, about the other night. What I did."

"Oh. That. You don't have to apologise."

Dan looked into her eyes. "Don't I?"

Catherine blushed. "No, it's not your fault. Spiritual warfare, right?"

"You know it's more than that."

"Yes, I know."

"Catherine."

"Yes?"

He moved closer to her. He wanted to take her hands. "I've never told anyone this before."

"Don't...."

"You don't know what I'm going to say."

"I do, and before you do, I need to tell you something."

"Let me go first. I...."

"No...."

"Catherine, I...."

"I'm engaged."

"What?"

145

Catherine suddenly became very aware of her surroundings; they were standing in the middle of the pavement, alongside a busy road, people hurrying past. "I'm engaged. I didn't tell you, because there was no need to tell you." Dan didn't know what to say. "You think I gave you the wrong impression, don't you?" She began noticing the disgruntled expressions of the pedestrians who had to manoeuvre around the pair. Dan exhaled and looked into her eyes. "But if it's of any consequence I do like you. In a more than a friend way. But it's too late for that."

"I'm guessing he gave you the necklace?" Dan said, after a long pause.

"Yes."

"What about your engagement ring?"

She held her finger. "It's being resized."

"Oh. Why get engaged at all?"

"How do you mean?"

"If the end is nigh?"

Catherine shrugged her shoulders. "I, we, take one day at a time. We try to live in the present."

"Right. What's his name?"

"Jered, Jered Birnbaum."

"American?"

"Yes. He's a wonderful man, Dan."

"Sure he is. Have you spoken to him about all this?"

"He's not reachable at the moment." She felt the empty space on her hand. "He wanted to marry before he left, but it's been so hectic. He and a friend, well…." She considered her words. "I'm not sure when I'll see him again."

"Not reachable? In this day and age?"

"Yes, that's what I said." She started walking, leaving Dan perplexed.

He caught up with her and they strode back to Abdalla's house with Catherine recounting what had happened to her at the police station and the hospital reception. Dan stayed silent as she talked. He was finding his feelings for her hard to control. He wanted to embrace her and never let go. He longed for her soft voice to tell him what he wanted, needed, to hear.

When they reached Abdalla's road they saw a police officer standing by the front door and a dozen or so TV reporters and cameramen gathered on the pavement.

"Big story." Dan sighed.

"Yeah."

"This way." He led Catherine down a narrow path that emerged in front of a row of garages. "He says it's a bit of an antique. A collector's item."

"Oh, right."

Dan stopped at a garage and inserted one of the three keys on the chain into the lock. The door squeaked as it rose on its retracting hinges. Inside was a late twentieth century, British made, metallic blue vehicle.

"Wow. They don't make them like that any more," Catherine said.

"No, they don't." Dan ran a hand over the bodywork, unlocked the driver's side and put Catherine's suitcase in the boot. "No GPS either."

"Have you got a licence?"

He gave her a wink. "Let's hope we don't get stopped."

"What about insurance?"

"It's covered."

"Okay. Dan, I've thought of somewhere to go."

"I said I know somewhere." He settled into the vehicle and released the catch for the passenger side. Catherine got in.

"We could go and see your mother."

Dan looked at her, and then tried the engine. After four attempts the engine choked into life. "I didn't think it would start." He put the car in gear and drove out on to the path. "We'll have to get some petrol."

"That's very, very expensive. They have almost have run out of that stuff."

"I know, but that's what these old cars run on. And they would have run out years ago if they hadn't dug up Antarctica."

Catherine nodded her head sadly. "Dan." He got out to close the garage. "Dan," she repeated, when he was back behind the wheel.

He stared ahead. "Is she really alive?"

"Yes."

"I don't believe it."

"I've found her Dan. It wasn't easy, but Abdalla gave me some information that someone called Fereshteh had given him."

Dan froze. He felt the blood drain from his face, as he thought back to that awful day. "We have to put this city in the rear-view mirror." He shifted the car in gear and drove them away.

The ward was quiet as everyone settled down for the evening. Abdalla sat up in bed reading the Bhagavad-Gita, trying to take his mind off all that had happened. He had spent the afternoon in reflective meditation, hoping for answers to his questions. Just by reading the paper he could see the enemy's grip on the world was getting tighter, the sinister veil was dropping. With Beacon faltering, he wondered if it was really possible that they could win.

Abdalla placed the book down and remembered the day when everything had changed, the day he heard Fereshteh's words about Dan. Shortly after that, he'd had a vision and taken his commission, which was now falling into ruin. If Catherine could get a message from them out to the world, maybe they could salvage something. Perhaps they could still be a symbol of hope, of light, shining out into a world soon to be totally eclipsed by evil, by darkness.

"Sleep time," the nurse said, working her way clockwise around the room making sure that everyone was comfortable for the night. Abdalla glanced up at the clock on the wall. It was only half past nine. "How are you feeling?"

"Very sore."

"Well, the doctor will see you in the morning. Oh, a real book." She took the paperback off his lap. "Is this one of those religious ones?"

"Yes."

"Glad to see someone still reads things like this. I heard that soon they won't be available to download any more." She put the slim volume on his bedside cabinet and switched off his light.

"Hmm. Not interested yourself then?"

"No, love. I'm happy to see people have their beliefs, but I don't think they should bother others with it."

"I hear that a lot."

The nurse plumped up Abdalla's pillow. "There you go."

"Thanks."

"Goodnight, love."

"Goodnight."

The nurse walked to the next bed. Abdalla got himself as comfortable as he could. His chest was tight and he couldn't lie on his right side. He didn't think he was tired, so he put on a set of headphones and listened to the hospital radio. Before he knew it he was asleep.

After filling the tank with petrol, Dan parked up in a vast and almost full service station car park. They got out and began walking over to the huge building.

"How much money have you got left?" Dan asked Catherine.

"A couple of hundred."

"Should keep us going. Abdalla gave me some too."

"How much?"

"Not sure. I didn't count. I'm starving."

The automatic door slid open. They went in and headed for an eatery. Hordes of people mingled about the stores and ate in a large seating area, where a dozen or so outlets offered a myriad of dishes.

"What takes your fancy?" Dan asked, the aroma of fried cooking already in his nostrils.

"Anything vegetarian, really. I haven't eaten all day. Even for me that is a stretch." Dan laughed. "What are you having?"

"Well, it could be one of each."

They ordered and sat down at the nearest table to eat. Dan was amazed to see Catherine scoffing down her meal.

"You are hungry."

"Yeah," she said, sucking up a straw-full of banana milkshake to wash down her veggie burger and fries. "So, are you going to tell me where we are going?"

"Well, I hope it's still there."

Catherine sighed and took a handful of fries, dipped them in ketchup and stuffed them into her mouth. "Okay, I'll bite. What's still where?"

"When I was younger a friend and I found this little hut, hidden away in a forest, in the ground. It was stocked full of tinned food and stuff."

"Oh?"

"Yeah, but it didn't look like anyone had been in there for years. It would be the perfect place to hide out."

"Okay. Do you think we'll be followed?"

"I hope not." Dan chewed on his burger.

"Why don't we go and see your mother?" She studied Dan's face to see his reaction. There was none. He continued to eat. "Did you hear what I said?"

Dan nodded his head and took a gulp of cola. "I did."

"Well?"

"Well, what?"

"Don't start that. It could help you."

149

"Help me?"

"Yeah, help you find out who you are and where you came from." Dan carried on eating, showing no emotion. "What's wrong?"

"Do you know what it's like growing up feeling unwanted? I had no idea why I had been adopted. Well, not until much later."

"When did they tell you that they weren't your real parents?"

"When I was quite young. They didn't want to keep it a secret."

"That's good."

"I guess. It's better than it coming out on my sixteenth birthday or something. Plus I didn't look anything like them either."

"Oh?"

"They were both quite short, and well, I'm not."

"No, you're not. Aren't you in the least bit interested?"

"Yeah." He'd finished his meal. "Okay, how did you find her?"

"You can find anything on the Internet, if you know where to look."

"That doesn't surprise me." He thought back to his own experiences. Catherine let out a huge groan. "What?"

"I need to post a message on the Beacon site."

"What are you going to say?"

"I really don't know. I just don't know if I can find the words."

"Well, don't ask me. I don't think I can help." Dan took a few fries from Catherine's plate.

"Hey! Actually I'm done." She offered her leftovers to Dan, who took them. "No pointers then?"

"Sorry."

"Both meals we've had together have been really unhealthy," Catherine said, changing the subject. "I'll have to cook for you one day. I'm a good cook."

"You like singing your own praises."

"No one else is going to."

"Not even, what's his name?"

"Jered."

"Yeah, Jerry. Do you, you know, live together in New York?"

"What do you mean 'do we, you know, live together'?"

"You know."

Catherine laughed. "We share an apartment, but no funny business."

"What? Really?"

"Of course. It's hasn't got anything to with our faith, just that I. we, wanted it to be special."

150

"Must be tough."

Catherine shrugged her shoulders. "Anyway, I am absolutely shattered."

"Okay. Let's see if we can get a bed for the night."

"Sounds good, and then I'll tell you what I found."

"What you found?"

"Out about your mother."

Dan nodded. He was still unsure.

They left the service station and went back to the car.

"How long until we get to this place?"

"It's not far. It's just I'm not sure I can find it in the dark." He looked up at the night sky.

"Why don't we stay in a hotel overnight and go tomorrow?"

"We could do."

"There's one over there." Catherine pointed to a building on the other side of the car park.

"Okay. Good idea."

Dan took Catherine's suitcase from the boot of the car and they walked across to the eighteen-storey hotel. The door glided open and they walked through into the lobby area. Approaching the electronic check-in screen, a female human hologram flickered into life.

"Welcome to Best Rest Hotels," it said, in a smooth calming voice. Catherine reached forward and pressed the 'Greeting and advice not required' button on the display.

"Ah, I hate those things."

"Quite hot though."

"Dan! It's a computer programme brought to life by light." She shook her head. Dan smiled. "Let's see if they have got any rooms." Catherine entered their requirements on the check-in screen. "Yep. Oh, they only have a room a double en suite. Shall I use my card or cash to pay?"

"Better make it cash." Dan handed her some notes, which she fed into the machine.

It counted the money, issued a proof of payment and dispensed a plastic keycode. Catherine took the receipt and Dan scooped up the keycode.

"Number twenty," he read.

"Lead the way."

Dan picked up her suitcase, and headed for the secure entrance that led to the accommodation. He waved the keycode over the keypad. The door clicked. He held it open for Catherine and they went through.

A hallway stretched out in front of them. Dan checked a map on the wall.

"Second floor. Stairs?"

"Of course."

"This way then."

Catherine followed him up and they were soon inside their room. She surveyed their new surroundings. "Basic but acceptable." The décor was simple, like the rest of the hotel. Their space was furnished with a bed, a sofa, a kettle and a dressing table.

"I'm glad it meets your approval."

"Hmm. Where are you going to sleep?"

"The bed."

"Hey!"

"Why can't the woman take the sofa?" Catherine placed her hands on her hips. "Okay, okay. I'll take the sofa."

"Good. Right, I'm having a shower. I feel completely yucky." Catherine lifted her suitcase on to the bed and flipped it open.

"Okay."

"See you in a minute."

Catherine went into the bathroom with her toiletry bag and locked the door. She undressed and stood beneath the water. She started to cry as she remembered the friends she had lost and the situation she was now in.

Dan sat on the sofa, listening to the hum of the shower. He lent forwards and flicked on the television. The news came on; an extraordinarily brief report about widespread famine across Africa. If only the rich nations of the world would spread their resources, he thought, then there wouldn't be any famine, and no one needed to go hungry, ever. But he knew that wouldn't happen any time soon, and it was down to the good nature of the individual to support charities. As Catherine had told him: 'We are God's body, hands and feet'. Dan was reminded of a quote his father was fond of repeating: 'When I feed the poor, they call me a saint, but when I ask why the poor are hungry, they call me a communist'. The bulletin swiftly moved on to their central story about a celebrity couple's new hairstyles. He changed channel and started watching a bawdy sit-com.

Dan turned off the television when the shower stopped and settled back on the couch, trying to appear blasé. He heard the sound of wet feet moving around the bathroom. The door unlocked and Catherine came out, wearing only a towel, wrapped tightly around her slender body. Her wet hair stuck to her skin, and Dan noticed that her eyes were bloodshot.

"Are you all right?"

"Sure. I'm fine." She dumped her clothes on to the bed and picked up a towel from the pile to dry her hair. "Are you all right?"

Dan couldn't help but stare at her. "Fine."

"You're not perving on me are you?"

"Perving? No, of course not."

"Good. Did you have the TV on?"

"Yeah."

"Anything happening?"

"No, not really."

"Okay. Now, turn around, I want to put my nightie on."

"I'm not missing that."

"Dan!"

"Okay, okay. I was joking." He twisted his torso round on the sofa.

"Jokes are supposed to be funny." The curtains were open slightly and Catherine's image was reflected in the glass. He saw the towel fall away, but to his own surprise he closed his eyes. "Okay. I'm decent." Dan shifted back around. Catherine was now wearing a blue, knee length, frilly nightie. "What do you think? It's vintage."

"Of course it is."

"Hey! Why buy new stuff when you can recycle? Right." She yawned. "Well, I think I'm going to go to bed." She closed her suitcase and placed it on the floor. "You don't mind do you?"

"I suppose not."

"I got hardly any sleep at the police station." Catherine pulled back the duvet and climbed under it.

"Those beds in the cells aren't very comfortable are they?"

"No, they're not, but it wasn't just that...."

"No...."

"I think I cried all night. Anyway...."

"Yeah...."

"Well, I can sleep with the light on, but don't make too much noise."

"I'll just have a wash and turn in."

"Okay. Goodnight."

"Goodnight." Catherine began mumbling to herself.

"What?"

"Sorry. Praying. Would you like to do it together?"

"Pray?"

"Yes, what else?"

"No, I'm okay."

"Goodnight then."

"Yeah, goodnight."

Dan stood up and walked to the bathroom. "You've only left one towel and it's tiny!" He held it up.

"Oh, sorry…." Catherine muttered, pulling up the duvet around her. "Goodnight." She screwed her eyes shut and clenched her teeth. She wanted to cry again, but resisted. The images of her friends and the times they had spent together came back to her.

Dan shook his head and stepped into the bathroom. After his wash, he dried off as best he could and dressed. Catherine was fast asleep when he reappeared. He wasn't at all tired. Looking down at her he felt a familiar yearning. He exhaled, and despite his promise to look after her, he picked up his coat, left the room, exited the hotel and headed back over to the service station.

All the stores stayed open twenty-four hours, seven days a week so that, like the cities, the service stations never slept. He needed to get some clothes and it didn't take him long to find some functional items and a sturdy pair of boots, which he put on, throwing the trainers he had been wearing away. He also bought some toiletries and a rucksack, which he stuffed all his purchases into. He then wandered around the building, enjoying the anonymity that came with these places, with staying in motorway hotels. Anyone could be anyone. That suited him. In here he was just another anybody. They didn't know him and he didn't know them.

Dan got himself a coffee and sat down. As he stirred several sachets of white sugar into his drink, he looked up and caught the eye of a woman sitting alone at a table a few feet away. She smiled. He smiled back. She was attractive, maybe a little older than him. Dan watched her sip her drink whilst reading a paper. After a few more surreptitious glimpses at each other, Dan picked up his coffee and went over. "Is this seat taken?"

The woman smiled at him, and swept her dark brown hair behind her ears. "I think you know it's not."

"May I?" The woman smirked to herself and shrugged. Dan sat down. "I'm Dan."

"Nadia."

"So, what's…."

"A nice girl like me doing in a place like this?"

"Yeah, something like that."

The woman thought for a second before replying. "I'm a sales manager. I travel up and down the country three weeks out of the month. The rest of the time I'm based in Reading."

"Sounds exciting."

"No, it doesn't, but it's okay. I like seeing different places, although the driving can be tiring. There are so many cars on the roads these days."

"There's always a jam somewhere."

"Yep, and usually it's where I'm heading."

"So, must be tough on the family."

"No, I'm single."

"Oh right, that is a surprise." Dan looked her up and down. Her face was tired, but attractive.

"What about you?"

"Me?"

"Yeah, what do you do?" Nadia crossed her arms and leaned them on the table. "Are you single?"

"I'm in-between jobs at the moment, and I'm also in-between relationships."

"Oh, I see. What do you do?"

Dan smiled to himself and thought of something to say. "I'm kind of a trouble shooter."

"Oh really? Interesting. So, why are you here? For the night life?"

"No, just travelling with a friend."

"But not a girlfriend?"

"Oh no. She's just a friend."

"Good." Nadia moved her hand across the table and touched Dan's. "You're not shy are you?" Dan didn't reply. "Isn't it what you want?" Dan pulled his hand away and took a gulp of coffee. He looked at her. "I've got a room in the hotel next door." She reached forward again for his hand.

Dan was taken aback by her brazen attitude. Her question made him think. Is that what he wanted? A part of him did, it desired that connection, but another part of him was thinking about Catherine. "I'd better get going."

"Oh?"

"Yeah. I'm supposed to be looking after my friend." Dan stood and knocked back his drink. "Nice to meet you though."

"And you. Are you sure you don't want to?"

"Must be going."

Dan picked up his bag. As he walked away he chastised himself. Was he mad? He glanced back. Nadia had gone. He looked around, but she was nowhere to be seen.

Returning to their room, he entered quietly so as not to wake Catherine, who was still fast asleep. He viewed the outline of her slim body, in its foetal position underneath the duvet. He stood next to her and tucked up the cover where it had fallen away.

She mumbled as he began to make up his bed on the sofa with spare linen. He undressed down to his boxers, turned the light off and settled down. He thought back to Nadia. He could be with her right now, but something had changed; he couldn't go through with it. He fell asleep to the sound of Catherine's breathing.

∞

I mentioned an appendix at the beginning, but I think it's now about time I offered an explanation to some of the devices of the future. This is no easy task. The advances in technology have been astounding. It will be hard for you to fathom most of these innovations as they rely on the microchip and electricity for power. So, let me start by trying to explain the microchip, which will lead to another indispensable device of the future, after which I shall list alphabetically.

Microchip: A small square of metal of semiconductor material carrying integrated circuits, especially one having logic circuits for computing. The size could be as small as a grain of sand.

Computers and Laptops: An electronic machine that performs high-speed mathematical or logical calculations or that assembles, stores, correlates, or otherwise processes and prints information derived from coded data in accordance with a predetermined programme. A keyboard, much like a typewriter, allows the user to enter information, which is viewed on a screen that looks much like a pane of glass.

3D: A technique of recording three-dimensional visual information, creating the illusion of depth (you will remember Duboscq's famous 3D photograph of Queen Victoria). Autostereoscopy made it possible for the recording to be viewed without the use of special headgear or glasses.

Aeroplane, plane: A winged flying vehicle that is heavier than air and powered by propellers or jet engines.

Atomic Bomb: An explosive weapon of great destructive power derived from the rapid release of energy in the fission of heavy atomic nuclei. Used twice in combat during the twentieth century and once during the twenty-first. Several countries had the weapon, which, bizarrely, they used as a deterrent against hostile action.

Automobile, also car (Jaguar and Ford, make of), jeep, 4x4 (four wheel drive), van (transit, type of) and lorry: The advances in the automobile have also been remarkable. The cars of the future are sleek, aerodynamic and are capable of speeds in excess of two hundred miles per hour.

Bio Trees: After man's decimation of the rainforests, fake trees, erected on sterile farms, with no benefit to nature around them, were needed to absorb the carbon dioxide in the atmosphere.

Call Centres: A centralised office used for the purpose of receiving and transmitting a large volume of requests by telephone. Operated by a company to administer incoming product support or information enquiries from consumers. Outgoing calls for telemarketing, clientele, product services, and debt collection are also made.

CCTV (close circuit television): A plethora of cameras positioned in *all* public places that record visual images of moving and stationary objects.

CD (compact disc): A compact laser disc for reproducing recorded sound when it is played on a specially designed record player (CD player) – a beam of light, the laser, senses variations in the height on the surface of the disc and converts them into electronic pulses and sound. Information could also be recorded on to it. Digital technology made them redundant by the middle of twenty-first century.

Credit/debit card: Issued by banks authorising the holder to buy goods or services on credit or funds taken directly from an individual's bank account. A personalised number (the PIN) was required to pay with the card.

Digital radio: Sometimes just called 'radio'. A system of broadcasting sound and written information using electronic signals which represent a series of the numbers 0 and 1 (binary code). The 'radio' was the equipment used to receive these signals. Binary code is also how other electronic equipment, such as computers, worked. These technologies had developed from earlier analogue devices, which had relied on variations in electromagnetic waves.

Download: Information (music, documents etc) taken from the Internet and transplanted to a device, usually a PDA.

Duvet: A type of bedding - a soft flat bag filled with synthetic material. Duvets reduce the complexity of making a bed, as they consist of a single covering instead of the combination of bed sheets, blankets, and quilts.

Electronic paper: Like regular newspapers but made from a thin, durable, plastic. The 'news' is stored in microchips and viewed on the screen or page and 'scrolled' through. Can be kept and updated daily with wireless downloads, or discarded/recycled. The news could also be downloaded to a PDA.

Genetically modified: A plant (or animal) that has had some of its biological make-up changed scientifically, for example to produce the perfect crops.

GPS (global positioning system) or satellite navigation: A system that can show the exact position of a person or object by using signals (digital/binary code) from man-made satellites in orbit around the Earth.

Holograms: A technique that allows the light scattered from an object to be recorded or created by a computer programme and later reconstructed. Also makes the image appear three-dimensional.

I.D. (identification) card: The plastic I.D. card was compulsory around the world. Displays your name, date of birth and a photograph.

Ignition screen: Replaced the key as the starting mechanism in an automobile. Programmed to recognise the owner of the vehicle's finger or thumbprint and prevent theft. Same technology also used to gain access to the vehicle.

Internet/World Wide Web: Accessed via a computer, laptop or PDA anywhere around the world at anytime. Much like an encyclopaedia, but virtual, that is, has no physical presence. Could be edited and contributed to by all who could access it.

Keycode: A replacement for the regular metal key. A thin plastic strip coded with microchip information.

Keypad: The lock of the future. A small black glass screen coded with microchip technology. The correct and unique Keycode would open the electronic lock the Keypad was attached to.

Lift: A mechanical apparatus usually consisting of a large metal cage or box hoisted and lowered by a series of chains and pulleys. Used for moving objects, and people, up and down between floors in buildings.

Multimedia: A term used to describe the collation of media communication (news, weather reports etc) and entertainment (music, books, films etc). Available through the PDA.

Motorways: Like a single track of road, but imagine ten of them side by side. Up to ten lanes going in either direction - the minimum was two. The speed limit was one hundred miles per hour.

PDA (personal digital assistant): An indispensable device of the future. No bigger than the palm of the hand, essentially a smaller version of the laptop. A plastic scriber could be used to write on the screen, or you could use an on-screen keyboard. The device incorporated the 'mobile phone', which was like the regular telephone, able to receives and make calls, as well as text, sound, or picture messages, from and to anywhere around the world, and entirely portable. Also contained integrated television technology so callers can see one another when speaking, and the 'music player', a device that holds digital music. Able to record speech, capture photographic and moving images, access the World Wide Web and digital radio, send e-mails (electronic mail) and facilitate downloads. An implantable microchip later replaced the PDA.

Refrigerator/fridge and freezer: Apparatus used for reducing and maintaining the temperature of a chamber below the temperature of the external environment.

Self-service checkout: Most stores were automated, that is staff weren't needed to complete the transaction of goods and you would 'serve yourself' by swiping an item's barcode (a code of the form of vertical lines and numbers) into a computer and inserting your payment cash or card.

Service station: A huge building incorporating refuelling points for vehicles (electric battery, petrol, bio-fuels) and a multitude of stores, which sold everything imaginable.

Shower: An area in which one bathes underneath a spray of water. Modern showers contained amenities, such as computers, radios, televisions, telephones and refrigerators.

Solar-powered: Power or energy obtained by direct conversion of radiation from the sun, either by its heating effect or by use of photoelectric cell to generate electricity.

Spaceship: A vehicle capable of flight both within and outside the Earth's atmosphere, which made putting people on the Moon and Mars possible.

Stores: A generic term for all types of shops. Items were tagged (micro-chipped with information), and once purchased at the self-service checkout, this tag would provide the key to leave the store. If on approaching the exit the electronic barriers detected un-paid-for goods, these barriers would swiftly close and the authorities were called. Only a few people were employed to restock shelves and deal with any problems. Stock levels were computerised, so that if an item was close to selling out, the computer would reorder it. Some stores, of course, did still rely on a greater number of employees, but these were slowly dying out. Giant warehouses stored food supplies. Products such as freeze-dried coffee, teabags (tea leaves held in small porous paper bags, enough for just one cup), and frozen meat and pre-prepared meals kept in fridges and freezers, were very popular.

Television: An electronic apparatus that receives the transmission of visual images of moving and stationary objects, with accompanying sound, as digital code, and is capable of the reconversion of received code into moving pictures.

Videophone: Much like the telephone you know, but with a screen to allow you to see the other caller. Also sends text, sound or picture messages to other videophones or PDAs.

Website(s): Accessed via the Internet/World Wide Web, websites are virtual pages (webpages or links) of information on specific subjects, organisations or people.

Wireless: A connection to another device that needs no wires. All PDAs and most computers are capable of this.

If I have missed anything out, then I do apologise. I'm sure you will appreciate that the innovations of the future are endless.

27

Dan's eyes opened and darted around the room. It took a moment to figure out where he was. The bed was empty and neatly made. The bubbling sound which woken him was the miniature kettle on the dresser reaching boiling point. He was about to call out when Catherine came out of the bathroom, wearing a floral dress and with a toothbrush in her mouth.

"Morning." Dan smiled and sat up. She dropped a tea bag into each cup. "Tea?"

"No, coffee."

"Oh. Okay." She picked out one of the bags and emptied a sachet of coffee into the mug. Dan got up, took another sachet and added it to the other one. "Caffeine fiend." Catherine poured the boiling water.

"Yep."

She walked back into the bathroom, spat out the toothpaste and gave her teeth a final brush.

Dan opened a small plastic tub of milk and tipped it into his drink. "Want some?"

Catherine quickly picked up her tea. "No. I try not to take that horrible processed stuff when I can, especially not from little plastic pots in a motorway hotel."

Dan laughed. He sat down on the sofa and Catherine joined him, her skin brushing against his. They looked at each other. Catherine's blue eyes reflected the sunlight streaming through the window.

"It's a lovely day outside, for once. I've been trying to write a message to post on the Beacon website."

"Any joy?"

"I just can't find the words. But I have downloaded the directions to where your mother is on to my PDA."

"Not that again."

"Dan, it's your mother!"

"Can we talk about this some other time?"

Catherine paused. "Okay, okay."

"Good. We should get going. We'll have to pick up some supplies on the way."

"Well, I'm ready. Where did you get those clothes?" She pointed at the plastic bags on the floor by the sofa.

"Oh, I slipped out last night."

"You're supposed to be protecting me!"

"Yeah, I know. Sorry."

"Very trendy, but not as nice as the clothes I got you in Liverpool." She removed a pair of cream jeans from the rucksack on the floor and tossed them over to him.

"Next time you can be my personal shopper."

After dressing, they left the hotel. The car, to Dan's relief, started first time and they pulled back on to the motorway.

"Look what I got when I paid for the petrol yesterday." Catherine dug a CD out of her handbag.

"What's that?"

"Old music. There's no connector for my PDA's music player, and the radio just plays rubbish."

"So that's why you didn't pay at the pump. I'm surprised they still sell CDs."

"Service stations sell everything. Apart from decent clothes." She gave a smirk.

"Very funny. What's on it?"

"1980s hits."

"1980s?"

"I know, I know, ancient. Prefab Sprout, Ultravox, Europe, Nik Kershaw, Belinda Carlisle, Ratt, Tiffany, Rick Astley...."

"Some of those names sound familiar. My mother used to listen an oldies radio station when I was young."

Catherine continued down the tracklisting. "Mel and Kim, White Lion, ABC, Heart, Spand-au Ballet, that's a funny name." She unwrapped the packaging, opened the case and took out the CD.

"Other way," Dan said, watching her attempt to put it into the car's CD player.

"Oh, right." The CD slid in and the music began. Catherine started to move her head to the beat. "This is pretty good, well retro!"

"It's not bad. I reckon they're playing proper instruments too."

As the car sped along the motorway, Catherine nudged up the volume.

Abdalla was sitting up in bed reading. He had just reached the end of an article about a devastating oil spill in Antarctica.

"How are you feeling this morning?" a young female doctor asked.

"Sorry?" Abdalla said.

"How are you feeling today?"

"Fine. A little sore."

"That's to be expected. Well, I'll be round later to check up on you."

Abdalla smiled back at her and she moved from his bed space to the patient next to him.

In the corridor the police officer who had been stationed on the ward handed over to PC Boender.

"Anything happen?" Boender asked, straightening his jacket and looking around for one the nurses, Kathy, who he had been talking to the day before.

"No, nothing," replied his colleague, putting down an electronic magazine she'd been reading.

"Well, you can go home now."

"Thanks, have fun."

The officer departed and Boender checked for change in his pocket. He was thirsty. He took a fleeting glance to see if Abdalla was all right and then wandered down the corridor to the vending machine. He studied the options, slotted two coins into the machine and made his selection. Whilst it dispensed the almost hot liquid into a plastic cup, he saw a door to his left open slightly, and then close. Boender picked up his drink and went over.

163

"Hello? Is that you, Kathy?" He opened the door, and as he did a hand shot out and grabbed the back of his head. He was pulled in. The room was a small store cupboard. Simon lifted Boender off the floor. The striplight above them flickered on and off. "I don't believe...." Boender dropped his cup as his eyes fell upon his attacker.

"Good...."

Abdalla yawned. Stretching, he tentatively swung his legs out of bed. He needed the bathroom. He wrapped his dressing gown around him, stood up and shuffled out of the bay and on to the corridor.

It wasn't until he was almost at the toilets that he realised he hadn't seen a police officer. He looked around. Finding the male cubicle free, he went in and shut the door. Almost as soon Abdalla had secured the lock the handle was depressed again. He hadn't seen anyone else in the corridor. Again someone tried.

"I won't be a minute."

But again the handle went down and this time it stayed down. A force pushed. The door broke open. Abdalla's eyes widened. Simon stepped in, foaming at the mouth.

"I won't tell you anything. In...."

Simon rammed his hand over Abdalla's mouth. "Oh, you'll tell us, you'll tell us everything...."

The door was slammed shut.

28

Catherine tried to ring the hospital, but her PDA battery had run out of charge. She turned the music again in an attempt to drown out the despondent thoughts circling through her mind, thoughts she had been suppressing for the last few days.

She put the PDA back into her handbag. "I hate these things."

"I know, you said you hated technology."

"I did, didn't I?"

"It's probably for the best, anyway. You can be traced if you use your PDA."

"I hadn't thought of that. Are we nearly there yet?"

"Yeah, almost." Dan flicked on the indicator to leave the motorway and the car descended a hill. "You see that forest over there?" He pointed straight ahead. Catherine saw a vast expanse of trees.

"Wow."

"And somewhere in the middle of that lot is a little cabin. Well, I hope it's still there."

"Right."

Dan turned left at a roundabout. "There was a local shop."

"Was?"

"Can't imagine it's still there now. It was a while ago."

After the roundabout, Dan took a right and then a left and they found themselves travelling into open countryside. After four miles, the car entered a village. To Dan's surprise the store was still trading, albeit now a franchise of an international chain. He pulled over and parked.

"Now this is a quaint old English village."

"I guess it is."

"How are you doing?"

"Okay. You?"

"I'm trying not to think about it."

"That's what I thought."

"I'm good at forgetting." She bit her nails. Her face suggested she was reliving the last twenty-four hours.

Dan changed the subject. "Right, let's get some supplies."

"Okay."

They crossed the road and went into the store, passing through the electronic barriers.

"Well, what will we need?" she asked, perusing the shelves in front her.

"I really hope it's still there," Dan said, under his breath. "One of everything I guess."

"Everything?" Catherine picked up a packet of dog biscuits that was on special offer.

"Well, not everything." Dan took a basket and made his way up an aisle. Catherine couldn't help but glance down at the papers. They all had headlines about Beacon. Dan noticed and called her over to him.

"What?"

"Crisps?"

"Crisps? Can't we get something healthy?"

"Of course. Give me a hand then." Dan held the shopping basket out to her.

She pushed it away. "Hey! You hold it, I'll fill it."

"Deal."

Catherine led the way and she crammed the basket full, resisting the urge to buy a paper. At the self-service checkout she scanned their purchases into the till as Dan packed. She paid and they returned to the vehicle and resumed their journey to the forest.

"Have you got any trainers?" Dan asked.

"Trainers? No. Why?"

"I was just thinking that heels aren't really suitable for hiking through the forest."

"Now you tell me."

"Sorry."

"You'll have to carry me."

"Carry you?"

Catherine looked at her shoes. "These are…."

"Vintage?"

She pulled a face and turned up the music.

Twenty minutes later the trees either side of the road were becoming much denser.

"We're here."

Catherine gazed at the tall evergreens around them. "We are?"

"Yeah. We're going to have to hide the car."

Dan checked his mirrors and with no one behind or in front, he slowed and took the car off the road and into the forest. The vehicle bounced along the uneven ground.

"What are you doing?" Catherine asked.

"We're hiding. We can't leave the car lying around waiting to be found, either by the police or…."

"Simon."

"Yeah. Simon."

Dan found the perfect spot, at the bottom of a slope that led into a sizeable hollow. He parked and got out. "I'm just going to cover the tracks. Can you get our stuff out?"

"Sure." Catherine jumped out on to the soft soil. "Smells…." She tried to think of the appropriate word.

"Earthy?"

"Yeah, earthy."

"Funny that. Right, I'll be back in a minute." He picked up several branches and, using them like a broom, brushed over the vehicle's tyre tracks. Catherine took out their luggage and supplies and waited for him to come back. The forest seemed impenetrable to her. She couldn't see the road, but could hear the sound of traffic. The trees were tall, thin and straight. They grew in perfect symmetry. The ground was covered in dried pine needles. Further in the trees were placed even closer together and it was a lot darker where the branches overlapped and daylight couldn't get through.

A few minutes later Dan returned.

"Are you okay?"

"Yeah."

"You looked spooked."

"I am a little. I suppose we're going deeper in?"

"Yes. I only hope I can remember the way, otherwise we'll be lost."

"Don't say that."

"Okay. Let's get going." Dan picked up their belongings.

"Can you manage it all?"

"Sure. I think you'll have your work cut out staying on your feet."

"Okay." Catherine tentatively followed, watching where she stepped. Dan strode forward like he wasn't carrying a suitcase, two full bags of shopping and a rucksack. As she expected, they were soon weaving between the trees and she was totally disorientated.

"You can't possibly know where you're going."

Dan stopped to let Catherine catch up. "Do you know what?"

"What? Ow… I've broken a heel."

"Probably just as well. Break the other one off."

"Huh?"

He dropped the luggage. "Give it here."

"But they're Jimmy Choos."

"He should have kept them."

"What?"

"Give it here." Catherine removed her shoe and handed it over.

Dan snapped the heel off. "That will make it easier for you."

"Thanks a lot. What were you going to say?"

"I was going to say that you might be right."

"I am?"

"Yes, I'm not sure where I'm going."

"Really?"

"I thought there'd be a clearing somewhere."

"So where does that leave us?"

"Lost."

"You can't be serious."

"Let's keep going. I'm sure it's around here somewhere."

"If you're sure."

"No, not really."

167

Catherine followed as Dan led them through the forest.

Half an hour later Dan stopped.

"No clearing, but I think the hut is just over there." He pointed at what appeared to Catherine to be some more trees and undergrowth.

"I can't see anything."

"Exactly."

Catherine watched on, puzzled. She blinked and he was gone. "Dan?" Moving closer, squinting to find where he had disappeared, it wasn't until she was on top of it that she saw the concealed entrance to the cabin. "Dan?"

Dan emerged. "Here we are. Come on in." He held back the overgrowing shrub that hid the door.

She hesitantly entered and found herself in the cabin. "This is impressive."

"Isn't it? Doesn't look like anyone has been in here since me. Can't imagine Chock could have found it again." Dan lit two oil lanterns that hung from the walls.

"What? What is a Chock?"

"Just an old friend."

"Oh, a person. Right. How can you tell?"

"Tell?"

"That no one has been."

"Because everything is how we left it. Our sweet wrappers are still on the floor." Dan picked one up and handed it to Catherine, who grimaced and dropped it on the table. "Well, get yourself comfortable. I'm going to get a fire going."

"I'll try." Catherine pulled out a chair and sat down at the table, whilst Dan set about lighting the stove with paper and wood that had been stacked up neatly for that purpose. "Who built it?"

"I have no idea." Dan unfolded a screwed up piece of newspaper. "This is dated October 2008!"

"Oh, let's have a look." He passed her the front page of a now out-of-print broadsheet. "Well, look at that; global recession and pollution, wars, famine. I've always said that the beginning of the twenty-first century was when the first ripples of the end began."

"Have you?"

"Of course, that's when it started. The first sign of what was going to come. That's when the darkness started to grip tighter, preparing its end game, and that's when organised religion had to get real and wake up to the world around it."

"Right."

"It took a while of course and initially only a few bold souls were brave enough to stand up and show the way. Thank God they did." She sighed. "Yep, that was the start. Would you believe that white, western, heterosexual people asserted a monopoly on spiritual enlightenment back then?"

"What? You're kidding. That's crazy."

"I know, I know. Scary. No wonder things got screwed up."

"There we go." The fire was alight.

"Oh. That makes all the difference. Cosy."

"Should warm the place up. I'll put the kettle on." Dan took a bottle of mineral water from the shopping bags and poured some into the metal pot. He washed it out and threw the unwanted water out the door, then refilled.

Catherine reached for one of the plastic bags. "Well, I'm starving."

"Cool. You make us lunch. There's some cutlery here."

"Is it clean?"

Dan looked at the tin plates and the knives and forks. "I'll give them a good once over."

Catherine stood up and went through what they had bought. She prepared a salad on the clean plates and they sat down to eat.

"Do you think people will see the smoke?" Catherine asked.

"No. Not this deep into the forest. The smoke will get circulated through the trees."

"How long are we going to have to stay here?"

"Until it's over."

"How will we know when it's over?" Dan continued to chew on his salad. "How are we going to know it's over?" He tried to think of something to say, but Catherine realised. "We're bait aren't we?" Dan carried on eating. "Did you even hide the tracks?"

"Yes, of course. Look…". He pushed his plate away. "Abdalla."

"Abdalla? Was this his idea? Hang on, that's what he said, 'you *both* know what to do'."

"We can't let more innocent people die. It was our idea."

"It was his idea, wasn't it?"

"What did I just say?"

"And what about Abdalla? Simon will go after him first." Her expression changed as she spoke.

"Is he going to tell Simon where we are?"

"Yes," he muttered. "I suggested I take you here. It's out of the way. No one will get hurt."

"What about us?"

"You'll be fine."

"Are you going to kill him?"

"I'm going to end it."

"I can't believe this." Catherine threw her fork down and walked out of the cabin.

"Catherine!" Dan punched the table in frustration and went after her.

Outside, he saw her heading into the forest. "Catherine, come back! You'll get lost." She didn't listen but carried on, her feet crunching over fallen branches and twigs. Dan sighed. He considered letting her go out of spite. He looked towards the sky. It was going to rain. He began to stride after her. "Catherine, stop." She turned, tears pouring down her face. "Are you okay?"

"Of course I'm not okay. All my friends are dead." She collapsed to the ground, her legs crossed; her hair fell forward. She continued to weep. "How can this be happening?" Dan sat down beside her and put his arm around her. The sensation of them touching sent a warmth through him. "This isn't how it's meant to happen." She stared at him, her eyes red and inflamed, her make-up smudged; she looked for an answer in his face.

"I know, but we have to do something."

"What's the point? They're going to win, aren't they?"

"I don't know. I hope not. Abdalla told me to make sure you rebuild."

"I just can't; not without him and Markus and the others." She closed her eyes and saw all her friends' smiling, sanguine faces.

"You can."

"I'm not strong enough." She rested her head on his shoulder.

"Catherine, I've never met anyone as determined as you."

A gentle drizzle began to fall.

"Oh, it's always raining in this country."

"Let's get back to the hut."

She slumped sideways on to the forest floor. "Leave me here."

Dan pulled her up again. Dirt was stuck to the side of her cheek. He wiped it off. A crack of thunder echoed around them and a downpour followed. "Come on." He hauled her to her feet and they made their way back to the cabin.

By the time they returned, they were both soaked through. Dan shut the door behind them and dropped the wooden catch, before setting about refuelling the wood burner.

"Bring yourself closer to the fire," Dan said, noticing Catherine shivering. She moved over. "Have you got any towels?" He opened her suitcase.

"Yeah. I liberated them from the hotel."

He smiled. "Thief."

Catherine shrugged her shoulders. "Nothing matters any more."

"Come on, Catherine. Look, we'd better get out of these wet clothes." Dan pulled off his shirt and wiped himself dry. He threw a towel over to Catherine and she began to undress. Dan turned the other way.

They were soon sat huddled around the stove, towels wrapped around them, trying to warm up.

"So, we're just going to sit here and wait?"

"Yes."

"Do you think he'll kill Abdalla?"

"I hope not."

"I couldn't go on without him, Dan. He started it. He's the rock."

"I know. If Simon finds us, then we can assume he has. Abdalla wasn't afraid of dying."

"But he can't die."

Rain bounced off the tin roof.

"It's lashing down out there."

"Yeah. Dan?"

"What?"

"Do you think you can?"

"What?"

"Deal with Simon?"

"I'm not sure, but I won't let him hurt you."

A bulky figure leapt from the back of a lorry speeding along the road. It hit the wet tarmac hard and rolled. After lying still for a few seconds the form rose. Driving rain flowed off it. The contours of a body were distinct under the wet clothing. Simon marched off the asphalt and into the forest.

29

It was warm. He could taste dust in his mouth. There was a lot of movement going on around him. Along with the dust, he tasted blood. Dan was exhausted. Every part of him ached. He moved his head to the side and opened his eyes. He squinted as the sun's rays blinded him, and sand blew against his face. He tried pushing himself up but he had no strength left in his body. He began to hear noises. It sounded like fighting. It sounded like animals clashing. Screams, shouts, gun shots, metal against metal. It sounded like chaos. Again he attempted to get up, but it was no good. He felt a soft hand on his back and heard his name spoken by a familiar voice. With her at his side he somehow managed to move. She knelt down. He looked at her. Her dark hair was long and wavy and it flowed in the breeze. She was without make up; her eyes were crystal in clarity, she was wearing a dirtied white robe. Catherine smiled at him. He glanced down at his body and saw that he was covered in blood. "I'm here," she told him. "I love you." Before Dan could respond a dark shadow was cast over them. He looked up and saw a hideous, and instantly recognisable face, towering over them. "Your replacement," he said, raising a four-digit hand.

Dan sat upright in the chair he had been sleeping on. His swift movement woke Catherine.

"What is it?" she asked, sitting up.

"Just a dream. I think."

Catherine yawned. "Oh, I thought it might be...."

"No."

"Are you sure it wasn't a nightmare?"

"Maybe, kind of."

"Tell me about it?"

"The dream?" Dan got up and stoked the fire, adding more wood.

"Yes."

"No, it's nothing."

"Go on."

"I was in a desert, I think, and there was fighting. I had been wounded." The fire crackled into life. "You were there."

"I was?"

"Yes."

"What was I doing?"

"I'm not sure, nothing really."

"Nothing?"

"No, you were just there."

"Oh, okay." She yawned again and stood up. "What time is it?"

Dan looked at his watch. "Almost six."

"We've been asleep all afternoon."

"I know. Must be dinner time."

"But we haven't done anything! Dan," she continued in one breath, "what do we do about, you know…."

"What? Simon?"

"No… going to the bathroom?"

Dan laughed. "You've never been camping have you?"

"Yes, I have, but on proper sites, with toilets and shower blocks. Oh, shower…."

"You're a city girl."

"Yes, I am. Well, it sounds like it's stopped raining."

"Yeah." Dan went over to the door and opened it. Outside it was still light, but only just.

"I take it you need to go?"

She pulled some toilet roll from her suitcase. "Yes."

"I think we'd better put some clothes on."

"Oh." Catherine looked down at the towel wrapped around her. "You're right."

They redressed into their clothes now dried by the fire, and stepped outside. It was cold, and the heavy rain had made the ground sodden.

"It's horrible out here." Catherine's shoes squelched on the ground.

"You'll be all right." Dan led her away from the cabin and scanned round for a suitable spot.

"What was that?"

"What was what?"

"I thought I heard something."

"I didn't hear anything."

"Are you sure?"

"Yes. What did it sound like?"

"Snapping."

"Might be a deer."

"A deer?"

"Yeah. Roe deer, muntjack."

"Okay." She gingerly followed Dan.

There was another snap. They both heard it this time.

"Did you?"

"Yeah. Keep still." They froze and their eyes shifted around the trees; what light there was in the dense forest was fading fast. "Can you see him?"

"You think it's... *him*?"

"It *is* him."

"Then Abdalla's...."

Dan didn't reply; he kept his eyes focused on the woodland, scanning from side to side. Catherine also looked through the trees, fighting back tears, but she couldn't see anything.

"We'd better get back to the cabin."

"Yeah. I don't need to go any more."

They turned and started to make their way back. As they did, they heard another snap, but this time it was louder, closer.

"We're not going to make it."

Dan stopped dead in his tracks. "You're right, we're not going to make it."

Catherine looked in the direction Dan was staring. From between the trees marched the colossal form of Simon.

"Your friend pleaded with us to spare his life. He told us where we would find you. He betrayed you!"

Catherine's heart sank. She thought of Abdalla. "Right." Her voice was indomitable. Fixing her gaze on the man closing in on them, she straightened her coat and moved forward to meet him.

"Catherine, no!"

"I can do this." Catherine raised her hand as Simon advanced. Dan watched on stunned, waiting for Simon to attack. "In the name of the God of love," she shouted. "I command you to leave!" Her words brought Simon to a halt. "In the name of the God of love," she repeated, "I command you to leave!" Simon fell to his knees. His body started to convulse. "Out! Out! Out!" Catherine stepped closer to him as he shuddered under the words. "In the name of the God of love, I command you to leave!" she again ordered, with spittle flying over her lips as her zeal increased.

From Simon's mouth a dark cloud manifested, followed quickly by five others. Catherine and Dan watched on astounded. With the demons released Simon appeared normal again, although utterly drawn and fatigued. His body had reduced in size and his eyes, which had been so full of hate, now had their lucidity restored. Catherine and Dan looked at each other. The six vapours circled around Simon and then dove back into him. His body shook, his form swelled, and his eyes once again clouded over. Before Catherine could restart he swiftly rose from his knees and knocked her out of the way. She flew through the air, hit the ground and rolled until she smacked into a tree. Simon advanced and Dan braced himself as Simon's clenched fist made contact, knocking him to the wet earth.

"You're coming with us."

Dan rubbed his jaw. "Really?" From the ground he levitated up, back-flipped and landed on his feet.

Simon lunged forward, but Dan got the first blow in. Simon stumbled backwards. Dan sent a wave of dirt and leaves flying into him. He ducked out of Simon's way and kicked him in the back. Simon crashed to the ground.

Dan jumped on him and put his arm securely around his neck. "I'm really sorry." He continued to choke Simon, but Simon jerked his head back, head-butting Dan.

Dan rolled off, landing on his hands and knees. Simon kicked Dan as hard as he could in the stomach and Dan spun over, collapsing into a heap. Simon reached down and grabbed Dan by his hair. Raising Dan's head, Simon punched him. Dan fell and Simon repeated the process until he was sure Dan was unconscious, his fist covered in blood.

Simon turned his attention to Catherine; she lay helpless. She was the last remaining person from Beacon who he had been directed to kill, and then the war would be over, a prophecy perverted, victory assured. They, the evil spirits inside him, were going to enjoy it.

He swaggered over to her; the demons beneath his skin, sensing the imminent conclusion, twisted a foul dance of celebration. Simon picked her up by the collar of her jacket; she began to come round. Catherine screamed as she regained consciousness. Simon's eyes fell upon the crucifix. He sneered, and despite his aversion to it, managed to rip it from her neck, throwing it aside. Simon held her aloft. She could smell his pungent breath and see every line of evil on his face. He snarled at her, his mouth foaming with pure odium. She was going to die.

There was an odd noise. Simon's face suddenly changed from wrath to shock. He dropped Catherine. She landed with a bump and gazed up. She saw why he had let her go. A wide pointed branch had passed through him. It protruded from his chest, which began to smoulder. She was covered in his blood. Simon toppled over. Catherine noticed a bloodied Dan on his knees behind him. Dan blew out an exhausted and relieved breath and timidly got to his feet. Catherine turned to Simon. The six vapours emerged, howling and screaming, from his mouth. Dan hastened to Catherine and dragged her away. The six apparitions looped the trees, their bawls echoing around the dark forest. Dan held Catherine close, unsure of what the spirits might do. They ascended, whirling and screeching as they rose, before they tore themselves apart and burned up.

"Are you okay?" Dan asked.

"I think so," she said, trembling. "What did you do?"

Dan held up Catherine's crucifix. "Blessed a puddle of water, and dipped the tip of the branch in it."

Catherine, shocked at what she'd just witnessed, took the necklace and cautiously crawled towards Simon. Dan followed her.

"Dan?" She indicated to the branch.

Dan nodded and pulled, as gently as he could, the branch from Simon's chest. Simon groaned as the smouldering object left his body, leaving a charred wound. Catherine ran her fingers through his hair and stared into his eyes. He was free, kindness had returned to his face and she was reminded of when they had first met.

"Sunayani," Simon mumbled, meeting Catherine's gaze.

"It's okay." Catherine held his hand, gripping it tight. He felt cold.

There were no more words from Catherine, just tears. She didn't know what to say and a few moments later Simon was gone.

"Catherine."

"What?"

"He's...."

"Did he have to die?"

"He was going to kill you. Besides." Dan sighed. "I don't think his body would have recovered, and would he have wanted to live?"

Catherine released her grip and wiped her eyes. "What now?"

"It's over."

"Is it?"

"Yes." Dan took a deep breath. "It's over."

"What now?"

"We, you, can go back."

"To what?"

Dan knelt down beside her. "You've got a job to do. There are people out there relying on you."

"I can't." She shook her head and started sobbing. "I can't. Not without Abdalla."

Dan took her hand, pulled her up with himself, turned her towards him and placed his hands in hers. "Let's get out of here."

"What about Simon?" She looked down at his body.

"We'll have to leave him."

"Leave him?"

"What else can we do?" Catherine didn't reply, but just stared at her friend. "We'll make an anonymous call to the police telling them where they can find his body."

"Won't they think finding him like this is strange?"

"I'm sure they will, but they might just be pleased they can wrap their case up."

Catherine reluctantly agreed and they made their way back to the cabin.

30

It was dark by the time Dan drove them back towards the village. After concealing the cabin, they had changed out of their bloodied clothes and Catherine had finally gone to the toilet. They then found the car stuck in the ditch, unable to get traction due to the heavy downpour, leaving Dan to push it out. Before hitting the road, they'd covered the tyre tracks, and eventually set out just as it started raining again. Now they sat in silence, both reflecting.

Passing the village store, Catherine called out. "Stop the car."

Dan slammed on the brake. "Why?" The car juddered to a halt.

Catherine swiftly alighted and Dan tried to make out what she had seen. A few minutes later, she returned soaking wet and crying. She produced an electronic newspaper from a plastic bag and tossed it on to his lap.

"What is it?" Dan viewed the headline: 'Hospital Cult Killings'. He continued to read the report, then stared at the picture of Abdalla. He had been a friend, a father figure.

"PC Boender is dead too."

"That's why we had to end it."

"Why didn't anyone see anything?"

"He may have appeared physically big but he, they, move with stealth. You know those little flashes, those black images you can sometimes see out of the corner of your eye? That's them." Catherine held a hand to her head and wiped her face. "What else you have got in there?"

"A battery for my PDA and...." She took out a bottle of bourbon.

"Whiskey?"

"Dan, I just exorcised six demons from the body of a friend, before you killed him with a branch dipped in holy water. I'm having a drink."

Dan tried to smile. "I can't argue with that. I guess I'd better make that phone call."

They drove further down the road and stopped when they saw a phone box; it was in a dilapidated state, its exterior glass panels and video screen shattered, and all remaining surfaces covered in graffiti.

Dan got out and as approached the box he wrapped his hand in the sleeve of his jumper as a precaution. The door creaked open and he picked up the receiver. With one finger protected by the sleeve of his sweater, he dialled 999. It began to ring.

"Which emergency service do you require?" answered a male voice.

Dan tried a Scottish accent. "Police."

"Police. How can I help?" asked a female voice. Dan wasn't too sure what to say. "Hello?"

"Yes, hello. The, erm, cult killer is dead. You'll find the body in Delamere Forest."

"Who is this please?"

"It's on the B5152 side."

Dan hung up. He considered what he had said and whether that was enough information. He hoped it would be. Exiting the booth, Dan rushed back to the car; he found Catherine absorbed in the thin electronic screen.

"How can anyone believe this stuff?" she asked, drying her eyes.

"You shouldn't be reading it."

"I know. I know." She sniffed and chucked the paper on the back seat. "What did the police say?"

"I just told them where to find his body." Catherine nodded her head, upset that they had to leave Simon. "Let's get out of here. Where to?"

"I don't know." She reached for the bottle. "Just pull over somewhere."

31

The sound of Catherine being sick woke Dan. His eyes focused on the clock on the dashboard. It was almost nine am. He turned and saw the now empty bottle of bourbon on the rear seat, resting on top of the sleeping bag he'd found in the boot and which Catherine had slept in. Looking out of the window he tried to recall how they'd ended up in a field in the middle of nowhere. He did remember; he'd just driven until the car ran out of petrol.

"I don't feel too good." Catherine held her stomach, sat back in the car and pulled the sleeping bag to her. "Have we got any water?"

"No, I'm afraid not. I think I'm a bad influence on you."

She coughed. "You must be. Where are we?"

"I'm not sure." He viewed the flat desolate fields and the hills in the distance. "Shall we listen to the news?"

Catherine shrugged her shoulders. Dan turned on the radio and managed to find the Government news station, just as the hourly report started.

"Good morning, Britain. I'm Peter Bennett. This is the news at nine o'clock on October the 3rd, 2095." The presenter's tone of voice was a mixture of gravitas and pomposity. "Police have found a body, thought to be that of the man suspected of perpetrating the cult killings." Catherine sighed, shaking her head. "Live from the crime scene in Delamere Forest, Cheshire, Amardek Ulinskas."

"Thank you," said an equally severe voice. "With me now I have Detective Inspector Osuobeni, who is in charge of the whole, despicable case."

"He's the policeman who interviewed me," Catherine said. Dan nodded his head.

"Detective Inspector Osuobeni, thank you for joining us. I believe you can, officially, confirm that you've found remains?"

"Yes, at approximately eight o'clock yesterday evening we received a call reporting a body located here."

"And is it that of Simon Moulson, the man thought to be responsible for the cult killings?"

"At present, I'm afraid I can't comment on that."

"But this is a significant moment in the case?"

"Yes it is, and I would urge the person who made the call to contact us again, as I believe they may have further information."

"Are you looking for anyone else in relation to the cult killings?"

"No."

"Really? What about rumours of a list?"

"List?" Osuobeni asked.

"Yes, a random list reportedly containing names of those involved with the cult?"

"Erm... I have no knowledge of that."

179

"Detective Inspector Osuobeni, thank you. Well, this morning there are still many unanswered questions surrounding the cult and further suspicions that Simon Moulson, whose body is thought to have been found here yesterday evening, may have had an accomplice."

"What is he talking about?" Catherine asked.

"Scare-mongering."

"Amardek Ulinskas, Delamere Forest."

"Thank you, Amardek. In other news, World Union Presidential Candidates…."

Catherine lent forward and switched off the radio. "Unbelievable," she sighed, "unbelievable."

"Not really."

"No, I suppose not."

"How are you feeling?"

"Terrible. I'm sure Osuobeni will want to talk to me." She slumped back and held her head in her hands. Dan stared out of the windscreen at the countryside. "Funerals!"

"What?"

"I'll have to arrange the funerals."

"Won't the families sort that out?"

She thought for a second, with a mixture of relief and sadness. "Yeah. I guess."

"But Abdalla didn't have any family, apart from us, Beacon."

"That's true. I suppose you may have to then."

"I wouldn't know where to start." She took her PDA out of her handbag and slotted in the new battery she'd bought the day before.

Dan twisted around to face her. "Hang on."

"What?"

"If you turn that on, they, or anyone, will be able to trace you, us."

"Does it matter now? Simon's dead. The demons are gone."

Dan thought for a second. "I suppose not."

The PDA came to life, telling her that she had thirty-two missed calls. "He's phoned me, and so have loads of other people, tons of emails too, and texts."

"Who? The detective?"

"Yes. I'll call him back."

"What are you going to say?"

Catherine switched the device to voice only and called his number. "I'm not sure." Dan listened in. "Hi, it's Catherine Halston. Yes, I'm fine. I know, I know. He meant so much to us all. Where? I've

180

been staying in, erm, hotels. I just listened to, watched, the news. Have you found Simon?" Catherine shot a glance towards Dan. "How did he die? Okay. You're not sure. No, I won't. Thank you. Bye." Catherine hung up. "They said his death was suspicious."

"They're right. Anything else?"

"No. He seemed relieved it was over."

"Good. Because it is."

"Not for us."

"Us?"

"Me, I mean, but… I just can't think about it now."

"What are you doing?"

"Checking my messages." She held her PDA to her ear. "People from Beacon asking me what's going on. Oh…."

"What?" Catherine started to cry. "What is it?"

"A message, a message, from Lian and Jean-Paul's daughter."

Dan took the PDA and listened. It was a stream of abuse. "Didn't she agree with Beacon?" Dan asked, after the call ended.

Catherine wiped her eyes and took back the PDA. "I thought she did. I'm sure she was supportive at least."

"It must be the press coverage."

"I just… just can't believe it."

"Did the others have children?"

"No." Catherine listened to the next message. "It's from Jered." Her mood lightened and she switched the PDA to visual.

"Found a phone has he?"

"Looks like it. Do you want to see the message? You can see what he looks like."

"No, you're all right."

"He's left a number I can contact him on. I'd better call him back. He says he knows I'm safe."

"How?"

She gave him a wink. "How do you think?"

"Oh, right."

"You don't mind if I call him do you?"

"Why would I?" Dan got out of the car and studied the horizon. Above, grey clouds were obliterating the early morning blue sky. He tried not to listen as Catherine spoke to her fiancé, recalling every detail of the last few days. Dan sat back down in the driver's seat when she'd hung up. He found her mopping away tears.

"How's Jerry?"

"Jerry is fine, looks tired though. He's glad we're all right. That call is going to cost me a fortune. He says I should go back to the States."

"I agree."

"Are you trying to get rid of me?"

"No, but the two of you must try and get Beacon back on its feet."

"Yes, but Abdalla's funeral first."

"Okay."

"Oh, I've got loads of messages." She stared back at her PDA as it started bleeping. "I can't deal with them now, my head…." She looked like she might faint.

"Are you all right? You've gone pale."

"It's just… everything. I'll be okay. Look, shall we go?"

"Go?"

"Yes."

"We're out of petrol."

"Oh."

"And if we could go anywhere you'd be going back to the States."

"But…." The rumble of an engine stopped her sentence.

Dan looked round and saw a tractor coming into view across the field. "Perhaps he could tow us?" He got out of the car.

"How do you think they got to Simon?"

Dan waved to the farmer. "How do you mean?"

"He had a love filled heart. He was full of light. I don't believe that would have changed. Demons only attack those who have a hard heart, the greedy, the selfish, those types."

"I don't know, Catherine. Something must have changed."

"I wonder what?"

"I don't think we'll ever know."

"I guess not." She paused, thinking. "Thank you by the way."

"What for?"

"Saving my life."

Dan smiled and walked towards the approaching vehicle.

The farmer towed their car to his smallholding and sold them, at a premium price, four litres of petrol. Catherine sat quietly, lost in her thoughts. The only action she made was to slot her 1980s compilation into the CD player. As Dan drove them out of the countryside and back on to the motorway, he caught the odd mutter from her as she sang along with the tunes that he was starting to tire of. Catherine let the upbeat music soothe her. Her throbbing head was swimming. There were the calls and emails that would be unbearably hard to reply to. She felt alone and without direction, and praying made no difference.

They made it to a service station, refuelled the car properly and decided to get something to eat.

Inside, Catherine headed straight for one of the stores and the electronic papers. Dan had stopped her loading up a news site on her PDA in the car and now, realising too late, rushed to stop her.

"Why do you want to put yourself through that?" He joined her as she scrolled through a publication.

"I don't know. Well, I do. It's our name they're dragging through the gutter."

"You don't need to read that rubbish."

"I want to see how they are reporting finding Simon's body." Dan shook his head. The headlines were split between the discovery of the body of the police's number one suspect and the forthcoming international elections. They both read the story about Simon. "This article says that the funerals of Sunayani, Erica, Harry, Jake and Lisette have already taken place."

"That's not surprising is it?"

"I suppose not. It says that the families wanted private funerals." Catherine was disappointed. "And that *cult* members were asked not to attend."

"That doesn't surprise me either, but it might not be true. You know what the papers are like."

"It also says the same goes for the funerals of Markus, Jean-Paul and Lian, which are taking place soon."

"I'm sorry, Catherine."

"Look there's a profile on me! I thought people were staring!" Dan looked over her shoulder and saw a full-page spread on her under the title: 'The Secrets and Lies of the Cult of Death'. There was also a helpline for those personally affected by the sect and what to do if you were worried if a family member was involved. He grabbed the tabloid from her hands and flung it back on to the rack. "Dan!"

He led her away by the arm. "Let's get some breakfast."

"All right, all right."

Dan let her go. She wiped a few tears away and they walked across to the food hall.

Dan ordered a cooked breakfast and Catherine had cereal. They found a table in the busy seating area and sat down. A giant 3D television, which almost filled the whole wall, was on and most people had their eyes glued to it. Dan had his back to the screen and was concentrating on his meal. Catherine watched, pecking at her food.

"A one-world government," she muttered to herself. An apprehensive shiver crept through her body, and she took a long deep breath. "It's coming."

"What?" asked Dan, mid-chew.

"Nothing."

"So what are you going to do about Abdalla's funeral?"

"I think I'll just contact a funeral director. I wouldn't know where to start."

"Have you decided when you're going back to the States?"

"Well, after his funeral obviously, but I thought we might...."

"What?"

"We might go and see your mother." Dan carried on eating. "What do you think?" He didn't reply. "Dan?"

His eyes stayed focused on his plate. "I don't know," he finally said. "I haven't thought about it." That wasn't true. He hadn't stopped thinking about the possibility of meeting his mother, but it felt like an unreal prospect. The enormity of the proposal seemed lost on Catherine, with her self-assured outlook.

"Okay." Catherine was surprised that Dan didn't appear more excited by the idea. "But if I were you...."

"But you're not. Can we drop it? Once and for all?"

"Sure. Sorry. Oh, I'm not hungry." She pushed the bowl away.

"Right, well, I'm finished too."

Catherine dug her PDA from her bag.

"What now?"

"I'm phoning Osuobeni."

"Why?"

"To find out about Abdalla's body."

"Okay."

She dialled the detective's number. As the call waited to connect, Dan found himself subconsciously imagining what his mother might look like.

"Hi, it's Catherine, again. Yes. I'm okay. Not great, but okay. Erm. Do you know what is happening with Abdalla Miller's body? Oh. Has it? Really? I didn't realise. Okay. Okay. Thanks. Yes, I'm going back to America as soon as the volcanic ash cloud clears. Okay. Thank you. Bye."

"Well?"

184

"He said his body was claimed by a relative."

"A relative?"

"I didn't think he had any."

Dan tried to think. "Hang on."

"What?"

"He was married."

"He was?"

"Yes, they divorced. I remember my mother talking about him. It was Abdalla's career that split them up. Abdalla was always working."

"Would he claim the body?"

"Perhaps he thought, like us, that no one else would. I guess maybe they still loved each other."

"I suppose. We should try and find out when the funeral will be."

"I guess."

"He'd want us to be there."

"Does it matter?"

"What do you mean 'does it matter'?"

"I mean, does it matter?"

"Huh?"

"I think I'd prefer to remember Abdalla as he was, you know?" Dan helped himself to some of Catherine's muesli. He grimaced as he tasted the sugar and salt free cereal.

"But we need to pay our last respects."

"I know, but I can't imagine he'd be too bothered."

Catherine smiled and thought about Abdalla, his kindness, his light, his love. "I still think we should go, Dan."

"I've been thinking about what you said," he replied, to change the subject.

"You have? Thinking about what?"

"About seeing...."

"Your mother?"

"Yeah."

"Oh, well, I do think that would be a good thing to do. We could go together." A few seconds passed. Catherine waited for him to reply. "I don't have to come."

"I'm not...." Catherine's face fell. "I mean, it would be great if you'd come with me. It's just that...."

"What?"

"It's just... daunting."

"I understand that. When do you want to go then?" she asked, without pausing for breath. Dan laughed. "What?"

185

"Nothing. I'm not sure. What about Abdalla's funeral?"

"Perhaps you're right."

"There has to be a first time."

She gave a flicker of a smile. "True. Perhaps we should stay out of the way and pay our respects when the dust has settled, so to speak."

"I think that would be the best idea."

"Okay. Just let me finish my coffee, my head is still swimming, and then we'll hit the road."

"Where does she live?"

"Some place called Herne Bay."

"That's in Kent."

"Yep. The directions are on my PDA."

"Yes, you said."

"People are gawping at me."

Dan shook his head from his daydream about his mother, and saw a couple of people staring at them. "Ignore them."

"I'll try." Catherine's thoughts began to wander. "Markus and I used to go to this place in New York...." She stopped, realising that they would never be doing that again.

"What made you say that?"

"Just...."

"What?"

"Things I'll never do again." Catherine glanced around: so many people, so many lives. She began to doubt herself, and her belief. It was impossible to make people do or believe anything with just words. Actions spoke louder. Seeing was believing. She knew that for most, it would come down to simply choosing light over darkness, and with that decision unquestionable attestation would come.

Dan changed the subject. "How long do you think it will take us to get down there?"

"What? Oh. Sorry. Erm, according to the directions on my PDA, from where we are now, Sandbach, it will take four and a half hours to get to Herne Bay."

"Sounds about right."

Catherine checked the time. "Which means we won't get to see her today."

"No."

"We'll have to stay somewhere. I'm not sleeping in the car again."

"At least you got to lie down."

"I would have slept anywhere after all that whiskey."

"I'm sure we'll find somewhere. I might have brothers and sisters. Well, half brothers and sisters. Do you really think my mother will want to see me again after…? Perhaps this is a bad idea, you know, just turning up?"

She touched his hands. "Don't be nervous."

"I'm not that nervous, more apprehensive."

"I don't think she'll know to be honest."

"What do you mean?"

Catherine put down her mug. "Oh."

"Oh what?" Dan's eyes narrowed. "What aren't you telling me?"

"Well."

"Yes?"

"She is in a, erm, private hospital."

"Hospital?" Dan's tone was tense.

"A small psychiatric hospital."

"What?" A few people turned around at his raised voice.

"Relax."

"Tell me."

"Okay." Catherine took a deep breath. "She's a resident of a place called The Limes Retreat. She's been there since she was sixteen."

Dan stared at her in disbelief. "Are you serious?"

"Yes, I even called last week to make sure it was all right to visit. Don't worry, she won't know who you are."

Dan shook his head and stood up, spilling his coffee across the table. "Don't you ever think?" Everyone now had their eyes on them.

"What?"

"You're unbelievable." He turned and walked out.

Catherine swiftly followed, uttering a muted apology to the other customers for the disturbance.

She managed to catch up with Dan in the car park and grabbed his arm. "Dan, wait."

"What?" He faced her; for a moment she felt scared of him.

"I'm sorry. I didn't think. I just thought it would be good for you." Dan continued back to the car. "You can't go on living the way you have been."

"Well, according to you guys that isn't going to be a problem. There's only a few years left!" A woman with two young children passed by, looking concerned by their conversation.

Catherine caught up with him. "Dan, let's just get down there and see how you feel? There's nowhere else for us to go."

187

"There's nowhere for me to go. Why don't you just go back to the States?"

"Volcanic ash?"

"Get on a boat."

"If that's how you feel…." Dan didn't respond. Catherine brushed past him and headed towards the car. Exhaling, he looked up at the sky. The grey clouds were turning black.

Dan joined Catherine in the vehicle and they sat in silence.

"What do you want to do then?"

"Load up your directions," Dan replied a few minutes later.

Catherine reached for her PDA and brought up the details. "Here they are."

Dan started the car and they rejoined the ten-lane motorway. They continued their new journey in silence, punctuated only by Catherine giving instructions.

It was almost eight in the evening when they drove into Herne Bay. It had begun to rain again and a strong wind was blowing in from the North Sea.

"We should try to find somewhere to stay," Catherine said, observing the buildings they were passing. "If I had thought about it earlier I would have booked somewhere online as we drove down."

"I'm sure there will be rooms, it's out of season."

They drove on a little further and spotted a bed and breakfast. The neon sign in the window indicated there were vacancies.

They got out of the car. Dan took Catherine's suitcase and his belongings from the boot, and they approached the entrance. Dan rang the doorbell. After a short wait a white-haired lady opened the door.

"Hello?"

"Hi," Dan said. "Have you got a room?"

"We have a double. Is that okay?"

Dan looked at Catherine. She stood expressionless. "Yes, that would be fine."

"Wonderful, come in." The woman stepped. "How many nights?" She moved them through the hallway to a little box room that served as a reception.

"Erm, four?" Dan said, adding the extra days to make it seem like they were staying for a long weekend, but also because he wasn't sure exactly how long they would be there for.

"Yes, that's fine. I'm Trixie."

"Dan and Catherine." Trixie smiled, but frowned when she noticed Catherine's dour appearance. "She's had some bad news," Dan said, covering for Catherine's manner.

"I'm sorry to hear that, dear. Well, I won't keep you too long. Actually, you look familiar."

They both thought back to Catherine's profile in the paper.

"She's just got one of those faces," Dan said.

"Yes, people often tell me I have one of those faces too. Well, if you'd just fill out this form." She slid a PDA across the small counter.

"Thanks." Dan filled out the electronic form on the screen, substituting their true details with false ones.

"That will be five hundred euros." Dan counted out the money and handed it to her. "Right, this way." She picked up two keycodes and led them towards the stairs. "Room two on the top floor, one of our better ones. We don't get that many visitors out of season. What brings the pair of you to the coast?"

"Just visiting family," Dan said, carrying their belongings up as Catherine followed behind.

"Anyone I'd know?"

"I don't think so."

"Oh," she said, disappointed at not finding out more. "I know most folk around here." Trixie unlocked the door and let them in. She switched on the bedside lights and showed them the features. Dan nodded politely. Catherine just stared at the dark pink carpet. "Here are your keycodes, this one for the front door and the other for your room. Breakfast is served between seven and nine."

"Thank you," Dan said.

"Well, I'll leave you in peace."

"Thanks again."

Trixie left, closing the door behind her. Dan checked the room out. They had a view overlooking the seafront.

"I'm glad she didn't remember where she'd seen you. She would have probably kicked us out." Catherine didn't reply. "Are you all right?" He turned to see that she had got straight into bed, still wearing her soaked clothes.

"Goodnight," she mumbled, dragging the duvet up around her.

"Goodnight." Dan sighed and drew the curtains. There wasn't a sofa to sleep on, just an uncomfortable looking armchair. "You can share the bed if you want," Catherine said, almost on cue. Dan thought for a second, then walked over to the bed, kicked off his shoes, and pulled back the duvet. He climbed in. Catherine moved across to him.

"Hold me." Dan put his arm around her. Catherine laid her head on his chest, and they slept in that position all night.

32

The first thing he saw was Catherine looking out of the bay window. Her hair was wet and she just had a towel wrapped around her. She sipped on a cup of tea.

Dan yawned. "Morning."

"Morning." She turned towards him.

"How are you feeling?"

"Awful. Not ill awful, just, you know."

"Yeah, I know."

Dan pulled back the duvet, stood up and stretched. He joined Catherine at the window and felt an urge to put his arms around her, but resisted. Instead, he observed the windswept coastline. The previous evening's bad weather appeared to have blown over, but the grey clouds remained.

"Do you want to go then?" she asked, her tone maudlin.

"Well, we're here now, but you should really do that message."

"Don't." She crossed her arms. "I just don't know what to write."

"Have you...?"

"Prayed?"

"Yes."

"Yep. Nothing. I know it's too late."

"It's not too late and that doesn't sound like the Catherine I know and...." He stopped himself from saying any more.

"Yeah, well." She didn't notice his omission. "Things have changed."

"We've both lost people we care about."

Catherine didn't reply. Below, she saw a family, a man and a woman with three young children. They walked along the seafront all holding hands. Why can't that be me, Catherine thought, me and Dan – Jered, me and Jered - down there with our kids, carefree and happy, with our whole lives in front of us. But that would never happen. She unexpectedly felt the enormity of what was to come resting upon her shoulders. She broke down, dropping the cup; its contents spilt on the carpet and she collapsed, crying, to the floor.

It took Dan an hour to get Catherine back to something resembling her normal self. They dressed, left the hotel and were soon driving along a road that wound around the coast.

"How are you feeling?" Catherine asked, noticing Dan becoming tense.

"Trying not to think. What about you?"

"Pretty much the same. Maybe a little better. It's not hit me like that before. That this is the end."

"But something better is coming, right?"

"I hope so." A single ray of sunshine broke through the clouds and hit the side of her face. Dan was relieved to see a radiance return to her. "But not before…. Look, we don't have to go."

"What?"

"I'm sorry about how I've handled this."

"No, it's okay. To be honest it's a bit easier knowing that she won't know who I am, even though that's tragic in itself." He sighed. "I can't imagine what she went through."

"The lady I spoke to said that she was comfortable most days. She doesn't get any visitors."

"Did you tell them who I was?"

"I just said you, we, were distant relatives, who'd only just found out about her."

"Right."

Catherine looked at the directions on her PDA. "I think we might be nearly there. There should be a turning on the left."

"I see it."

The car veered off on to a narrow road. Ahead of them they saw a large old house. Dan parked on the gravel driveway; they got out and walked up to the entrance.

"Looks nice," Dan said.

"Yeah." Catherine knocked on the tall wooden door and a young man answered almost immediately.

"Can I help?" he said, stuttering over his words.

"Erm, yes, we're here to see Ms Blake," Catherine said. Dan surveyed the grounds. The garden looked peaceful. It was mostly grass with a few well-maintained, diamond-shaped borders, and a variety of trees framing them.

"Oh?"

"I phoned a few days ago, spoke to someone called Mayling?"

"Well, come in."

"Thanks." Catherine stepped forward. "Dan?"

"Sorry." Dan's eyes had been fixed on the sea.

They went into the hallway. The interior was smart; wooden beams painted black were prominent against plush red carpet and white walls.

"Wait here, please." The man went into a room marked 'office'. A few moments later a woman emerged and greeted them.

"Catherine?" the woman asked, her voice elegant, like her appearance.

"Yes, hello." Catherine shook her outstretched hand.

"Mayling Krieger."

"This is Dan," Catherine said, introducing him.

"Hello Dan." Mayling shook his hand too. "Well, I must say this is a surprise. We didn't think Kristina had any family left after her parents died."

"How did they die?" Dan asked.

"Oh." Catherine noticed the confused look on Mayling's face. "We've only just tracked their branch of the family tree down. We know nothing about our relatives!"

"Oh, I see, right, well, we'll talk and walk shall we? Jason, I won't be too long."

"Okay."

"He's a little bit, well, he is very useful around the place, and staff are hard to find. Nobody wants to work in healthcare these days. They prefer those call centres, I suppose."

"Right, well, lead the way," Catherine said, taking Dan's hand and giving it a squeeze. They proceeded to follow Mayling through the house.

Jason stood in the hallway and watched them go. There was a knock on the door. Jason shuffled over and opened it. There was no one there. Then, ahead, a dark vapour hurtled towards him.

"From what I've been told her parents died after a gas leak in their house," Mayling said.

"That's strange," Catherine replied, taking a good look around.

"Yes, it apparently happened just a few weeks after Kristina was attacked. You do know about that, don't you?"

"Yes, a little."

"Their life insurance policies more than paid for the care we've been giving Kristina here over the years."

192

"I was going to ask about that."

"We'll be able to keep her comfortable for the rest of her life."

"That's good to know." Catherine gave Dan a smile.

"Tragic, very tragic. She had a child, you know. You might want to contact the social services, if you're interested in tracing it, but, I don't know…" She stopped outside a room. "I personally think some things are best left in the past. But that's up to you. Well, here we are. I must warn you, don't expect too much. She's never spoken in all the years I've been here."

"We're not. We just needed to see her," Catherine replied, gripping Dan's hand tighter.

"That's understandable." Mayling opened the door and they went in.

The room was immaculate, if devoid of anything that reflected the occupant's life. Sunlight poured through a large window. Dan and Catherine saw a woman sitting in a chair, facing the gardens. She had a blanket covering her legs.

"Kristina?" Mayling said.

Catherine held Dan's hand even tighter and he clasped it back. The woman turned and their eyes fell upon her. Dan's heart leapt. For him it was akin to looking in a mirror. His mother was still young, in her mid-forties, her face thin and drawn. Her long auburn hair, which almost reached her waist, was simply cut and greying. She showed no emotion towards the two strangers in her room.

"These two people are relatives. They've come to visit you."

Kristina said nothing. She turned back towards the gardens. Dan had an urge to go to her, but was mindful of Mayling's presence.

"Right, I suppose I can leave you two alone with her for a few minutes, if you like."

Catherine glanced at Dan to get a measure of how he was feeling. His eyes were focused on his mother. "Thank you, that would be lovely."

"Okay, well, I'll just be down the hallway."

"Thank you."

Mayling left the room.

Dan let go of Catherine's hand and slowly approached his mother, eventually kneeling down beside her.

"Hi," he said, his voice soft. Kristina didn't react. Dan looked to Catherine. Her facial expressions urged him to continue. "I don't know what to say," he mouthed back. Catherine shrugged her shoulders. Dan moved his hand across to his mother's. The moment he touched her, she

193

turned to him, and when their eyes met, there seemed to be a connection. Catherine saw it, and began to well up. "Mum?"

Kristina gazed at him. She raised her hand to his face and stroked his skin. "Baby." A tear ran down her cheek.

Neither Dan nor Catherine could believe what they heard. Dan burst into tears, as did Catherine, and he rested his head on his mother's lap. Kristina placed her hand on her son's head and resumed her vacant vigil out of the window; the brief link to the present was gone.

Wiping her eyes, Catherine noticed Jason walking past outside. He was looking at them. She smiled. But the look she got back shot terror through her body. She blinked and he was gone.

After a few minutes they stepped out of the room and were greeted in the hallway by Mayling. "Everything okay?" she asked, checking the room to make sure Kristina was all right.

"Yes, fine, thank you," Catherine said.

"Yes, very sad, isn't it. I don't suppose she said anything to you?"

"No."

"Must be very hard to see a family member like that."

"Yeah," Catherine said, taking Dan's hand.

"Well, you're free to visit any time you wish." She gave Kristina one final glance and closed the door behind them. "Is there anything else I can help you with?" They started to walk back to the office.

"No, I don't think so."

"I can assure you that Kristina is getting the very best care."

"We can see that, and that's very comforting to know."

"Jason?" Mayling said, popping her head around the office door. "Jason? I wonder where he has gone."

"I saw him outside," Catherine said.

"Outside? What's he up to now? Is there anything else I can do for you?"

"No, I think we're good," Catherine replied, checking Dan, but he was impassive, his eyes bloodshot.

"Let me show you out then."

Kristina's door creaked open and footsteps trod over the cream twist pile carpet.

Jason sneered. "You've served your purpose." She recognised the tone of his voice and tried to scream, but he swiftly brought a pillow to her face. Her struggles were silenced.

"Are you okay?" Catherine asked Dan, as they sat in the car.

"Yeah," he said, nodding his head, wiping his eyes. "I'm okay. For a second she knew who I was."

"I know. I saw."

"And you were right."

"About what?"

"It did help." Catherine beamed. "I can't imagine what she went through." He shook his head, wishing that he could have protected her.

"I know. It doesn't bear thinking about, but at least she's being well looked after."

"Yes, that's really good to know." He paused. He wanted to return to her, to never leave her, but knew he couldn't. Not yet anyway. "Right." He rubbed his eyes and took a deep breath.

"What?"

"We need to get you to your laptop. Or we could park up somewhere and you could write it up on your PDA?"

"Oh, I don't... I can't write on those things. I need a proper screen, but I really...."

"No one else is going to do it, are they?"

"No, no one else has access to the site."

"There you go then."

"Are you sure you're okay?"

"Yes, I'm fine, and don't change the subject."

"I'm not."

"Good."

"But I can't write it."

"You should try." Dan started the car.

Catherine reached for her seatbelt and saw Jason watching them. "Dan, look."

"What?"

Catherine turned back, but Jason had disappeared. "Nothing, nothing, doesn't matter." She searched round.

Dan put the car in gear. "Okay." Releasing the handbrake, they drove off.

The road twisted beneath them. Catherine had again put the 1980s compilation on to distract her from her thoughts. She quietly sang along to the songs she now knew well.

"*Spare a little candle, save some light for me, figures up ahead, moving in the trees...*" Dan thought she had a good pitch. He watched her lips move as she sang. She looked beautiful. Everything about her was beautiful. *"I search for the time, on a watch with no hands, I want to see you clearly, come closer than this….* What are you looking at?" she asked, noticing his glances.

"You and your signing."

"Nah, I can't sing to save my life. Anyway, keep your eyes on the road. How are you feeling?"

"I can't stop thinking about her."

Catherine squeezed his hand. "I know it was hard."

"Yeah."

"Now keep your eyes on the road."

Dan did so, but with his thoughts returning to his mother and the life they had missed out on.

Catherine started singing once more. *"There's something out there I can't resist. I need to hide away from the pain. There's something out there I can't resist."*

Dan couldn't help but take another peek at her.

"Dan…."

"Yes?"

"You know what, watch the road."

"Sorry."

"Eyes forward."

"Yes, ma'am."

"These dreams go on when I close my eyes. Every second of the night, I live another life. These dreams… Dan, watch the road."

"Sorry."

"Every moment I'm awake, the further I'm away. These dreams go on when I close my eyes. Every second of the… Dan!"

Dan's eyes faced forward just in time to see a figure appear in front of them. He swerved, instinctively, closely avoiding the person. Catherine screamed as the vehicle shot off the asphalt, skidding into woodland. The car crashed into a tree, and the front windscreen shattered, showering them in glass.

"Are you okay?" Dan said, a few moments later.

"That was Jason!" Catherine mumbled, freeing herself from the seatbelt that had tightened around her.

"Jason?"

She coughed. "From the hospital." Smoke rose from the crumpled bonnet.

"What was he doing?"

"I'm not sure. We'd better see if he's okay." Catherine opened her door and hauled herself out, feeling shaken and unsteady on her feet. Dan did the same. They saw Jason striding towards them.

"Are you all right?" she asked. Jason didn't speak. Catherine and Dan looked at each other. They were both thinking the same thing.

"Run!" Dan grabbed Catherine's hand.

They fled over the sodden woodland floor towards a group of red-bricked buildings, and soon found themselves in what appeared to be an abandoned farm.

"Well, what do you think?"

"He seemed…." Catherine caught her breath and waved her hand across her face.

"Yeah. I agree."

They looked through the woods; there was no sign of him.

"Why are you running?" The voice was deep, strong, forceful. They spun around to see Jason standing behind them. He was staring at Dan.

"Jason?" Catherine said, optimistic that she might be wrong. "Are you okay?"

He laughed. "This *is* a poor excuse for a body. I've had better."

"Who are you?" Dan asked, taking Catherine's hand.

He threw his arms open. "It's daddy!"

∞

Your faith has always been strong, beloved. Mine faltered. Mr Darwin's work was to blame. But his science was right; only his conclusions were wrong. I have studied the Today Christians' viewpoint with great enthusiasm and I feel I must explain a little more.

The essence of their movement was to seek greater clarity by revisiting the original biblical texts, re-examining the traditional translations, and balancing scripture with the times it was originally written, so as to apply the contents to everyday life: facts and faith. It was a breath of fresh air to a religion that was dying, that was derided, that was insular and, to most, irrelevant.

Controversial issues to us such as evolution and same sex attraction (which also happens in other organisms) that had drawn up barriers for many in secular society, most probably erected by the enemy, were torn down.

The evidence from nature showed the Earth to be over four billion years old, which continues to evolve, and thus we should interpret Genesis as a poem about creation, when man became conscious.

Human beings were proven to be born unique, with different biological impulses. Some sections of society have been needlessly ostracised because mistranslation, or wilful misinterpretation, of the scriptures resulted in the demonisation of their sexual convictions. Genesis, for example, dictates that it is natural for a man and a woman come together to create a new life, and this has been interpreted by some to mean that homosexual couples must therefore be unnatural. But in fact the text is silent about relationships that do not lead to the bearing of children, or couples unable to have children, those who are too old, or who choose not to have children. These are not condemned as unnatural.

The city of Sodom's sins were its prosperity, pride and arrogance, and its failure to help the poor and the needy. Any moral person would oppose the brutal sexual crimes committed in that story, which details the common practice of conquering armies to dehumanise and demean the vanquished enemy through rape; a behaviour more about power and revenge than demonstrating true homosexual love. Jesus and five Old Testament prophets all speak of the destruction of Sodom, and not one of them mentions homosexuality. Indeed Jesus never does at any point.

Leviticus was an of-its-time, now outdated, holiness code, listing homosexuality alongside the wearing of garments made of mixed fabrics and the displaying of round haircuts as prohibited behaviour.

In Romans, Paul documents the great number of temples built in honour of the gods of sex and pleasure, with priests and priestess fornicating with a multitude of male and female temple prostitutes. This behaviour, perpetrated in the name of worship, cannot be equated to loving and committed relationships.

And finally, and some say most significantly, a mid-twentieth century translation of the examples of unlawful practices, as recited by Paul in Corinthians, refers to the malakois, the effeminate call boys of first century Greece, and the arsenokotai, clients of these unfortunates, incorrectly as homosexuals.

Reputable theologians agree that a great deal of text was wrongly mistranslated, added to and rewritten over the centuries, simply to suit the rulers of the day, so that they could control their citizens. The Today Christians finally provided the world with the most accurate version of the great book, which, as you know, tells the story of God's love for the world. To quote your favourite apostle, Peter: 'I now understand, that God has no favourites'!

One of the most enlightening aspects was the interaction with the other ancient faiths and the re-interpretation of their revered texts. There was no doubt that they were all connected, striving to find the same source, and that source was light, and love. Love, unequivocally, outshines everything else. Love doesn't discriminate. It is the key to spiritual illumination.

The Today Christians' tenets were: there is something sacred in all people; all people are equal before God; religion is about the whole of life; in stillness we find a deeper sense of God's presence; true religion leads to respect for the Earth and all life upon it; each person is unique, precious, a child of God.

But to continue; the next section, like ones before it, is one that I have constructed in my own mind, and it refers back to the very beginning of this account. But I truly believe that something of what follows must have occurred.

33

He had been staring at the computer screen most of the day. Harvey arched his back, yawned, and took a look around the office. All his colleagues had left for the day. He removed his black-rimmed glasses and rubbed his eyes, then cleaned the lenses with a piece of tissue. He squinted at the time on his desk clock. It was half past six. No wonder he was the last one here. Come to think of it, there had been people wishing him a good weekend earlier. He examined his spectacles. Much better. Slipping them back on, he returned his attention to the document he had been working on.

The videophone on his desk rang. He yawned again and answered the call. "Hello?"

"Harv?"

"Hi love." The image of his wife appeared on the screen.

"You look tired. Are you coming home?"

He clicked save on the document. "Yes, soon. How are the kids?" He picked up a framed photo of his wife and their two children.

"They're fine, Jodie's staying round Samaria's tonight."

"Ah peace! How's my little man?"

"Missing his daddy. When can I expect you?"

"I'll be half an hour."

"Harvey!"

"Sorry, love, I need to get this report done for Monday's meeting."

"Of course you do," she replied, annoyed. "I bet you're the last one there as well."

Harvey saw the cleaners alight from the lift. "Yeah, almost."

"Okay, so we'll see you soon?"

"Yes, I promise. What's for dinner?"

"Mexican."

"Lovely. Right, I'll see you soon."

"Okay, bye."

"Bye."

Harvey ended the call. He was always the last to leave in the evening, and sometimes the only one in the office on Saturday, but he had to put the hours in if he wanted to eventually become a partner in the firm and make the sort of money he craved. Harvey watched the cleaner wipe desks and empty bins, and then re-read what he'd written. It wasn't great, but it would have to do. He just had the summary to construct and then he'd be able to head home.

A little over an hour later, Harvey emerged from the square glass building. The Friday night drinkers were out, moving from bar to bar. Harvey crossed the road, making his way to the taxi rank on the corner of the next block. He had begun to cycle in, which was fine, but when he left so late, as he frequently did, the last thing he wanted to do was spend thirty minutes pedalling home.

"Steady on, Terry, steady."

Terry looked up from his pneumatic drill. "What now?" He turned the machine off, lifted up one of his ear defenders, and scowled at Steve, his foreman.

"I said take it steady, we'll end up in Australia at the rate you're going."

"Okay, okay." Terry started up the machine again.

Further up the road a man was approaching them. He was stumbling along the pavement, swaying from side to side as he went. He was holding something close to his chest and mumbling to himself.

Steve stood back from the hole they were digging to access a water pipe. He lit up a cigarette and looked at the young women out for a night on the town. He wished he were twenty years younger. He heard the drill stop.

"What's up?" Steve asked, peering down.

"I've found something,"

"Oh yeah?"

"Yeah." Terry handed him the object. Steve brushed off the dirt that was stuck to it. "What do you think?"

Steve put his cigarette in his mouth and had a good look at Terry's find. "It's just a coin."

"Valuable?"

"How should I know?" Steve said, removing some more dirt.

Harvey headed up a quiet side street. Ahead, he saw two workmen in their orange overalls. They had partially blocked the pavement with a red and white striped barrier, and were now obstructing the other half with themselves. Harvey considered walking around on to the main road, but thought that he could just squeeze past, if he made his presence known.

"I think it might be worth something," Terry said, taking the object back out of Steve's hands.

Steve agreed and tried to think of a way he could keep it. He took the disc from his colleague. "Well, back to work, mate. The others will be here soon."

"Okay, okay." Terry grabbed the coin again and ran his fingers around the contours. "I wonder what these engravings mean? Could be Latin or something?"

"What would you know about Lat-in? Let me have another look." Steve snatched it back. "Oi!"

"Back to work. I'll look after it."

"It's mine."

"I'll keep it safe."

The workmen stopped bickering when they heard the incoherent speech of the man approaching them.

"Tell me when, tell me when," he burbled. "Lord of darkness, lord of darkness, tell me when." The man walked under a street light and the two workmen could see he was a priest, his white clerical collar standing out against the black of his suit and coat. He was clutching, in his bony hands, what looked to be a stone bottle.

"What's up with that?" Steve asked.

Terry laughed. "Too much communion wine, or whatever they call it."

Harvey saw the priest as he attempted to go by the two workmen. "Excuse me," he said.

"Careful!" Steve said.

The priest suddenly stopped in his tracks, his face pale with fear. Steve and Terry looked on, bemused.

"Now?" the priest mumbled. With an unexpected frenzy he threw the stone bottle to the ground. It smashed in two. He turned and ran off screaming.

"Nutter!" Steve shouted.

"What the hell was all that about?" Terry asked.

Harvey turned to the workmen in bewilderment.

Then from one end of the stone bottle they heard an elongated whirling noise, culminating in an unearthly wail.

"What's that?" Terry asked.

"It's coming from the…." Steve said. His sentence was cut short as a dark fog emerged, increasing in size as it rose at speed.

Steve, Terry and Harvey all cursed. A black vapour shot up into the air with a howl that pierced their ears. They stood watching the form dance in the sky, circling above them for a few moments. Then it dived. The workmen ducked and Harvey ran down the street. The shape followed. He looked back to see it zooming up behind him. He could see its hideous features as it got closer. Harvey couldn't take his eyes off it and he couldn't outrun it. He tripped and fell, landing in a puddle. The vapour stopped and for spilt second hovered above him. Harvey shrieked as its face became clearer. Two red eyes glowed and a jaw opened, emitting a high-pitched shriek that resonated evil. He could do nothing as it leapt into his mouth. Harvey started shaking, his body violently convulsing before becoming still.

Terry and Steve cautiously approached.

"Are you all right, mate?" Steve asked.

"What was that thing?" Terry glanced around, wary of its return.

"No idea."

Harvey stirred and his eyes flickered open.

Terry and Steve's bodies were found two days later.

It was the banging shut of the front door that alerted Libby to her husband's return.

"Where have you been?" she asked, stepping into the hallway. Immediately, she knew there was something different about him. "What's wrong?"

"Nothing." His tone was blunt, his face blank, unreadable.

"Are you sure? You look...."

"I'm sure I do."

"You said you'd be home hours ago, I've been trying to call your PDA. George wanted his daddy to read him a bed time story."

"Quiet, woman."

"Excuse me?" She put one hand on her hip. Harvey stepped forward and grabbed her face; Libby's eyes widened in horror. "What are you doing?" He pulled her closer to him and studied her features. She could feel his eyes burning into her.

"You're not the one." He let go, brushed past her and walked through to the living room.

Libby stood rooted to the ground for a moment, shocked by Harvey's behaviour. Then she turned and followed him. "What's happened to you?"

Harvey reached into the sideboard and pulled out a full bottle of whiskey. He uncapped it and began drinking. "How I've waited." He dropped the empty bottle on the carpet.

"You're sick."

"I know. Now get out of my house."

"What?"

"This is my house isn't it?" Libby stared at him. "I have his memories and suffer his pathetic, yet selfish, greedy emotions and his fondness for...." He paused. "Hmm. No wonder I was gifted this body."

"What?"

"And I know he owns this dwelling. I don't need you."

Libby started to cry. "What's happened to you?"

"Leave, woman! Before I grow impatient and...." He stopped. "Well, before you can no longer do so for yourself."

Libby rushed out of the room and went upstairs. Harvey took out another bottle, sat down in an armchair and began to drink. His wife and son left minutes later, and he was alone.

He spotted her from a distance. Her beauty exuded, eclipsing all those around her. Forty-eight hours had passed and he'd been walking the streets, searching for someone, someone special, and now he'd found her.

Harvey went through the Sunday morning shopping crowds, getting ever closer to the girl. She was with friends. They joked and laughed. He studied her, fascinated by her charm. She was the one. She had the qualities, the beauty. She reminded him of why he was here now. It was in those long ago days when he'd first been dispatched to watch over humanity, that he'd discovered the allure of human females. He had those same feelings again as he watched her.

He knew she'd seen him out of the corner of her eye, but his human appearance was normal to her, and she would think nothing of it.

In the days that followed he trailed her, allowing her to see him when he wanted her to, sitting on the same bus, brushing by in a busy store, staring from the other side of the street. He enjoyed the game. He enjoyed denying himself. At night he'd look up at her bedroom window, waiting to get a glimpse.

Finally he could resist no more. When he'd seen her with her boyfriend he'd grown jealous. It angered him to know she was with another. She was his, she would only be his, and that night, with the calm sea below, he made sure she was.

34

Dan let the words echo in the silence that remained after they had been spoken.

"No hug? No tears? I was kind of hoping for those, after what happened with your mother." Jason laughed.

Dan backed away. He felt Catherine grip his hand tighter. "Catherine?"

"Run?"

"Yes."

Jason smiled and shook his head, as Catherine and Dan disappeared into the farm buildings.

"Is that really…." Catherine asked when they stopped.

"I don't know." Dan surveyed their surroundings. They were now in a barn; it was empty apart from a pile of rotting straw heaped up in one corner.

"How did he find us?"

"I've no idea…."

"What?"

"Maybe he was watching my mother?"

"That's right." They spun around to see Jason in the doorway. "Although you should have kept your PDA switched off too. I've waited such a long time. I hear we've had problems finding you. I'm disappointed that you haven't embraced your heritage. Your soul has been corrupted by goodness."

"Stay away." Dan motioned to Catherine to get behind him.

"But we've only just met." Jason walked forwards.

"I said stay back."

"Trying to protect your little woman?" Catherine was flung to the side of the barn, crashing into the wall. Dan was shocked at his power. "Impressed?"

"Disgusted."

Jason laughed. "Daniel, don't you know what you've been created for?"

"What do you want?"

"It's a shame your mother couldn't be here for this family reunion but...." He sighed. "She's no longer with us."

"What?"

"She's served her purpose. Once thirty years ago and now today."

"You killed her?"

"Yes."

Dan cried out in anger and launched himself at Jason, who responded by hurling Dan into the wooden wall of the barn. The vibrations shook thick dust from the beams.

Dan got back to his feet.

"You're needed, Daniel. You're an abomination. You're perfect." Jason took a deep breath. "A new dawn is coming." He clicked his fingers and four spectres appeared at his side. "My friends here will assist you. We can't waste any more time." The svelte apparitions, their appearances a shifting blend of distorted human and demonic features, crept forward. "Take him!"

Pouncing, two of them grabbed Dan. Their grips were strong and he tried to fling them off, but they were attacking him from within. He felt weak, paralysed, and slowly dropped to his knees, trying to resist them.

"This fight seems a little unfair."

"What?" Jason turned to see two individuals materializing in mid air, bathed in a golden glow. Descending, the radiance diminished. They were angels. Resembling the classical description, their skin was soft, taut over well-defined bone structures, and their physique

205

muscular and toned. They were wearing white, well-fitted shirts, short pleated skirts and behind them, emerging from their backs, a pair of mighty feathered wings. Both were over six feet tall. One appeared older, distinguished lines etched on his face, his short black hair flecked naturally with grey. The second had a youthful expression with light brown hair that hung, ruffled, in line with his ears. Around their waists were belts that bore scabbards containing swords.

The spirits jumped off Dan in terror.

"Kokabiel," said the older of the two angels, addressing Jason; his voice was rich, commanding. He drew his blade, its sharpened edges catching the fading light. "It's been a long time."

"Raphael, Uriel. Yes, it has."

"You four weren't going were you?" Uriel asked, approaching the apparitions with his sword drawn.

"Get him," Kokabiel ordered.

Dan was sidelined as the younger of the pair took the four entities on. The older angel squared up to Kokabiel, the fallen angel who had possessed Jason's body.

Kokabiel looked around. He stretched out his arm and from a dark corner of the barn a length of steel pipe flew to his hand.

"It's still not too late," Raphael said.

"I want to be on the side that wins."

Their weapons clashed, sending sparks flying.

Meanwhile Uriel was being backed into a corner. Dan watched on, his strength slowly returning to him. Uriel somersaulted forward; he landed, twisted around, and sliced two of the demons' heads off. Their separated parts disappeared in a blaze. Dan grabbed one of the others, holding its arms behind its back. Uriel stabbed the creature and it too burned up. The forth spirit knocked Dan to the ground and began attacking him. Uriel produced a dagger from his boot and threw it; the blade split the demon's head in half. It let out a cry as flames engulfed it.

Raphael and Kokabiel were matching each other blow for blow.

"Where have you been hiding all these years?" Raphael asked as they fought.

"Missed me?"

"You've been missed."

He laughed. "Concealed over the centuries by those who worship the lord of darkness, in the end it was a priest who set me free."

"And you fathered the final nephilim."

"Yes."

"But you've failed."

Kokabiel shot a look of disdain at Dan. "We can, we will, still win."

Raphael blocked Kokabiel's strike and slashed across his body, sending him backwards with a hit to the jaw. Wrenching the pole from his opponent's hand, he spun and thrust his weapon into Kokabiel's chest.

A look of surprise, then anger, then a sadistic smile, passed across Kokabiel's face. "You will find your place awaiting you in the bottomless pit," Raphael told him.

Kokabiel's black ethereal form lifted from Jason's body and was consumed by fire.

Raphael withdrew his sword with a look of sadness. He returned the blade to its sheath and dropped the steel pole to the floor. Jason, coughing up blood, tumbled backwards.

Uriel walked over to Dan and offered him his hand. Dan took it and was pulled up. Raphael knelt down beside Jason, whose eyes had returned to normal. Blood poured from his mouth and he tried to speak.

"Take it easy, my boy." Raphael held Jason's hand, as his body jolted and he was gone. Raphael gently closed the young man's eyes and got to his feet.

"Another casualty of an unseen war," Uriel remarked, joining his colleague's side. Raphael nodded.

Dan faced the two angels. "Who was he?"

"Kokabiel, one of the original fallen angels," Raphael replied.

"And he was my...?" He couldn't bring himself to say the word.

"He was."

"Catherine!" Dan broke away from his thoughts. He rushed over to her, sliding to his knees. Raising her head, he brushed back her hair and checked for a pulse.

"She'll be fine," Raphael said.

"Good." Dan rested Catherine's head back down and stood to face the pair. "So, I guess we might be related or something?"

Uriel chuckled, drawing a derisive reaction from Raphael.

"I'm...." Raphael said.

"Yes, I heard, Raphael and Uriel. Catherine is going to be so annoyed that she's missed you."

"She must write her message."

"It's not too late?"

"No, it's not too late," Uriel replied.

"What is happening?"

"There was an attempt to change things." Raphael fixed a knowing stare on Dan. "If you…."

"Yes…?"

"They were trying to pervert the prophecy," Uriel said. "You were key, but you know that, don't you?"

"They've been after me."

"We know, but even if they thought they had a chance, they didn't," Raphael replied.

"How do you mean?"

"Do you remember Fereshteh?"

Instantly her ardent face appeared in Dan's mind. "Yes." He was taken aback to hear that they knew of her.

"She was a fallen angel."

"What?"

"Just that," Uriel replied, "she *was* a fallen angel."

"She came back to us, reconnected with the light, unlike the fallen who must possess. She was tasked with protecting you. She was the one who made sure you were adopted into a strong progressive faith family, so their love would…."

"I understand," Dan said, sighing, bowing his head and thinking back on his childhood. "I understand."

"Nurture over nature," Uriel said.

"An army of darkness is still rising, however," Raphael said. "You are powerful, being the offspring of a fallen angel. You were born to be one of the unholy trinity and bring hell to Earth."

"I know. But it's still coming?"

"The end *is* coming, as prophesised." Raphael emitted a weary sigh and sat down on an over-turned box. "He sent many throughout the ages, whether they knew it or not, a diverse group. Those who chose to hear, heard wonderful music, those who chose to see, saw wonderful art, those who chose to read, read wonderful literature; prophets, artists, poets, writers, musicians, even comedians, all using their talent, their conduit to his spirit, to enrich a world already so full of his delight. His word is embedded in nature, in the moral compass of humanity, but the enemy has been chipping away at the human race for so long, that they've lost what it means to be human. They have forgotten that they are all one, with all that beautiful cultural diversity. No matter race, creed, colour, sex, sexuality, language or pathetic land borders. They're all one, all equal. And with regards to faith." Raphael sighed again. "It was never a matter of who was right and who was wrong, it never has been. It was the knowing that there was more. The believing,"

Raphael said, impassioned, clenching his fist. He shook his head. "I can't fathom the hate and intolerance inside many who call themselves people of God, their small-mindedness, their pettiness.... Perhaps we should have done more. I don't know."

"Perhaps you should," Dan said.

"Rules are rules," Uriel replied.

Raphael exhaled deeply. "And I can't believe what man has done to this planet that he declared good. The ecology has been raped. It's the darkness that has eroded the light and they've forgotten the one universal truth. Love. Absolutely nothing transcends that. Nothing. Ever."

"What's going to happen?"

"You know," Uriel said. "The enemy's shadow will fall."

"And Beacon?"

"Their light will shine out into a world of darkness. They came close to being destroyed. If that had happened it would have been a major victory for them, but you." Raphael paused. "Rather ironic that you should save her." He indicated to Catherine. "When you should have been.... Well, as I said, love is the greatest thing." Dan looked back down at Catherine. "Anyway. We're bending the rules even being here." Raphael stood and they both started to walk away.

"Is that it?"

"That is it."

Their powerful wings began to beat. They rose into the constraints of the building, gradually fading from view, bathed in the same warm light with which they had appeared.

Catherine moaned, moved to sit and held her head. Dan dashed to her side. "Are you okay?"

"Yeah. I'm getting fed up of being thrown about. Where's Jason?"

"It's over, really over."

"Over?" She brushed her hair back and spotted Jason's body. "You?"

"No. We had some help." Catherine gave him a puzzled look. "Are you sure you're all right?"

"Yes, yes, just a sore head. What do you mean, we had some help?"

"You're going to be so annoyed."

"Why? What happened?"

Dan grinned. "Angels."

"Angels?"

"Yes."

209

"You're joking?"

"No."

Catherine bit her tongue to stop herself from swearing. "Which ones? Michael? Gabriel?"

"No, Raphael and Uriel." Catherine looked hurt. "He killed my mother, Catherine."

"Oh, Dan." She leaned forwards and hugged him. "I'm so sorry."

"So am I. He'd been waiting."

"Was he your father?"

"Yes. They called him Kokabiel."

"Kokabiel?"

"Do you know that name? They said he was a fallen angel."

"Yes, yes, that's right."

"Then some demons showed up."

"Demons? Oh hang on." She thought for a moment.

"What?"

"My knowledge on such matters is a little flaky, but I think, that Kokabiel commanded over three hundred thousand spirits."

"Well, I'm lucky I only met four of them."

"But you're okay?"

"Yes, and Raphael told me to tell you that you *have* to write your message."

"I do?"

"Yes." He helped her to her feet.

"Right, then that's what I'll do. Can't argue with an angel, can you?" Catherine appeared instantly re-energized. "What are we going to do about him?" She looked over to Jason's body.

"Phone it in, I guess."

"I guess. Poor soul."

Dan put his arm around her and they headed out of the barn.

"I think this old thing has seen better days," Dan said, when they reached Abdalla's car; it was a write-off.

"What are we going to do?"

"Not sure." They heard the rumble of a vehicle approaching. "Get down."

"Why?" Catherine replied. Dan pulled her behind a fallen tree. "They can't see us. We're down a slope."

"I know but if they did, we might get linked to Jason's body."

"Oh. True. So, ideas?"

Sirens wailed in the distance.

"Police?" Catherine said.

An ambulance sped past.

"Might be going up to the hospital."

"For your mother?"

"Yeah."

"I'm so sorry, Dan."

"Perhaps...."

"Yes?"

"Perhaps she's in a better place now?"

Catherine smiled. "Without question, without question." She rested against the trunk. "So, what are we going to do with the car?"

"I'm not sure."

"I did notice something just now."

"What?"

"I think there was a pond."

"If it's deep enough...." Dan considered. "Let's have a look."

Catherine found the pond and they threw several stones into the water to try to ascertain whether a car could be submerged within it. The satisfying noises that followed suggested that it could.

Dan pushed the vehicle through the woodland, negotiating trees and shrubs, to the water.

"You're going to get wet," Catherine said, while Dan got his breath back.

"I think I'll survive." He took his shoes off and rolled up his trousers.

"Don't forget our stuff!"

"Oh, I had."

They took out their belongings and Catherine rescued her CD. Dan wound down the windows and they shoved the car forwards. It gradually became immersed in the thick stagnant pool. The weight of the water flooding in dragged it under.

"Well done."

"Thanks." She held her nose. "That water does stink."

"Let's get out of here." Dan put his shoes back on.

"What about the tracks?"

"We'd better cover them up and get the broken glass from the windshield hidden too."

"Okay. You do the tracks, I'll do the glass."

"Yes, boss."

Half an hour later they were walking back into the town through the forest. Catherine kept her distance from Dan, who reeked of the vile water. Just before they reached the main high street, Dan spotted a phone box. Smashing the video screen, he made another anonymous call to the police. They returned to the bed and breakfast, where they managed to avoid being seen by Trixie. In their room, Dan headed straight for the bathroom to wash. Catherine opened the windows and sat back on the freshly laundered bed linen. Everything that had happened to them re-ran in her mind. While Dan washed he tried not to think about his mother. In one day he'd gone from being without her, then with her, and then finally, totally without her again. He dried his legs and found Catherine lying on the bed.

"Are you okay?" she asked him.

"I think so."

"You smell better."

"Thanks. How are you?"

"Relieved that it's over."

"I think it's just the start for you, Catherine." He joined her on the bed. "You've got to rebuild Beacon."

She looked into his eyes. "I will, I will."

"The angels said it was over, but I suppose we'll have to avoid my mother's and Abdalla's funerals, just in case."

"Yes. I was thinking that too." Catherine placed her hand on his. "I'm so sorry." She leaned forward and hugged him. "I know she is in a better place now."

Catherine's PDA started ringing. She dug it out of her handbag.

"Who is it?"

"Oh, it's Mayling." They gave each other a glance. "I'd better answer it."

"You should try to act surprised."

"Yes, okay. Hello?" Catherine closed her eyes as Mayling explained what had happened. Kristina had been found suffocated and the police suspected Jason, whose body had been found with a fatal injury. It was hard for her to lie, but Catherine responded as best she could to what Mayling was saying. They talked for a while about the funeral and she informed Mayling reluctantly that they couldn't attend as they would be in America.

"I'm so sorry, Dan," Catherine said, resting her head on Dan's shoulder when the call had finished.

"It's okay."

For a few moments there was a hush. The warmth of the other's touch comforted them.

Dan brushed a hand through Catherine's soft black hair. "I guess this is it then."

"Yeah. I'm afraid so."

An hour later they left Herne Bay. Catherine had managed to get a last minute booking on a flight for America, flying out that evening. It was one of the first taking to the skies after a break in the dense cloud of volcanic ash that had smothered the country for the last few weeks.

After travelling by train into London, they took a packed tube to the airport. Throughout the journey there was an awkward silence between them. They both knew that in all likelihood they would not see each other again.

"What are you going to do without me?" Catherine asked, with more than hint of resignation at their impending separation in her voice. Dan shrugged his shoulders. He was holding the overhead rail, supporting Catherine, who had her arm around him. The train rattled through the underground tunnels. They didn't comment on their closeness, but were both more than comfortable with it. "You could come with me."

"I don't think Jerry would like that."

"Why not? You kept me alive. He has a lot to thank you for."

"I guess."

"I suppose you haven't got a passport or visa though."

"No, but that's never been a problem."

"Oh? Got a getting on a plane and getting through customs free power have we?"

"Something like that."

One of the commuters overheard their conversation and looked appalled. Dan and Catherine smirked at each other.

The tube pulled into the airport and with a little bit of pushing and shoving everyone disembarked. The concourse was packed with people trying to get home while they could. Dan carried Catherine's suitcase and they searched the departure boards for her flight.

"There it is. Twenty to ten. They're checking in." Catherine faced Dan. "Right then."

"Yes. I'd better...."

"Yeah."

"Well, thank you for… everything. You know, *everything*." She stood on her tiptoes and kissed him softly on the lips. Dan's heart almost stopped. "You will be okay won't you? I'll miss you."

"I'll miss you too. I'll be fine."

"You've got the money I gave you?"

"Yes."

"And you know how to contact me?"

"Yes."

"Okay, well. Bye then."

They embraced. Dan breathed her in for the last time and Catherine did the same. Parting, they looked into each other's eyes. Catherine bit her lip. Across the public address system a voice announced a final check-in call.

"You'd better go."

"Yeah. Well, take care of yourself."

"And you."

They gave one another a final lingering look and separated. Dan watched Catherine walk away. As she approached the gate, she suddenly realised she could take a photo of him with her PDA, but when she turned, he was gone.

Settling into her seat on the plane, Catherine powered up her laptop and opened a new document. She took a sharp intake of breath. 'Dear friends', she wrote, before stopping to consider the next line. 'First, let me apologise for not issuing this statement earlier. A continual flow of events prohibited this. You will no doubt be aware of the controversy surrounding Beacon, and the untruths disseminated by the secular media. I would like to present you with the truth'. Catherine carried on typing as the plane took off, heading towards a burnt-orange horizon.

35

Remnants of the lager swilled round in the bottom of a plastic pint tumbler. Dan watched the liquid rotate, then knocked it back and signalled to the barmaid for another.

The bar was dark and narrow with just enough room to fit a pool table at the rear, above which hung a giant 3D television screen. Dan looked around. He'd been there since noon, slowly drinking, in his continued attempt forget all that he knew.

The barmaid, Poppy, dropped a foaming pint of beer in front of him. He gave her half a smile, handed over a five euro note and told her to keep the change, just as he'd been doing all afternoon.

He wasn't sure which town he was in. Twelve months ago, after leaving Catherine at the airport, he had boarded a train from London to Liverpool and then, after an hour or so, randomly alighted. He'd been walking the streets ever since.

Dan watched two guys playing pool; they smacked the balls off the cushions with no intention of actually playing the game properly.

He glanced up at the screen above them. Celebrations. People cheering and waving, balloons, banners and hundreds of cameras flashing, and a man, immaculately presented, grinning from ear to ear, gesturing to the crowd, approached a microphone.

"What's going on?" Dan asked Poppy, who was mopping the floor behind the bar.

"Huh?" She looked around to see what he was referring to.

"What's going on?"

She reached down, and produced a remote control for the television and turned up the volume. "Where have you been? Mars?"

The camera switched to a news anchor sitting behind her desk.

"Today, the countries that form the World Union elected their first President."

The shot returned to the man, who had now ascended on to a huge stage. Dan recognised him as a former British Prime Minister who, before becoming a politician, had been a self-promoting academic and author of odious, hateful, misinformed and arrogant works such as 'The Case Against Religion', 'A New Dawn: The Enlightenment of Man', 'The Secular Bible' and 'A World Without Consequences: The Beauty of The Self'. He was a leading figure in the anti-theist movement, regularly appearing on multi-media interfaces lambasting faith in all its forms. Behind him there would always be an oversized banner with the symbols of the world's major religions crossed out. "This is an historic day," the man said, to rapturous applause, as a blonde-haired woman clung to his arm. "A new dawn is rising over the world, a new beginning, a strong united World Union! Today I make this promise – prosperity for all!" The multitude exploded in ovation.

"Didn't you vote?" Poppy asked.

"No." Dan appeared puzzled at having missed the whole event, but in truth he had known. It had just never really registered with him, because he'd tried to remain drunk.

The man continued his speech. "Over a year ago, when I started this long campaign, you will recall that I was attacked. I just want to say if it weren't for my special advisor, with his guidance and support, I

215

wouldn't have pulled through to be here today. Alec." He called off stage. "Come on up here."

A familiar figure with a beaming white smile, dressed in a designer black suit, marched on to the stage, waving at the delirious throng. Dan couldn't believe what he was seeing. He immediately felt sick to the bottom of his stomach. Then the camera focused on the woman holding Alec's hand. It was Anya.

The picture went back to the news anchor and she began to cover the story in detail.

Dan didn't, couldn't, move.

"I voted for him. I think he'll be good," Poppy said, returning her attention to washing the floor.

Dan's voice faltered. He muttered something almost inaudible to hear. He stood up, his stool scraping on stone, and exited the bar, leaving the barmaid bemused at his whispered comment.

Outside it was a fresh evening. People were leaving work and making their way home. Dan was motionless for a few seconds. A thousand thoughts were racing through his mind. He wiped away the layer of sweat that had formed on his brow, and then started walking.

∞

And that is how he ended his story. Another year had passed for him since that day in the bar. Now he slumped down, the hours of drinking finally taking its toll on his body. As I wrote previously, he had told me his story over the course of two weeks. I felt guilty for encouraging him to continue, for that encouragement meant keeping his glass topped up. Before I met him he had been stealing alcohol, since cash was no longer accepted. At first, of course, I did not believe him. Would you? It was beyond comprehension. However, I had lived in the nineteenth, twentieth and twenty-first centuries and had seen the cultural and political shifts, and the abolition and umbrage, through fear and intimidation, which all religions had suffered. Then there was the persecution: the allegedly accidental deaths of two witnesses (one of whom was incidentally named Jered) to unrest on the streets of Jerusalem, both of them leaders of believers representing the Old and New Testaments. There had for years been a steady encroachment on this historical and holy city, which was now a place where the buildings stretched towards the sky, built as obelisks to man and his greed and his new gods of money and power. They died protesting as the final part of the old city was raised to the ground to be developed, like the areas surrounding it, into the new political and financial capital of the world. It was the ultimate perversion of what was once such a sacred place.

And, of course, there was that giant of a man, unconscious through drink in front of me, who had shown me his supernatural powers as we stumbled home the night before. No demons appeared - he'd marginalized himself through a broken heart and his place had been taken in the unholy trinity, his successor nowhere near as powerful, thankfully, but still part of a movement that was castigating believers and enslaving the world.

I left him and returned to my lodgings. As I walked back it struck me how cold, although a warm early autumn evening, everything seemed. The streets were achromic. CCTV cameras were everywhere. People, tired, cheerless, separated, passed without looking at one another. The masked, black-clothed law enforcement officers, with automatic weapons slung over their shoulders, watched on. I went by a church, boarded up, waiting for the wrecking ball. Mosques had been set on fire, temples torn down, synagogues silenced.

That night, whilst taking supper, I watched the television. Every channel, and there were over one thousand, dripped with morally questionable programming. It was vacuous, shallow. This was indicative of art, music and film, which were mass-marketed, sterile, void of creativity. I suddenly realised how different, in all aspects, this period in time was from the years preceding it. I searched online for Beacon, but, of course, nothing; all religious outlets had ceased to be since the new laws had been introduced a year earlier.

For some reason my thoughts turned to the poor and unemployed. I was thankful I had a source of revenue that did not require me to work the minimum eighty hour week imposed on those in state employment. Furthermore new legislation had been introduced that forced those in poverty, or without a job, to relocate to one the new industrial cities. A few were brave enough to call them for what they were: labour camps.

Alongside believers, the unfortunate were forbidden to procreate. Those few in society who were allowed to bear offspring could only do so legitimately by entering into a World Union genetics programme. Any children born outside this strictly enforced code of conduct had to be hidden, for fear they would be disappeared, as rewards for their destruction were great.

I then looked down at my hand. That chip, that sliver of titanium. The one used for all transactions, the one that contained all one's personal information, and the one that had made cash finally redundant and illegal. Everyone had one, implanted just beneath the skin. Something that had been voluntary had, since the World Union formed, become compulsory, essential. A police officer could approach you, scan the chip and instantly, on a PDA connected to a vast database, know everything about you, every detail; your birth, your occupation, father's occupation, mother's occupation, mother's maiden name, mother's mother's maiden name, your education and employment history, how much money you had, where you lived. An exhaustive list of facts was available. It also served as a multimedia interface. You downloaded to it. You could make phone calls through it. You could access the World Wide Web (a wrist-bound screen picked up the pictures, and sound came from another chip implanted in the ear). It was thought, if rumours were to be believed, that anyone's movements could be tracked via GPS. Those without the chip could not function within the complex legislature of society. Transactions for food, clothes, etcetera could only be made via the device. You ceased to exist without the chip. If you were found without one you would be interned. If you were unwilling to co-operate, a lengthy interrogation followed, and if you would still not comply, well, suffice to say, *all* crime after the World Union formed was punishable by death – immolation chambers were built in every populated area; there was no forgiveness, no rehabilitation. The theory was if you didn't want to live lawfully, with the chip that is, then you must have something to hide, and must be opposed to the new way of life, that you were probably a terrorist, or worse, a believer. This, along with constant expansion of regulations, drawn up and instantly enforced, made it impossible for a person of faith to function in the new society. Not that I could blame the population's acquiescence. They were swept along with all the changes, which had been surreptitiously happening for decades, even before the World Union had formed. With no honourable axis to guide them they fearfully lived the only way the World Union allowed.

Each country was now ruled over by a sub-government of the World Union. Life was controlled and everything, including oxygen, was taxed. Even the beauty of nature was removed; green areas were concreted over, wildlife destroyed.

218

There was no privacy. There was no assistance if you were in need. Access to medical care, or knowledge (albeit what the World Union wanted you to know), was beyond the reach of most. If you were a burden on your family through ill health you were encouraged to go to an immolation chamber. Existence for those who weren't fortunate enough to be in the top naught point five percent of the world's population consisted of consisted solely of work, processed meals, and degrading entertainment. The billions strong workforce powered an economy that created a privileged environment for the few, the rich. Not only that, through humanity's subjugation, which he'd tempted and coerced, the devil had subverted what it meant to be human, the ultimate insult to God, reducing life to a pitiful, souless routine.

I thought I was going to be sick. I pushed away my plate of genetically modified and artificially grown food; processes that had become essential following the mid-twenty-first century food shortages, alongside the erection of bio trees to cleanse the air after the destruction of the rainforests. I had a sudden urge to get back to my own time. It wasn't perfect by any means, but it now seemed like paradise.

But before I set my course to return to you, my thoughts were drawn to the future again. It had never occurred to me to visit the world's final days; how could it have? I had had no idea when that would be, but now, if I was recalling correctly what Dan had told me, it would only be roughly two and a half years until the end of human history. An irresistible desire overtook me. I grabbed a knife, checking its blade for sharpness, before digging it into my hand. Blood issued forth from the self-inflicted wound. I prised out the chip that I'd procured on the black market (at considerable cost), and flicked it on to the table in front of me. Wrapping a cloth around my hand I studied the thin, centimetre square device. Then, with horror, I noticed something. Thirteen circuits divided and contained in three blocks: 6.1.6 - the number of the beast, the mark of the antichrist (666 was known to be a miscalculation.)

We met in the bar again the next day. It had been over two years since he had last seen Catherine. I asked him if he'd thought about finding her. He replied that he hadn't. I then felt obliged to tell him my story. To his credit he listened intently, although the drinks I was supplying (I traded my cocaine with the owner of the bar for a steady stream of alcohol) may have helped. When I had finished my tales he simply knocked back his twentieth double whiskey and smiled. I asked him if he wanted to see the future. His reply didn't surprise me, as he hadn't believed what I had said. He simply shrugged his shoulders and muttered 'sure'. Before he could order another drink I helped him up and we made it back to my lodgings. He seemed unimpressed when I showed him the capsule.

"A wardrobe?" he said.

"It's Regency," I replied, rubbing the rich coloured wood. "Mahogany. Wax finish."

He gave me a dubious look. Upon opening it he saw that it was decorated with wires, buttons, levers and other technical instruments.

"O-kay," he said. I again sensed his scepticism. "How does it work?"

"Are you really interested?" I was hopeful that he was, and that I could explain its principles: for it's not the capsule that moves, but time and space around it.

"No, don't worry." My heart sank a little. "I'm not sure we'll fit."

He was right. The capsule wasn't built for two, but I was confident that with a little manoeuvring and creative positioning we would be able to embark. And so, a few minutes later, I had set the controls, hopeful that the chosen destination and the time would be correct.

Exiting the capsule we looked out upon a desert landscape. The heat was intolerable. We were overlooking a valley and below us, two armies, one of darkness, one of light, advanced towards one another. My body was shot through with fear and trepidation, my hairs stood on end. We had made it. We turned around to see the city of Jerusalem, the tall opulent buildings unmistakable. Heading the army, a most terrifying trio, unmistakably the unholy trinity. We saw the devil. My heart almost stopped as we looked upon the obscene creature. Alongside him, the antichrist, the World Union President, and the false prophet, Alec Lars-Coe.

"Catherine," Dan said. He left my side and rushed down the slope. My first reaction was to attempt to stop him, except I knew nothing would be able to, and certainly nothing I could utter. All I could do was watch on.

Catherine looked exactly as Dan had described her to me. She was beautiful, although her face was drawn, a little heavy, perhaps because of the years of persecution she had suffered. Her dark hair was long and flowing. She, like those with her, dressed in threadbare garments. I assumed they had been called back to God's promised land,

220

to what was once a holy conurbation, to defend their belief. The dehumanised occupants of the city now faced the realisation that the written prophecy was coming to pass. They were rapt with fury. Despite their best efforts their way of life was coming to an end; all the money and hate in the world couldn't protect them.

All that Dan had told me over those days and weeks now made sense. He was conceived by the last of the watchers, a fallen angel, who had been waiting for the designated time, specifically for the purposes of fathering a child who would go on to be one of the unholy trinity, alongside the devil himself and the antichrist. Dan was destined to be the false prophet, who would have used his power to influence and delude humanity, and to confirm to them the authority of the antichrist. But the love and faith instilled in him by his parents had prevented that. The re-appearance of Anya confirmed to Dan that he had been manipulated. Her apparent death was plainly meant to bring anger to his soul and convert him to their cause. But although he suffered from an intemperate personality, he had resisted the darkness.

 And more importantly, he then fell in love with Catherine. Paradoxically, it was he who was there to save her, and consequently Beacon, from the very forces he had been born to serve. Alec had taken his place, no doubt lured by greed and power like countless others through the ages before him.

 Despite the efforts of the devil's agents, their bluffs, double bluffs and triple bluffs, regardless of their grip on the world growing ever tighter since the emergence of ego and slowly cutting the human race off from the light, ultimately, at the end, without Dan's powers, they could not change the prophecy of John. He, the devil, would lose.

It appeared Beacon had recovered and had established a haven for believers in one of the very few countries not tied into the World Union and its economy. Its members must have lived an impoverished existence, unable to trade or travel outside its borders, yet by implementing their values they seemed to have formed a community that endured through subsistence food production and the equal distribution of what little they had. I'm positive that their ideals and acceptance of the other ancient religions that also dwelt in the light brought believers together. Together, as I saw before me, they stood their ground against an enemy that, for just a little while, was on the brink of defeating them and establishing hell on Earth.

I can only imagine what was said when Dan and Catherine met again. I could make out surprise and joy on her face. If I believed in fate then I would say it was fortune, because as Dan reached Catherine, a bullet fired by an aggressor, hit him, instead of her, as it would undoubtedly have done had he not appeared.

It was a one-sided, chaotic battle. I observed, helpless and scared. God's army held hands and stood united as the enemy attacked. Only Dan, with his great strength and super-human ability, and a few others, fought back physically, protecting those around them. An hour must have passed, after which I saw Dan's wrecked body fall to the dusty earth. Catherine dashed to his side. Alec, the false prophet, approached. He towered over them. In their last moments, Catherine and Dan both looked up. Dan's eyes fought an impending death, his strength gone, and Catherine's were wide and hopeful. They, and I, saw the atmosphere become charged with electricity, which sent the unholy trinity, their demons, the possessed and their followers scattering, as a fearsome bolt splintered a gap in the sky. From deep within the fissure a brilliant pure white shone out, heralded by a spectrum of colours arching onwards. In the foreground, leading a thousand-strong flock of magnificent angels, and astride a mighty white horse, was love personified, who meant all things to all people, and whose love, light, freedom and kingdom, had come.

I hurried back to the capsule, struggling to tear my eyes away from the spectacle in front of me.

I awoke back in my study, the grandfather clock chiming midnight, with moonlight illuminating the room. It appeared that on my return I had been flung from the machine, which now lay in ruins, smashed to pieces. My supply of cocaine that had been hidden in bags in the wardrobe now covered the study, having exploded on impact. Easing myself up from the floor, I found that my head had been resting on the pages of the Bible. The title 'Revelation' stared back at me.

My darling Joyce, this is the end. You know what proceeded. If only you could have seen for yourself what becomes of the human race, you would weep, as I do now.

I am grateful for the paper and ink that was supplied to me. I trust you will receive this manuscript and believe what I have written.

I regret with all my heart that I did not share my journeys with you earlier. I hope to be with you again soon, but if that is not to be, let me convey this wisdom that I would urge humanity to embrace:

'A new command I give you: Love one another. As I have loved you, so you must love one another.'

John 13 34

Faithfully yours,

Buford J Tretheway

Professor Buford Jacinto Tretheway

Acknowledgements

'These Dreams' by B. Taupin/M. Page

Disclaimer

(1)
The theology represented in this novel is a blend of perspectives, primarily Progressive Christianity, but with a touch of the Religious Society of Friends (Quakers), and the author's own opinions based on his research. It also amalgamates the Futurist and Idealist views with regards to the Book of Revelation.

The author acknowledges the differing, fervent values of the diverse denominations of the Christian church and of the individual Christian.

It is the author's hope that the central message within this fictional narrative will serve as light to those on a spiritual journey.

(2)
Any resemblance to actual persons, living or dead, is purely coincidental.

James D Quinton lives in the UK

Also by the same author

Fiction

Touch
The Victorian Time Traveller

Poetry

Street Psalms
The City Is On Fire And Has Been For Weeks